Our Lady of the Various Sorrows

Voices of the Dead: Book Two

Victoria Raschke

Our Lady of the Various Sorrows -
Voices of the Dead: Book Two

For further information, please contact:

1000 Volt Press
info@1000voltpress.com

www.victoriaraschke.com

Cover design and book layout: keifel a. agostini.
Find him at keifelagostini.com.

The book is typeset in Brisio Pro. The font was chosen specifically for the shape of the letters and support of Slovene character sets.

Second Edition
ISBN: 978-1-7347422-1-3

for my parents Doris and Bill

What is remembered, lives.

ACKNOWLEDGEMENTS

This book has been ushered into the world by many hands.

I am lucky to have a dedicated and sharp group of early readers. Janet Neely, Mystie Thongs, Heather Smith, A.J. Scudiere, and D.B. Sieders, thank you for making me a better writer.

Griffyn Ink's indie publisher badass, Eli Jackson, and her growing band of writers, held my hand through many firsts and continue to keep me on the straight and narrow when I whinge about marketing and writing blurbs and pretty much anything else that isn't writing.

The physical book and its digital doppelgänger wouldn't exist without two very important people. Jennifer Goode Stevens reined in my tendency to wax poetic with her top-shelf editing and proofing. And keifel a. agostini makes me look good, quite literally. His book design and layout is always better than what I thought I wanted. I'm thankful everyday that he is both my partner in this publishing adventure and in life.

Thank you (again) to A.J. Scudiere for her forensic and medical knowledge. A special thank you to Tisa Šenekar and her canine companion Dakota for trekking to the Ljubljanica springs with a video camera so I could see it more clearly. Thank you to Irena Šumi and to all the Šenekars: Aleksander, Tiha, Brina, Bistra, and Tisa, for Slovenian language help, playing host and tour guide, and sharing their stories and knowledge. My understanding of Slovenia and its history are richer because of them and I hope that translates for readers as well.

There are too many to list, but thank you to the friends and family who came out to events and book signings, and who bought books for yourselves and to give to other people.

Your support means more than I can say. A special thank you and my love to Julian and Ishara for being the adults we all hope our children grow up to be.

A note on Slovenian pronunciation

Slovenian uses a few extra characters.
č is pronounced like the ch in church.
š is pronounced like the sh in shirt.
ž is pronounced like the second g in garage.
Familiar letters are pronounced differently.
e is most often pronounced like a in bay.
i is most often pronounced like the e in be.
j is pronounced like a y.
r without a paired vowel is pronounced like the ir in skirt.

CAST

Jo Wiley - the owner of Renegade Tea, the dead are corporeal in her presence

Faron Črnigad Wiley - Jo's son, who may be keeping his own secret

Helena Belak - Jo's former lover and current spirit guide

Matjaž Belak - Helena's brother, whom Jo is avoiding

Avgusta Belak - Helena and Matjaž's bad-tempered mother

Vesna Kos - Jo's best friend and business partner who can see auras and the future

Brother Leo Kos - Vesna's uncle and a witchfinder, Jo's friend and confidant

Gregor Bregant - Jo's surrogate older bother and business partner

Ivanka Novak - the oldest of the newly orphaned Novak sisters and Faron's girlfriend

Veronika Novak - the middle Novak sister with a chip on her shoulder

Ana Novak - the youngest Novak sister, the quiet one

Dušan Črnigad - Faron's long-absent father and an enigma

Goran Kralj - a professor of more esoteric things than European domestic arts, Jo's neighbor

Gustaf Lichtenberg - Jo's Observer and neighbor

Frédéric Berkane - Renegade Tea's cook and resident voice of reason

Henry - a ghost of the Slovenian Alps

"The world breaks every one and afterward many are strong at the broken places. But those that will not break it kills. It kills the very good and the very gentle and the very brave impartially."
Ernest Hemingway, *A Farewell to Arms*

CHAPTER 1

The Violent Femmes enumerated the reasons for taking a drink or drugs, Jo had never figured out which, from a speaker attached to her ancient iPod. She wiped the dust off the dresser with a rag and bent over to open the bottom drawer. It was empty save for a few dust bunnies and the scent of stale cupboard. She took her phone out of her pocket and placed it in the drawer. For the next week, or two, or four, it took for her to come back to some semblance of herself, she had no intention of talking to anyone and didn't want the temptation. Not that there was much of one.

The chorus from "Whatever Lola Wants" floated through her thoughts. She appreciated the announcement but not the presence it preceded nor the drop in room temperature.

When she turned around to look at her spirit guide, Helena Belak looked exactly as she always did. She had enough power as a shade to alter her appearance after death. The toga-like dress she'd been murdered in was no longer crumpled and soiled, as it had been the first time Jo had seen her after death, and Helena's head was straight where before it had sat misaligned on her broken neck. Her dark hair hung to her jawbone in its shiny bob, and her amber and green eyes greeted Jo with reproach.

"I don't understand why you think exile is going to do you any good." Helena's gaze moved about the room, stopping at the worn bedside table topped with a neat stack of sketch books and a box of charcoal pencils.

"I don't know that anything will do any good. I just want to remember what it's like to be alone."

"Well, you found a good place for that, love."

"Not exactly." Jo stared at Helena.

"You don't expect me to leave you here all by yourself, do you?" Helena's ability to deadpan remained unaltered by death.

"I know better than to expect you to do anything. I am asking you to give me some time and some space." It sounded so much like a conversation between lovers at the end of a relationship. They had been entangled in life, though "lovers" was not the best description of what they had been. Their relationship had ended, but not by their choosing. Death had parted them, and then brought them right back together.

Helena arched her eyebrow. "I don't think it will do you any good. I think you need to be around people. Living people. *That* will get you out of that muddled head of yours."

"You've made it clear who you think those people should be." Helena had spent the last few months trying to throw her into the path and bed of her brother, Matjaž. He and Jo were friends — friends who were at least physically attracted to each other — but there were too many reasons for her not to get involved with him. Helena's insistence itself served as a barrier, but it was one her brother had no clue about.

Helena pursed her lips. "I'm right. You're just stubborn."

"Whatever." Jo turned back to the dresser and wiped the drawer handles down. She'd already cleaned the rest of the bedroom, but it still smelled musty. She crossed to the window, ignoring Helena even though she could feel her eyes boring into the back of her neck, to try to figure out how to open it.

"You'll freeze."

"It isn't that cold out, and you won't notice." Jo pushed the window open despite its protests. She hardly noticed the cold herself.

"I'll go. On two conditions."

"Why do I feel like I'm not going to like these conditions?" Jo wiped down the window sill with her rag, pausing at the corner to avoid turning around again and facing Helena. It was still light out, and Jo could see down into the valley to the road leading into the gorge and the national park.

"You might or might not."

Jo waited for Helena to speak again.

"One, you set proper wards. You have no idea who or what is here."

"Already done." Gregor had made her promise before he'd driven off. She'd spent the next half hour walking around the house, lining each window sill and threshold with Piran salt.

It had been Gregor's idea for her to get out of Ljubljana and into the countryside. He was her surrogate brother, best friend, and business partner, though he'd been taking the big brother thing a little too seriously for Jo's liking. He'd purchased the house and farm after its owners had been murdered by a demon, with plans to turn it into a *gostilna* with rooms. In Gregor's estimation, it was the perfect place for her to "escape" to and sort herself out.

Jo turned around and leaned against the open window frame. "What's the second condition?"

"When you've finished your dark night of the soul nonsense and go back to Ljubljana, you'll call Matjaž. And–" She put up her hand to stop Jo from interrupting her. "And you'll at least consider what I've said."

Jo let out an exasperated sigh. She couldn't in good conscience agree to the second condition. And she couldn't lie and say she would, because Helena would know. Her Aunt Jackie, Jo's source of information on her recently discovered ability to speak with the dead, said it was one of the things about having a guide — you always had to be truthful. Jo was certain, though, it didn't work both ways. Helena was as coy in death as she had been in the part of her life Jo had known, and Helena was queen of the lie of omission.

"I can't agree to that. We've had the same conversation at least twenty times. It's part of why I need you to leave me alone."

Helena mocked a pout. "I'm not leaving unless I get my way." She smiled the same sly smile that used to give Jo butterflies.

Now that smile let her know there was no way she was winning this argument. She sat on the edge of the newly made bed. "What does 'calling' him mean exactly?"

"A date. For coffee. Or tea. Invite him to the teahouse while you're working. But you have to go somewhere alone afterward."

"Why do you think it will make any difference?"

"Because I know you two have a connection. If you'd quit throwing work and your high horse in the way, you might realize it, too."

Jo already knew it. She had spent the last few months saying no to Matjaž. No explanation. She'd seen him a handful of times, always with Gregor, as they talked about plans for the *gostilna* and Matjaž's firm's handling of the renovations. His occasional smile in her direction catapulted her back to the night he had kissed her on the dark path at the edge of Tivoli Park, when they had both been grieving and raw over Helena's death.

But most people were best kept at arm's length, including Matjaž. Jo's darkness had always been on her periphery. Now that it had a name, it was easier to keep people at bay; it was for their safety.

"Has it not occurred to you that my 'high horse' has more to do with you than with me?" Helena started to speak, but Jo cut her off. "You slept with my son — while you and I were seeing each other. You kept secrets from me. You talked about me with your brother in some effort to, what? Pawn me off on him? I don't need you, of all people, to play matchmaker. You slammed the door on any interest I might have had in Matjaž with your incessant bullying." Jo stood again and paced angrily from the bed to the window and back. "I'm not interested in anyone. No one needs to be involved in this." She waved her hand around her head to indicate her life and all its complications, including her spirit guide, and plopped back down on the edge of the bed. Jo had a list of omissions, too, though. She didn't trust herself with her own thoughts on who she was interested in, let alone Helena.

"You're lying. At least about not being interested in anyone," Helena said. "You may believe you're better off alone, or with that troupe of posers you collect at Niko's gallery, but I think you're wrong about that, too."

"Whatever interest I may have had in your brother is pretty much academic at this point. He's your brother, and now he is a business partner. Either would be off limits."

"You are beyond stubborn; you're selfish."

"Selfish? Selfish would be dragging him into this fuckery. I can talk to dead people and am a magnet for bad, weird shit. Do you really want Matjaž to know what I am? Do you really want him to know you're still here?" And most of all, had Helena, of all people, forgotten that Jo's "gift" meant she left dead people in her wake?

"He's already involved." Helena sighed and sat on the bed.

"No. He isn't. He's in the dark about you and about me. And he'll be happier and safer to stay that way."

Helena took Jo's cold hand in her colder one. "Just say you'll call him, and I'll leave you to your wallowing. I will not let you drive a wedge between yourself and the world, though."

"I will call him. I will invite him for coffee. You will not be there. And then I will go back to my fucked-up little life and leave him to his quiet one."

"It's a deal. And this isn't a condition, but when you get

back you might want to consider talking to the people who care about you."

Jo pulled her hand away, back into her own lap. "Please, just go. I agreed to your extortion, and now I don't want to talk to you anymore."

"Hardly extortion, dear."

"Believe what you want."

"Like you believe barricading yourself in the mountains and being a Class-A bitch to everyone will somehow protect the people you care about?"

"We're done. Go. Now. Do not contact me until I am back in Ljubljana. However long that is. If I hear even the opening note of that fucking song, I will push you through the first available door into the Next, even if I have to follow you through to do it."

Helena stood up. "That's not funny, Jo."

"I didn't intend for it to be." Jo stood up next to her and tried to unclench her fists.

"I meant about threatening to kill yourself."

"It wasn't a threat."

"Jo ..."

"Look. I'm not going to off myself. I just want to be alone. Really, truly alone."

"Wish granted." With that, Helena was gone. No pop or ruffle in the cold air.

Jo threw herself back across the bed. Her mended ribs twinged with the sudden jolt, another reminder of an event she'd rather forget. Whatever control she'd had of her temper had abandoned her weeks ago, and to keep from biting off the heads of everyone around her, she'd stopped talking. Apparently, her courtesy came off as bitchiness. She didn't have the energy to actually be bitchy. Well, except to Helena. And she had brought out the worst in Jo lately.

Aunt Jackie had been right when she'd said it was best that a spirit guide not be someone close. It clouded everyone's judgement. Jo wished someone had informed Helena of that before she'd taken the mantle of Jo's guide for herself.

She got up to close the window, but only halfway. She'd rather the room be cold than smelly if she was going to sleep in it. There were more blankets if she needed them; Gregor had insisted on leaving her with enough supplies for a polar expedition.

———

Being alone was like putting on a pair of forgotten shoes. They were hers, but they were stiff and unfamiliar. She expected her thoughts to be interrupted. She anticipated another's intrusion. But there was no one to interrupt or intrude.

As the days slipped by, there was routine. There was coffee made on the antiquated cookstove. The fire, banked the night before, needed a poke and more wood to boil the water on the griddle plate. It took some getting used to, but tending the fire became part of the ritual of her day as quickly as a walk in the winter-barren landscape or the hike into town. The thing she could not adjust to was being completely alone with her thoughts. They never took her anywhere good.

When she had gone for a walk the first day she was there, the low thrum of the unquiet dead had followed her along the trail. The area had been the site of bloody, frozen campaigns, and those who hadn't crossed into the Next still lingered. Jackie's ongoing instruction in controlling and developing her ability as a *Vox de Mortuis*, a Voice of the Dead, included a way to ward herself. She had knitted a tam with the items necessary to hide her light. When she wore it, the hat blocked the silver beacon that shot into the sky from the top of her aura and signaled to the dead, and to all who could see auras, what she was. Jackie said the ward was to be used with caution because it prevented even her spirit guide from reaching her if there was danger. Jo figured out fairly quickly she could still connect to a single shade if she wanted. Like many aspects of her late-blooming ability, this appeared to be unique to her.

The other Wiley women had been Voices since birth, but Jo's gift had landed on her suddenly and without warning the night of Helena's murder, when Jo was well into adulthood. Jo took her outlier status as permission to be contrary in other ways, like using the exclusion ward against her own guide.

She also refused to think about marrying a steward. Her father, when he had appeared to her, told her it was a bane for Voices to marry a man to provide for them. He had not said it was a bane against madness, even when Jo had pointed out marrying for protection was sexist and antiquated. It was possible he didn't know. His marriage to her mother had not saved Mary from madness, and his early death had hastened her descent. Aunt Jackie took the traditional wisdom with a grain of salt, being unmarried herself. But she also treated the whole Voice thing like an elaborate parlor game, except when the Observers were mentioned.

Gustaf Lichtenberg, Jo's Observer, bent the rules in his own way. They had been neighbors for almost eleven years, both living above the teahouse she owned with her best friends. He was only supposed to keep an eye on her to make sure she didn't abuse her power, but he'd taken it upon himself to educate her in the history and lore the *Vox de Mortuis* families had lost as their numbers dwindled. She, her mother, and Jackie were the only ones left. Perhaps that's why he'd taken such a keen, if rebellious, interest in her.

She stirred the coffee in the *ibrik* on the griddle plate and waited for it to come to a boil before stirring it down again. Her teahouse — aptly named Renegade Tea — would be fine in her absence. They might even be better off, if Helena's assessment of her behavior over the past few months was correct. She winced to think she had caused more pain to those she loved. She couldn't change her ability — Jackie had made it clear there was no "off" button — but she didn't have to compound their injuries with her shitty attitude.

That was why she was holed up in the mountains. Alone, she could gnash her teeth and wail instead of doing her poor imitation of a Stoic. Alone, she hoped, she could crack open the shell she'd crawled into and mourn the dead, even the one she could still talk to.

She hadn't meant to threaten her own life in her conversation with Helena, but the comfort she'd found in the thought scared her. There had been too many days when the weight of this pointless "gift," of everything that had happened, and of everything that could happen pressed down so hard on her that she would have happily walked through the first door into the Next that opened for her. It was appealing, except for the thought of what it would do to the people who cared for her. Her ability naturally turned her toward the dead and the past. She had to focus on the living and the present to survive, or at least to not follow her mother into the darkness.

Jo scrolled through her iPod playlists while she took the coffee off the eye to let the grounds settle. It felt like a Leonard Cohen kind of morning, but he might also help her dig a deeper hole to stew in. She tapped the Quiet Mornings playlist Gregor had made for her, and Cloud Cult's "Breakfast with My Shadow" spilled out into the room. Gregor could be a bit on the nose sometimes, but she appreciated his attempt at continuing the mix-tape communication of their early friendship.

Other than the constant companion of her dark thoughts, she'd gotten her wish about being physically alone. She should have been more careful about what she wished for, or at least more specific about what she needed. There was no one she could talk to who knew what she was, who wasn't also directly involved. And she didn't need a fixer; she needed a sounding board. Where was a therapist specializing in demon dreams and woo-woo fallout when she needed one?

The coffee grounds settled, and she poured her drug of choice into a mug she had brought from her flat. It was good to have the familiar with her, even a small connection to the reality beyond the thick walls of the farmhouse and the mounting snow. Where she was now wasn't her reality. Her reality was never this quiet.

CHAPTER 2

Faron sat on a chair near the window sill. Two dead flies lay legs-up on the wood. He chose the less mangled of the two and touched its crunchy wing with the tip of his finger. An unseen current passed between them, and the fly fluttered and buzzed off the window sill, dazed but alive.

Ivanka touched him on the shoulder. "Come to bed."

He continued to stare at the other fly. Its wings were broken and a leg was missing. He had learned enough to know it would come back to life only to struggle and die again because it was mangled. He stood and turned to Ivanka. Her eyes were soft with compassion as she looked up into his face, but he could see the worry, too. She had reason to be afraid of things beyond her understanding. She had reason to be afraid of him.

"Maybe it only works on small things, things without souls." She took his hand.

"Who knows what has a soul and what doesn't?" He pulled away and walked toward the bedroom.

"Where are you going?" She tried not to sound accusatory,

but the edge was there. He ignored it.

"To bed. Like you said."

She followed him and walked to the wine crate she used to corral her clothes in the room she shared with him in his Uncle Rok's old apartment.

He watched her undress and neatly fold her T-shirt and leggings before placing them in the crate. She slid her underwear down her legs and tucked them into the laundry bag.

He stopped her on the way to the bed, which was a futon mattress on the worn wooden floor, and pulled her into a hug. "I don't mean to be such an asshole."

"I know." She leaned away from him and looked up into his face. The worry was still there. "You should talk to someone. What about that priest guy your mom talks to?"

"Brother Leo? No." It came out harsher than he'd intended.

"Okay. Then let's find someone else. I can't help you."

She was right. It was unfair for her to be the only other person who knew and be the one person he had tried to help and failed. Saving her father hadn't been an option; there wasn't enough of him in one piece to try to resurrect. Her mother had been whole, but she hadn't come back when he touched her.

Leo would know what he was, he was sure of that. He also saw the way Leo looked at his mother. Whatever he told him would go straight to her, and Faron wasn't ready to talk to her about this. She had enough on her plate.

"I'll find someone. Maybe Lichtenberg."

"Do you trust him?"

No more than he trusted anyone else, but Lichtenberg's loyalty seemed to be only to himself and his order of watcher weirdos. He was also a pro at keeping secrets, and he probably already knew what Faron was — whatever that was. "No, but I don't think I've got many other options." He hugged her to him. "I don't really trust anyone but you. And Mom, but …"

She pulled away and smiled up at him. Her smile was a rare thing since the night her parents had been killed.

"But she's got her own stuff to deal with?"

He nodded.

"I still think you should tell her. She promised not to keep secrets from you again. You aren't returning the favor."

He knew that, too, but his mom had been through enough. She tried to hold it together, but he'd seen her on the mornings she was at the shop alone for hours before anyone else came in. She looked tired and sad all the time. Everyone had kept secrets from her, and she'd buried friends — partly because of those secrets.

And still he was keeping things from her.

"You're right. I should tell her." He ran his hand down Ivanka's dark hair to where it fanned out over her bare shoulder. "When she gets back." He stepped back and pulled his shirt over his head. He threw it over the chair he used for a nightstand and followed it with his jeans. "Let's get some sleep. You've got to be up early to make bread."

———

He walked Ivanka to work before heading to the library

and class. When they got to the teahouse, the door was unlocked. Fred must have come in early. Faron followed her in, to be sure. He tried not to be overprotective, but it was hard now that they both knew that the monsters under the bed were real.

Fred came out of the kitchen drying his hands on his apron. "Good morning." His greeting lacked its usual enthusiasm.

A man sat at a table in the darkened, far corner under the mural of a clipper ship surrounded by burning crates of tea. He set his teacup down on the saucer soundlessly and looked at Faron with interest.

"Ivanka, let's get started. I think this needs to be a private conversation." Fred motioned her into the kitchen. He walked by the shop iPod on his way and tapped on the music. Tom Waits, something Faron's mother liked.

Ivanka looked at Faron with an "are you sure?" expression. He nodded.

He'd never met his father, but he'd seen him on television and on magazine covers at kiosks.

Dušan Črnigad stood and extended his hand. "It is good to see you, Faron. You look well."

Faron didn't take his hand but nodded as a greeting.

"Would you like to talk here or go for a walk?"

"Let's walk."

His father collected his teacup and saucer and took them back to the kitchen. Faron could hear every other word of Fred introducing Ivanka and Dušan over Waits' mourning about a grapefruit or something. He put his hands in the pockets of his jeans. He didn't want Dušan to see them shaking, whether they shook from fear or anger. Nothing good could come of a visit from his father.

Dušan returned, and the two of them walked together into the courtyard. Faron waved at Goran, who was watering the evergreen topiaries in front of his antique store opposite the teahouse. A thought flitted across Goran's face, but it didn't linger long enough for Faron to figure out what it meant.

"Where to?" Dušan extended his arm toward the entrance.

"I guess down the embankment. There are a few places to get coffee."

Dušan nodded. His hair shifted slightly. It was long, past his collar, and still dark, like Faron's, except at the left temple where it had gone completely white. Faron was taller than he was, but just. They were built the same, long and lanky with broad shoulders that made them both seem taller than they were. He was dressed in a slim-fitting black suit, like the ones he always wore in pictures, with a stiff, white shirt, open at the collar.

Faron led the way out onto *Zajčeva* and down to *Breg,* where he turned left toward the Three Bridges.

"Is the woman your girlfriend?"

"Yes."

"She is quite beautiful and very protective of you. She was giving me daggers when Frédéric introduced us."

"Hmm."

"I see I will be doing most of the talking this morning."

Faron clenched his fists in his pockets. "You've done very

little over the years. Seems fair."

Dušan laughed. "You are very much like your mother. I am glad of it."

That was not the reaction Faron had expected.

They walked through Prešeren Square, where an accordion player was murdering a Beatles song across from a violinist banging out a folk tune. A few people glanced at his father, their faces shifting to surprised looks of recognition, but no one spoke to him.

They crossed the main bridge, and Dušan steered them toward a gate with steps leading down to a bar that faced the river below street level. It had been the old fish market, and it was empty save for the two of them and the bartender. His father nodded at the man. "*Dva, prosim.*"

They sat at a table and stared at each other for a few minutes before the bartender returned with two skinny glasses of water and two cappuccinos on a steel tray. He placed the water and coffees on the table with a small box of sugar straws and disappeared into the back.

"I know your mother trades in tea, but I prefer the stronger stuff." Dušan ripped the tops off three packets of sugar and dumped them into his coffee.

Faron sipped his cappuccino.

"I can imagine what you are thinking."

Faron looked up at him over the rim of his cup. "I doubt it."

His father laughed. "You have every right to be angry."

"I hadn't planned on asking your permission about how I should feel."

"Nor should you. I do realize I have been distant and unavailable."

It was Faron's turn to laugh. "Distant and unavailable? That's putting it mildly."

"Perhaps. I would not have had much to offer you had I stayed. Your mother has clearly done an admirable job."

"Is that your idea of an apology?"

"No. I have no intention of apologizing for my actions. I am sorry if you were hurt by them, but there was nothing to be done about it."

"Then why are you here?"

"Yes. Why I am here. You are very much like her. Direct and to the point. I have always admired that about Jo."

"She's too good for you."

"I will not argue that. The reason I am here is I suspect you will have questions for me now your mother's talents have emerged. If you are indeed like her, I suspect you have not mentioned yours to her."

Faron almost dropped his cup into its saucer. "How can you–"

"I knew what your mother's family was, even if she did not. I expected you to have some mixture of our abilities."

Faron continued to stare at his father.

"Unlike your mother, I cannot speak with the dead, I can only raise an army of them to do my bidding. It is not very useful in this modern world. Can you speak with them, like her?"

Before Faron realized he should have lied, the truth tumbled out. "I can bring things back to life."

It was Dušan's turn to be speechless. He regained his composure quickly. "What kind of things?"

"Fallen leaves, insects, mice. If they aren't too broken." He wished he'd kept his mouth shut.

"Since when?"

"Just within the last year."

"Have you reanimated anything larger than a mouse?" Dušan looked at him as if he expected a particular answer.

"No."

"But you have tried."

"Yes, Ivanka's mother. But it didn't work." Faron stared down into his coffee cup. He had given his father what felt like a weapon.

Dušan shook his head. "It would not have, but I am impressed you tried."

Faron pushed the cup away.

"Have you told anyone else?"

"Only Ivanka."

Dušan nodded. "Good." He pulled a phone in an expensive-looking leather case from his pocket and tapped out a number. "Gustaf. Perhaps you would like to join us? You were quite wrong."

———

His father had decided the rest of their conversation

required something stronger than coffee. He ordered three neat glasses of single-malt scotch when Gustaf Lichtenberg arrived. Faron had never had anything to drink that cost more per ounce than he made in an hour, and definitely not before lunch. It burned in a satisfying way as it went down and steeled him for whatever was coming next.

"And you have not told your mother?" Gustaf looked at him like a skin cell under a microscope.

"She's been through–"

His father cut him off. "Do not underestimate your mother. She is made of stronger stuff than you can possibly know. Still, I am glad you have not told her yet."

None of this made sense to Faron. How could his father know he would have some ability? And what kind of scary asshole could raise an army of the dead?

"It's not unexpected your son would have some semblance of your ability, Dušan. Though I assumed without knowledge of it or any training there was nothing of concern. Necromancers require more pomp and circumstance than Voices." Gustaf turned to Faron. "And you did not think this was worth mentioning to your mother?"

"It seemed too crazy for anyone to believe."

His father nodded. "Was there anything that triggered it? Somewhere you went? Something you did?"

"I don't think so." Faron wasn't going to tell them where he had been the first time it had happened. It was too embarrassing.

His father finished his whisky and set his glass down soundlessly on the polished table. "There had to be something.

You need to remember. It is important." He picked up Faron's phone from the table and turned it to Faron to unlock it. "I will add my contact information. Call me as soon as you remember."

Faron tapped in the code and his screen, a photo of him on the top of Triglav with Rok, popped up, obscured by app icons.

His father turned the phone around and touched in his contact information. "Does your mother still see Rok?"

"You should ask her that." Faron bristled. He was not going to tell him anything about her.

"I should. When will she be back?" Dušan finished and slid the phone back across the table.

"I don't know. She said she'd be back when she was back."

"She has gone to Tolmin to be alone. Not that it is possible for one like her." Gustaf finished his whisky and centered the glass perfectly on his napkin. "She will be delayed in her return in any case. There are storms forecast for the mountains, and the roads will be impassable with the snowfall."

Faron wanted to kick Gustaf under the table. His father had no right to any information about his mother she didn't give him. He downed the dregs in his glass and nearly dropped it onto the table. His hands were still shaking. It was definitely anger.

"I have no desire to interfere in your mother's life. To talk with her, yes, and soon, if possible. But not to interfere." Dušan folded his hands in front of him on the table and looked up at Faron. "Does she know how protective you are of her? I doubt she would welcome it."

Faron gritted his teeth but couldn't think of anything coherent to say.

Gustaf rescued him in his way. "Let us leave Faron to his day. I believe he has class to attend."

Faron stood and slung his backpack over his right shoulder. "I do." He pushed his chair in and turned to leave without another word.

The two men were sitting, their heads bent together over the table, when Faron looked back before closing the door to the bar and taking the steps back up to street level.

He stood on the cobbles and tried to take in the late-morning blur of people going about their business. All those people unaware of what he was or what he had come from. He started back up the river toward the library and the university. He wouldn't get any reading done today, but he wasn't going to be late for class.

———

Veronika pushed her soup around in the bowl. Her sister Ana sat across from her. Of the three sisters, she looked the most like their mother. She and Ivanka, their oldest sister, had their mother's thick, dark hair. Veronika's was mouse brown when she didn't dye it orange or green.

Olga, their aunt, picked up the basket of rolls and tried to hand it to Veronika. "Bread? You've hardly touched your soup."

"I'm not really hungry." She took the basket and set it in front of Ana.

"You're never hungry." Ana spoke under her breath, but

Veronika heard her.

"Leave her be. She'll eat when she is." Olga went back to her soup, and the table returned to the silence that hung over almost all their meals.

No one, including Veronika, talked about their parents. It was almost like they never existed. She knew the story about how they died was bullshit; she'd seen her father's death. No one ever talked about that either.

They also didn't talk about the fact that their grandparents never spoke to them anymore and pretended not to know them in the street. Everyone failed to mention that Veronika and Ana had been foisted on their aunt while their sister Ivanka moved in with Faron. He, with his mother, was responsible for making her and her sisters orphans in the first place.

"Finished?" Olga stood and collected the bowls.

Veronika nodded. She got up and started back to her room.

Ana grabbed her wrist. "Do you want to watch TV with me?" Her sister's face was still chubby with childhood, but she was taller every day.

"No. I'm going to read."

"I don't know why you are so interested in those dusty books."

"What dusty books? Have you been in my room?"

Ana looked guilty. "No, but I can see you reading when you leave the door open. It's always some old book. They must be dusty."

"Well, stay out of my room." Veronika needed to find a

better place to keep her growing collection. It was probably stupid to put them on the shelf where Ana or her aunt could see them. Not that Olga ever went in her room. Her aunt had made it clear she wasn't their maid and would not be cleaning up after them.

Olga made sure they had clothes and got to school on time. It wasn't like she was mean; she just didn't seem to care much about them. She didn't have any of her own kids and joked about being married to her job, first as her father's business manager and now as Gregor and fricking Jo Wiley's business manager.

Jo Wiley couldn't stay away from her family. Ivanka worked for her, too, at her stupid teahouse. All their friends hung out there, and no one seemed to know or care that the woman was evil or attracted it. Whatever. They were all so blind.

Veronika closed the door to her room behind her. She pulled her altar out from underneath her bed and removed the black cloth she used to protect and hide it. Nothing looked disturbed. If Ana had been poking around, she hadn't found everything.

The books would have to go under the bed, too. She rummaged around in her closet looking for a crate or box they would fit in and still slide under the bed rail. Her socks and underwear were in a plastic basket on the shelf. She dumped them out on the bed and stood the books, spines up, against each other. The books and basket cleared the rail. She pulled out the spell book she'd been reading and set it on the floor. There wasn't any more of the cloth she'd draped over the altar, but she did have a ratty old black T-shirt. She laid it on top and pushed the crate back under the bed.

Cross-legged on the floor in front of her makeshift altar, she lit a cone of incense and a red candle and turned to a page on breaking up lovers. She wasn't as powerful as her teacher, but maybe she could at least make Ivanka come back and live with them.

CHAPTER 3

The dead do not dream because they do not sleep. Of all the things of life he missed, dreaming bothered him most. Not that his dreams in life had been pleasant: images of war and loss, the loss of friends and lovers and, finally, his sanity and autonomy. But there had been good dreams as well. They were now as distant as his life, though. He had been dead longer than he had lived.

He had come to this place when he died, and now he could not leave. He had served nearby during the war. He had loved there. And like many others, he was lost there. His job had been to tend the wounded. Instead he had been an unwilling Charon transporting the dead.

He still saw every face behind his eyelids. He saw young men's bodies torn and shredded, or their flesh burned from the cold. He had years to forget, but could not.

He could not forget other faces. Those of his wives and his children and the friends he outlived and the friends he left behind — they haunted him. Almost all were gone now. He was alone with the countless and unknown dead who could not leave these mountains.

It was torture by a horrific beauty. It would not end until they were mourned, but the mourning of a ghost did not satisfy the unnamed and unknown. He felt their exhaustion in what he assumed was his soul. He had to have one, there was nothing else left to feel pain.

———

The first day he saw her in the distance, she hiked up to a flat, open area near a war monument. She sat on a rocky outcropping, the valley spread out before her, to eat a sandwich out of brown paper. She looked lost in thought and methodically chewed each bite. When she finished, she screwed up the paper and shoved it into a pocket in her clothes. She walked along the path toward him, pausing to look up at the mountains. She wore an ugly, flat hat, and her dark blonde hair flowed from underneath it. She stopped and turned to walk back the way she came, her loneliness drifting off her and over him on the thin mountain air.

———

He saw her again the day of the snowstorm. She walked past him and off the trail into a small wooded area near another of the shrines to the dead. She spread a blanket on the ground and knelt in a clearing among the trees. He thought she might be praying. She took a spoon out of her coat pocket and dug a shallow hole in the frozen ground in front of her. She tipped a small thing into it and packed the pile of earth she had excavated back over it.

She rocked back and sat on her heels. When she brushed her arm over her brow, she knocked the strange, flat hat off. A shimmering plume spun up from the top of her head. She transfixed him as the hum of all the lingering dead on the mountainside crescendoed. He went to her and found he was walking on the ground. The frozen, winter-browned grass hiding beneath the snow crunched under each footfall. The sensation of his own feet hitting the ground jarred its way up his legs. She turned, and surprise flickered across her face. She reached for the hat but clutched it in her hand.

"Hello?" His voice sounded. It was strange to speak, and stranger still to hear the words rattle in the bones of his head.

"Hello." She pushed her hands against the blanket and stood. She still clutched the hat in her hand, like she was trying to decide whether she should put it back on.

"You can see me?"

"Yes. And hear you." She put the hat back on. The thrumming around them stopped. "And now only you."

Curious. "And you are?"

"Jo." She extended her hand. "And you?"

It had been so long since he had thought about his name, he found he was protective of it. To say it out loud was a betrayal of who he had been in life. He thought of another, instead. "Henry." He shook her hand, shocked by the contact of flesh on flesh.

"Henry." In her mouth it sounded like a foreign word, a meaningless but musical sound.

"What kind of magic is this?" He flexed his fingers out, the bones of his wrist cracking.

"No magic. Well, at least not any trickery." She folded up the blanket and tucked it under her arm.

"It has been a long time since I've felt … present."

"I have that effect on people." She laughed. It was a high, clear sound in the cold air. "Or at least dead ones."

"You are a strange creature, Jo." She was, and intriguing. Not beautiful so much as memorable or striking. "I've watched you the past few days."

She tilted her head back in surprise. "It must've been very boring."

"Not boring. I've wondered what you were up here looking for." Had he said too much? She cocked her head at him as if she were trying to decide whether to answer his half-asked question.

"Henry, would you like to join me for dinner? I have eaten every meal alone for two weeks. I could use some company."

He looked up into the darkening sky. A storm was gathering in the distance, and the sun was setting. "Yes. I will join you for dinner."

"We should go. I'm not much of a weather forecaster, but that cloud looks dark and snowy."

He nodded. "Lead on."

She took his arm, and they walked in silence to a farmhouse perched on a hillside. The muscles in his legs lengthened and contracted with each step. How had this woman made him flesh? He could feel the wind as it picked up and blew against their backs. He could not feel the cold, but the woman rubbed her upper arm and quickened her steps. She opened the door and walked into the dark room beyond. He stopped at the threshold, unable to cross.

She stopped. "Oh, I forgot. Henry, welcome to my home. Please, come inside."

With her words, he stepped over the threshold. She sprinkled salt from a bag hanging near the door over where he had walked. He followed her into the main room of the house.

———

He watched her move around the kitchen. She poked the fire awake in the stove and put a pot of rice on. As the rice cooked, she opened a bottle of wine with a knife she pulled from her pocket.

She held the bottle out toward him. "Red okay?"

He nodded. Why did she think a ghost could drink wine? Why did he think he could not? The chair underneath his thighs felt like a chair.

She handed him a glass and held hers up. "A toast."

He held his glass up close to hers. She looked him in the eyes. It was still unnerving. A living person could see him. When she looked at him, it was as if she could see into him, as well.

"To new friends." Her gaze suggested things other than friendship.

They clinked their glasses together and each took sips.

The wine washed over his tongue, over every tastebud in his mouth full of teeth. Summer and warm leather and ripe plums. Wine had never tasted so good when he was alive. Or he had forgotten?

"Do you like Indian food?" Her back was to him as she

chopped onions with an admirable precision.

"I am sure I will."

She laughed. "Good. It's pretty much what I brought provisions for."

With all the chopping done, she pulled a pan from a lower cupboard. She tossed a handful of spices into it when it had warmed on the griddle plate. The air filled with the aromas of cumin and turmeric and cinnamon. She crushed a few leaves in and added oil and the onions. With that task completed, she scooped up the apples she had sliced and fanned them out on a plate. She sprinkled more spice and some apple cider vinegar over them and placed the plate in front of him.

"It's *chaat,* an appetizer of sorts. It'll tide you over until the dhal is ready."

The apple slices were crisp and tart and sang with the combination of spices she had dusted them with. He savored each bite, surprised by how acute his senses were. Had he experienced things as purely as this when he was breathing? He had thought he grabbed life around the throat at every opportunity. There had not been time for regrets.

Jo set a large plate with a pile of fragrant, slender-grained rice and a bowl of deep yellow stew filled with split lentils on the table. Two pieces of charred bread lay next to the bowl. There were no other plates. She sat next to him, beckoned him to eat. He watched as she ripped off a piece of bread, dipped it in the stew, and put the whole of it into her mouth. He followed her lead.

When the food was gone and the dishes washed, she picked up her glass and the bottle of wine and bade him follow her.

She moved back into the small sitting room they had come through. She refilled her glass and curled up in the corner of the couch.

"So what's your story, Henry?"

He sat in the middle near her and set his glass on the table in front of them. "First. What are you? How is this possible?"

"Long version or short version?"

"Short version for now."

Before she could start her story, the lights flickered and went out.

"So much for that, but I have lanterns." She set her wine down in the dark and pulled a small thing from her pocket. It shone a blinding light at the floor that she used to navigate to a cupboard in the corner of the room that groaned with books and the trinkets of life.

She produced two oil lamps and a box of long matches. A match lit when she struck it against the box. The wick sputtered and threatened to go out before it caught, and a blue and gold flame sprang up from the cotton. She put the glass chimney back on and curled back up into the couch, wine in hand.

"Where were we?"

———

Jo took a sip of her wine and looked at her guest. He was probably in his forties, or had been when he died. His hair was long enough to be rakish, and his beard had gone mostly gray. His eyes were intelligent and deep but not warm, or not exactly. There was pain in them, but he didn't much seem the type to share that. They had that in common.

"I am a *Vox de Mortuis*, a Voice of the Dead."

"And what does that mean exactly?"

"It means I can see and speak with shades, like you, and that in my presence you are solid enough to make a dent in the couch."

He nodded, but his expression was one of confusion.

"There are only three of us in the world. It's not a very common ability."

"Perhaps that is a good thing."

"I think so. I wouldn't wish it on anyone." She took another sip of wine and continued to appraise her unexpected guest. He was attractive in a Ralph Lauren, all-American way, and yet vaguely Bohemian. She was more interested in the Bohemian bit. He was familiar, but she couldn't say why.

"The living are difficult enough to understand."

She laughed. "Yes. Yes, they are." She didn't even understand herself these days.

"It must have been hard when you were a child."

"It's a relatively new thing. But, enough about my weirdness. What about you? Who are you, Henry? If that is your real name."

"It isn't, but it will do."

"It will if that's what you prefer." She pulled a blanket off the back of the couch and wrapped it around her legs. The fire usually kept the room warm, but her guest sucked the heat from the air, almost as much as Helena did. That didn't stop her from edging a little closer to him as she settled the throw over her.

"For now at least. I hadn't expected to ever speak again, let alone have anyone ask me my name."

She nodded.

"I was a writer. I traveled. I lost my mind, and I blew my brains out in the end."

Jo shivered. She was grateful to whatever gods allowed a gunshot suicide to not appear to her in his death form. He was a strong shade to be able to project a different visage.

"I thought honesty was best here."

"No. It is. It's just usually when shades first appear they look like they did when they died and, well, I'm glad you don't." Maybe it was different with suicides. She hadn't met the shade of one yet.

"Is there a mirror?"

"A small one in the bathroom. Do you want me to come with you?"

He stood. "I don't, or didn't usually, invite women to join me in the john, but I think this is a special circumstance."

She got up and led him with a lantern to the small bathroom off the main bedroom. She handed him the light and motioned for him to go ahead. He stood in front of the mirror and ran his hand over his beard.

"How old were you when you died?" He was fit in a man's man way. Shades were usually pale, but his skin looked as if it had been heavily bronzed in life.

He put his hands on the edge of the sink and pushed away,

looking down at the cracked tile on the floor. "Early sixties going on dotage."

"You look more fortysomething now."

"Those were good years. Or at least better ones."

"You don't look too bad for a shade. Feel better?"

"I don't know how to answer that question."

She took his cold wrist. "Let's go back to the couch and you can answer different questions." She was sure he wouldn't have an answer for why the shade of a suicide would find his way to her, now. Maybe the whatever gods were responsible for that, as well.

He looked up at himself in the mirror one more time. "It's best not to dwell on the past."

"I'm learning that lesson."

He stood up straight and walked back toward the sitting room.

Once they were both back on the couch, closer than they had been before, she asked more questions, trying to parse out who her mysterious guest had been in life. She was drawn to his loneliness, and her thoughts spun out into where that might take the evening.

"What did you write?" She poured more wine into both their empty glasses.

"Novels, stories. I worked as a correspondent."

"Anything I would have read?" She looked over the rim of her wineglass at him as she took a sip.

"Possibly. What did you study at school?" He was very

good at changing the subject. Almost as good as she was.

"Photography and history." She wasn't giving away any more than he was, but his nearness with the flickering lamplight and the wine were chipping away at her reserve.

"What do you do now? I don't see any cameras in your house." He turned facing her on the couch, his arm stretched along the back. He picked up a few strands of her hair and rubbed them between his thumb and fingers.

She took another sip of wine and moved closer to him on the couch. What *did* she do now? "I don't live here. I live in Ljubljana. I own a teahouse with a couple of friends."

"Why aren't you a photographer?"

"I gave that up." She'd had a mouth to feed, and photography had lost its luster for her. Picking up a camera had reminded her too much of Dušan.

"Why?"

"I don't have a good answer for you." She didn't want to pierce this fragile thing they were weaving with complaints about an old lover.

He nodded and ran his fingers down her arm. "And does owning a teahouse fill that same creative need?"

"Sometimes. I work there, too. Baking and scheduling bands. I've started sketching again. It seems to be filling that void." His light touch made her aware of other needs.

"What do you draw?" He brushed his thumb over her earlobe.

"People mostly. Faces. But sometimes buildings or landscapes or my friend's cats." She turned in her seat and shifted inside the crook of his arm.

"Do you have them here?" His voice deepened, and his words slowed in a languid, aroused way. She laughed. "Yes, do you want to come to my room to see my sketches?"

He smiled. "Is that an invitation to your bed, Jo?"

She turned her face toward him to answer, and he brushed his lips over hers.

"It might be."

CHAPTER 4

Leo took the cup Vesna handed him. "It's not that green tea, is it?"

"No. Irish breakfast. The one you like."

He nodded and took a sip. "Have you spoken with Jo?"

His niece shook her head.

"I'm worried about her being up there alone. That place." It was a beautiful natural area, but the memorials and the starkness of the mountains made it feel like a place of the dead to him.

Vesna curled her legs up under her on the giant couch. It was still a puzzle to him, how she'd managed to get it into the cramped flat.

"She'll be fine, I think." Vesna held her cup in the air while one of her cats, a sleek orange tabby, made itself comfortable on her lap.

"That doesn't sound very convincing."

"Jackie told her how to make that ward with the hat, and I think she needs to be alone, but ..." Vesna looked out the window, but her eyes were focused somewhere in the middle distance.

"But what?"

Vesna shook her head like she was coming back from somewhere far away. "She has been in a dark place. I thought she was getting better, but the week before she left she barely spoke to anyone, even at work."

He had thought she was dealing with things better, too, until the last time she'd come to visit. She had asked him again how she could have saved Katarina. She was convinced it was her fault she had died. He'd tried to reassure her that death was beyond her control, but she was still haunted by the possibility that there was a choice she could have made or an action she could have taken that she had failed to see. Jo had said that working with Ivanka every day at the teahouse was a reminder of her failures.

He interrupted his own thoughts to share them with his niece. "She thinks everything that happened is her fault."

Vesna sat up, and the cat protested in her lap. Vesna pushed her dark hair away from her face and tucked it behind her ears. "I think she realizes she couldn't have stopped it. I think it was seeing Veronika and Ana in the house. She keeps telling me about the blood on Veronika's face." Vesna paused. "I don't think that's the only thing." His niece started to say more but stopped herself, either for his comfort or her own preservation.

Death was inevitable. He and Jo had discussed that, but she clung to an idea that people got the death they deserved. And she didn't believe any of those killed by the demon, who had come for her, had gotten the deaths they deserved. She thought her duty to the dead meant she should have stopped it.

"She hasn't mentioned anything else to me."

"There might be other reasons for that." His niece cocked her head and arched her brow at him. "She's not going to get past any of this if she won't talk to anyone."

"She'll get there. She questions why Tomaž and Katarina didn't appear to her after they died." He put his hand on hers to reassure her, or maybe himself.

"I wondered about that. But don't you think they would have crossed quickly?"

He nodded. "I would have if what was left of my body was a–"

Vesna put up her hand. "I really don't need another description of Tomaž's death." She went a little green around the gills.

"I'm sorry."

"It's fine. I know you've dealt with more of this than I have."

"That should make me more circumspect about what I repeat." He took a sip of his tea and leaned back into the couch. He looked around at the flat. His niece's personality was on display in the photos and tchotchkes she managed to cram onto every surface. It was orderly though, even in its Victorian excess.

She nodded. "And how are you?"

She could see his aura, so there was no sense in lying to her. "I've had a lot to think about."

"Perhaps the thing you should most consider before you

break your vows is whether she feels anything for you." His niece wasn't being patronizing, though she had every right to be.

He had considered that, often in the early hours of the morning while he stared at the ceiling above his bunk. He had fallen in love with Jo. Her attempt at holding herself together and trying to soldier on had only deepened his affection for her. "I don't believe she does."

"I honestly don't know. I know she trusts you implicitly." A shadow of a thought flitted across her face.

"But?"

"I'm just worried about how she's coping."

"She's finding a new normal. Slowly." He was, himself, part of Jo's new normal, but he had no idea if it was a welcome part.

"She is, but I'm not sure she's chosen the best way to go about it."

"Ah. … I don't think I want to know."

"Probably not, but maybe she would talk to you about it. When I bring it up, she rolls her eyes and throws things at me." Vesna sat her empty cup on the table in front of them.

"She's being violent?" Jo could be testy and often threatened to kick people in the shins, but he'd never actually seen her hit another person.

"I don't think tossing a tea towel at my head counts as being violent."

He laughed. "That sounds more like Jo."

"It does." His niece wasn't laughing.

"That's not why you're worried about her."

"It isn't. She's in this reckless abandon mode, like she was when I met her." She shook her head. "I think she's forgiven Rok, but he isn't around to talk her down. Or keep her occupied."

"I don't think he feels responsible for her unless she's in real danger." Rok, Jo's longtime, Long-Lived friend with benefits was not his favorite person. It was pure jealousy, which shamed him, but he was still relieved the man had been in the wind for the past few months.

"You don't think picking up different people every other night at Niko's gallery in Metelkova is dangerous?" She looked like she could shake him.

"I got the impression Jo could handle herself where ... that's concerned." His skin crawled at the thought of her with random men, or women. The ones he knew about were bad enough.

"Not physically dangerous. She's not dealing with everything that happened. She's using sex, like she always does, to avoid having to face her own feelings — about anything." Vesna flung herself back against the couch.

"Then you should be happy she is up in the mountains alone." He was beginning to warm up to the idea himself.

"Not really. It's just another way to get away from what's going on here."

"So what is going on here?" His niece's concern was overblown. Jo spending time alone to heal and grieve, to do what she wouldn't let herself do around all of them, had to be a good thing.

"I wish I understood all of it. Faron is being secretive. His aura has changed, but I can't describe what's different. I figured it was just the shock of everything that happened and taking on some responsibility in his relationship with Ivanka."

Leo nodded. "That would change him."

"It's more than that. I can't explain it." She shook her head again, like she could shake the words she needed loose. "And I think Jo needs to get rid of Helena. That is not a healthy relationship."

"Do I sense a touch of jealousy?"

"Good grief, no. But Helena badgers her about getting together with Matjaž. It's probably why Jo is sleeping with half of Ljubljana."

He shuddered more than he would have liked at her words.

"And you're asking me if *I'm* jealous? You do realize even if Jo is interested in you, she isn't going to stop being who she is? If you can't accept that, you should go back to your closet and pray about it."

He had thought and prayed and gritted his teeth about it. He wanted to believe he had more control over his emotions. He did in most areas of his life, but not now and not where Jo was concerned. "You're right."

"Wait. Can you say that again? It's so seldom you admit it."

"*I'm* going to chuck a tea towel at you."

Vesna snickered, then looked at him with what Jo described as her "serious mom" face. "You should go see her in the mountains. Just go check on her. We'll both feel better."

"Didn't she specifically say she didn't want anyone to go up there?"

"She did, but she didn't mean it."

He frowned at her. "You've known her much longer, but I've gotten the distinct impression she says exactly what she means. Besides, there are storms forecast for the week. The roads will be terrible."

"See. An even better reason to go check on her. What if her electricity is out and she runs out of wood?"

"Didn't Gregor take her up there with a year's supply of everything? I was here when they left, remember?"

His niece huffed at him. "I think you should go. I just have a bad feeling about her being up there alone."

He wanted to go. Alone with her on a mountain in a snowstorm might be his best chance to tell her he loved her. "Yes, but you have to pay for a rental car. One that can get through the snow."

———

Lichtenberg caught him on the stairs. Leo was more at ease with him than he had been in the past, but every encounter gave the officious man an opportunity to piss him off again.

"Leo. One of the people I most wanted to find today."

Leo nodded a greeting in return.

"I have need to speak with Ms. Wiley. Do you know when she will return from her trip? She was very vague with me about her plans."

"She said she didn't think it would be longer than a month."

"A month? This cannot wait. I will call her. Thank you." Lichtenberg started up the stairs on the way to his apartment.

"You won't have much luck. Vesna said her phone goes straight to voicemail. She thinks she's turned it off so no one can get through."

"That is a very bad idea. What if she is in danger?" His expression hovered between genuine concern and deliberate manipulation.

"Gustaf, she has Helena if she needs anything. She's fine. I'm sure whatever you need to speak to her about can wait a few days."

"A few days, maybe, but not weeks." He stroked his beard.

"Why is it so important that you speak with her?" Lichtenberg being vague was never a good sign.

"Dušan Črnigad is in town."

That was part of it, but Gustaf was holding something back. He always did. "Faron is an adult. I'm sure Jo won't be happy Črnigad is here, but she'd hardly come rushing down from the mountains to see him."

"Wouldn't she?"

The man's smugness was infuriating. Jo had loved Dušan. She had told Leo that much, and he suspected the wound was deeper than she would ever admit to herself, let alone him. But that Lichtenberg thought to use the man's presence as a pry bar on him was delusional. "I don't know, Gustaf. I need to be on my way." He hurried down the stairs away from the little gray Austrian. He could feel his stare on his back until he turned on the landing.

He'd intended to pop into the teashop to say hello to Ivanka and Frédéric, but he didn't want to spend any more time in Lichtenberg's vicinity.

———

Gustaf watched the priest scurry down the stairs. The red tendrils of his aura drifted behind him and turned the corner a second after he did. An outsized aura for an outsized man. He didn't need to be able to see auras to know the man was in love and trying with everything he had to fight it. Leo Kos would never be the man he would choose for Jolene Wiley, but Leo's feelings for her made him easier to manipulate.

At the moment, Gustaf had bigger concerns than a lovesick priest. As dangerous as he had believed Ms. Wiley's unexpected and untrained powers to be, her son's were a more pressing issue. Gustaf had suspected Faron would have some supernatural gift after Jo had relayed the story of her affair with Dušan Črnigad to him. Gustaf had not told her then who or what Črnigad was. The Necromancer had taken advantage of her, and it only added to Gustaf's distaste for the man.

Črnigad had the Board at his disposal, and someone had informed him his former paramour might be of more interest to him now. But Faron Wiley and his ability were a much greater prize for a man with Črnigad's powers than a Voice could ever be. He needed to tell Ms. Wiley about Črnigad before he got to her or convinced Faron to reveal the secret he was still hiding.

CHAPTER 5

Henry traced the edge of the tattoo at the base of Jo's sternum. A solar eclipse, a solid black circle edged in white with coronal flames in orange and red. One flame, a solar flare, extended to her navel. Under his fingertip he could feel the beading of a circular scar covered by the dark moon of the eclipse.

She didn't speak and closed her eyes as he worked his way around the tattoo.

"You have a scar." He kissed a flame tip.

"Many." She sighed and arched her back.

He had noticed the three silvered lines under her left eye when they stood outside in natural light. The marks disappeared in the dim interior of the farmhouse. The scent of her skin reminded him of bakeries in a long-ago place and a feeling he couldn't find a word for. "This one is different from the others."

"An old god possessed me to save the world, or something like that." She said it as if it were nothing. As if it were the same as "I took a walk this morning."

He kissed the center of the moon. "It must have been painful."

She opened her eyes and raised her head to look at him. "The tattoo?"

"No. The god."

"Not like you mean." She closed her eyes again.

He kissed his way up her body, moved his lips over the tattoo again, between her breasts and up to the place where her jawline met her ear. "What do you want, Jo?" He kissed again, feather-light.

She arched her back, straining against him. "I want to forget."

She said it so softly, he almost missed it. He pushed himself into her, expecting to feel alive again. He expected the rush of power a woman's contented sigh conferred. He felt instead how alive she was. As he moved against her, as she opened herself to him, a silver fire enveloped him. He didn't know what she was, but he understood then what she could do.

He paused inside her. She opened her eyes. An exquisite anguish washed over her face as he crashed into her, hungrier, angrier.

She pushed him over and onto his back. "Not so quickly."

He closed his eyes again and thought only of being at the center of her and she of him.

Beyond the shimmering flames was a door. If he walked through it, he would walk back into life. He would live again in the world that had grown so foreign to him. He could mourn the dead in the mountains, release each of them, and himself, into the hereafter. He also knew to do so would consume the fire. For him to live, this woman would have to die.

Her eyes flew open and she stopped moving, terrified. She scrambled off him and out of the bed, pulling the duvet with her to cover herself.

———

"Go." Jo pointed at the door.

"It isn't what I want from you." He stood. Still naked. Where the fuck had his clothes gone?

"I don't care. Just go. I need to be alone." Her whole body was shaking with anger and something like shame, but sinister and more twisted even than that.

It was dark, but the moon reflecting on the snow outside filled the room with pale blue light. Henry's skin glowed in it, making him look more like the ghost he was than he had at any point up to that moment. He sat on the edge of the bed.

"I will go. If that's what you want."

Did she want him to go? Her head felt like it was full of cotton. Indecisiveness wasn't usually an issue for her. "Fuck. I don't know. Go sit on the couch and give me a minute."

He disappeared. She stood with the bedclothes wrapped around her. What the fuck was going on? She was still aroused and still wanted him. The thought was a gut punch; her own body was betraying her.

She threw the comforter on the bed and found a robe to wrap around herself. She grabbed a pair of thick socks and walked into the living room.

Henry sat on the end of the couch fully dressed. He was perched like a schoolboy who knew he was going to be scolded. No one needed to be scolded but her. She sat as far away from him on the couch as she could and pulled her socks on.

He turned to her. "Why didn't the god stay?"

"I don't know. It didn't feel like he wanted to." She didn't add the god had wanted her to go with him instead.

"Are you afraid of me now?"

"Shouldn't I be?" She should be, and yet she wasn't.

He didn't answer her. "What are you, truly?"

"I told you. *Vox de Mortuis,* a Voice of the Dead."

"But what does it mean?"

She repeated the line she used when she encountered new dead people who didn't know what to do with her. "I can talk to dead people, and the dead can speak through me. In my presence shades are corporeal and can interact with the physical world."

"How many shades have you 'interacted' with?" She felt him smile in the darkness.

"Only you."

"Did you know?"

"I did not. Gustaf left that factoid out of our lessons. I knew I could be a Portal for gods and demons, and even for shades, but not like … that. What did you see?"

"A door. And I knew. I've spent years waiting for a door to open. But I knew I'd have to walk through you, and you would die."

"Why didn't you?"

"Why didn't I commit murder?" He laughed. "That was not the door I've been waiting for."

———

Jo wrapped herself in a flannel robe. The sun was almost as high as it was going to get, and she was hungry. And besides, hiding in bed all day wasn't going to solve any of her problems. She poked the coals of the fire and put a couple more logs on to warm up the griddle plate.

Caffeine. Protein. Carbs.

She took half a dozen eggs out of the basket on the counter and cracked them into a blue earthenware bowl she'd found in one of the cupboards. She broke the yolk of the last egg with the tip of her whisk. How had she gotten back to the exact place she said she didn't want to be? Henry wasn't alive, but his presence put paid to her idea she really wanted to be alone. She had invited a shade into her carefully warded lair and tried to fuck his brains out. She liked to think she was smarter than that.

Before Helena died, before everything was turned completely upside down, she had cherished her solitude and the ability to pierce it at her own will. Her son was grown and lived on his own with friends. She could come and go as she pleased, eat when she wanted to, and sleep alone or not as the mood struck her. Now with Helena on the prowl, her time never felt like her own. She was at work or went to Niko's hoping the crush of people drinking and talking around her would keep everything else at bay. She rarely left alone. Niko teased her about using his gallery as a poaching ground and using sex like some people use alcohol. Vesna had tried to call her on it, too, and she'd brushed her off.

Henry startled her with his cold hands on her hips. He brushed her hair aside and kissed her neck. "Good morning."

"Good morning." She sidled away from him and got the coffee started. "Sorry, I'm not much good as company before I've had coffee."

"What's for breakfast?"

"Herb omelettes, toast, cheese, fruit."

"Do you make breakfast like this for all your guests?" He leaned against the counter and watched her.

He was fully dressed, even shoes. She had never figured out where his clothes had gone the night before. There was a lot to this dead whisperer business she would never understand. Like had he actually slept when she'd banished him from her bedroom? And where did the food go? Whether or not ghosts could shit was probably not a topic to ponder before breakfast.

When everything was ready, she made plates for them both and set them on the table.

"Milk?" She held a cup out to him. "Sugar?"

"Black."

She tipped warm milk into her cup and carried them both to the table.

Maybe Henry was her door, her way out. No. She'd been offered that before. She wasn't ready to slip into whatever the Next held. She needed to keep telling herself that.

"You don't seem like the type of woman who waits on a man."

She laughed. "Is that what you think is going on here?"

"Isn't it?"

"No. I was hungry and wanted breakfast. It would be rude not to make you some, too." She spread butter across her toast and took a bite.

"So I shouldn't get used to the effort?" He took a bite of omelette.

"You are dead, and eventually I am going home. There's nothing here to get used to." She waited to see if he was insulted.

"Then I will just have to enjoy the moment."

She nodded her head. "Me, too."

They finished breakfast in companionable silence. She piled the dishes, except for their coffee cups, in the sink. He followed her like a puppy but at a respectful distance, until she turned back to the bedroom to get dressed. He stopped her and put his hands on either side of her face.

"I don't know what to make of you."

"Your hands are very cold."

He stepped away from her, dropping his arms back to his sides. "Jo. It's such a funny name for a woman."

"I didn't mean to offend you."

"You didn't. I have almost forgotten that despite enjoying your excellent breakfast, I am not here."

"You are here. And it's short for Jolene." His presence made her shiver, in both ways.

"Jolene?"

"Yes. From a song."

"I don't think I know that song."

"What year did you die?" She touched the thickly cabled cotton sweater he wore. She still couldn't remember when he had gotten undressed, and it bothered her. She hadn't had that much wine.

"Nineteen sixty-something."

"It was after your time then. Dolly Parton wrote it. It came out the year I was born. My mother loved the sound of it, the name."

"It sounds nicer than Jo."

"Hmm. It wouldn't if you'd had it sung at you by every jerky boy you went to school with in the worst-possible, off-key way. Trust me."

"What's the song about? What does Jolene do that would make boys mock you with it? Not that young boys need much reason to mock."

"In the song, the singer is begging Jolene, who's this fiery redhead everyone is in love with, not to steal her man." She picked up a hank of her hair: "Not a redhead. And until college, I wasn't really interested in men." Or anyone.

"I think I see why you prefer Jo."

"Yes. Henry, whose real name I do not know, sometimes it's best to choose our own names."

He picked up the same piece of hair. "You would make a

good redhead, though."

"I'll have to take your word for it." She wrapped her hair into a bun and secured it with the elastic she had on her wrist. "I need to wash up. Anything in particular you'd like to do today?" She wanted a hot shower, but the power outage ruined that plan.

"I'm the guest here. What do you usually do?"

"Go for a walk and then sketch for awhile."

"I can do that. Would you make a sketch of me?"

"I'd like that."

———

They walked next to each other in the snowy woods near the farm. They had been too busy to pay much attention to the storm, but the fresh snow was a few inches deep. The sky held more. Outside he was more like a live person, as he and the air were closer to the same temperature. It was still strange to see only one cloud of breath when they spoke.

"When will you go home?" He looked off ahead through the trees.

"When I feel like I'm ready. The tattoo, the scar. The wounds inside have not been so quick to heal." It was good to have someone so far removed from everything to talk to. What did she care if he judged her? "I haven't been very good about not reopening them over and over again, either. The scar is going to be much worse."

"What happened to you?"

She told him the whole story, from Helena's murder and her realizing she could speak with and for the dead, to recovering at Gregor's house and finally escaping to the mountains to figure everything out. She skipped over the worst parts. She hadn't been able to describe it to anyone after that first day she'd woken up battered, in an unfamiliar room, at her friend's house. She left out the devastated faces of her friends. She omitted the horror of what had happened to her father's shade. There would be no Next for him.

"There's more isn't there?"

She stopped. "I can't talk about it. If I think about it too much, I'm there again. I don't want to go back."

"Shell shock. You have nightmares."

"Yes. When I'm alone."

"I never put much stock in all that Freud and Jung stuff, but I can tell you what I've learned in these mountains since I died."

She waited for him to finish.

"Whatever you don't deal with is what you are left with."

"And what are you left with, Henry?" She took his cold, gloveless hand in her mittened one.

"The faces of the dead whom no one named or claimed. I never actually came here in the war. I was near here, and I wrote about it. Writing exactly what I had seen was hard, like you said. And now I am here, and this is my own hell."

"I don't think I believe in hell. At least not one that we don't make ourselves."

"I made this one, then. I suggest you not do the same."

She took a deep breath. "When I was trying to find Faron, I went to Tomaž and Katarina's house. The demon had already gone. It ..."

"Maybe you should sit down. We can go back to the house."

"No. If I stop ..." She took a deep breath and looked off at the snow-covered mountain tops. She couldn't face another person and tell them what she'd done. Even a dead one. "The kitchen was like something from a horror movie. Two of their daughters were there. Veronika, the older one, had blood spattered on her face, like big red freckles, and she was too horrified to speak. She and Ana clung to me, and I couldn't do anything to help them. I took them to a neighbor and ran to the museum to save Faron. I left them. Mute and blood-splattered."

He took her by the shoulders and turned her to face him. "Is that the thing you are so ashamed of? You took them somewhere safe, and then you saved your son from some unspeakable thing."

Jo couldn't find any other words. It was close enough to touch but felt like it had happened to someone else decades ago.

"Jo." He pulled her into a hug, his arms around her were warm for a brief moment, like her father's had been when he'd hugged her by the river. "You can't save everyone."

She sobbed against him. Her tears stung her face in the cold. She didn't deserve the catharsis of letting go, and definitely not whatever absolution Henry was offering her. Still, it was good to not try to hold everything that had happened because of her inside of her, however briefly.

She stepped back and rubbed her arms. "Thank you."

"It's the least I could do. Breakfast was very good."

She laughed. "No really. Thank you for listening."

"You aren't cured. These things take time. I know this."

"We should head back. I'm cold." It took her longer to feel chilled, but when the cold finally got to her, it settled around her heart.

"Your face is pink."

"Thanks." She checked him with her hip.

"It suits you."

They walked out of the woods near the farmhouse. A black, all-terrain vehicle hulked in the driveway.

"Expecting someone?"

CHAPTER 6

"I don't care if he is your father." Ivanka shoved her pajamas into the laundry bag and turned on Faron. Her face was flushed. "You shouldn't trust him. Why now? Why is he here?"

"I don't know." He pulled a sweater over his head. "But you're late for work, and I need to get to class."

"You just don't want to have this conversation right now. I cannot believe you told him. And Gustaf! What a jerk. Has he been in contact with your dad this whole time?"

"I don't know. I don't want you to lose your job. Mom wouldn't fire you for being late all the time, but Vesna will."

She pulled leggings on and finished getting dressed without another word. She didn't need to say anything. Her anger rolled off her in waves as she shoved her arms into her coat. "Let's go."

Tension crackled between them on the silent walk to the teahouse. He knew she was right. He shouldn't trust Dušan, but he also didn't want to be in the dark about why he was there.

They turned into the courtyard. Vesna, Fred, Goran, and Gregor were all wrapped in their coats and standing on the cobbles in front of the shop staring at bright-red letters spray-painted across the front window. *"Bela Europa"* and "Go back to Afrika" screamed out from the glass and black-painted wood. The pots Fred and his mom grew herbs in were turned over and broken, and it looked like someone had punched the glass in the front door.

Vesna turned to greet them. "Good morning. Or at least it was."

"What the hell?" Who would scrawl such bullshit on his mom's shop?

Ivanka reached out for Fred's hand. "I am so sorry. We'll scrub it off right now."

Fred nodded. He didn't look angry, which was sobering.

"We have to wait for the police to get here so they can take pictures." Gregor had his phone in his hand and tapped out a reply to a message.

"How long will they be? This shouldn't be here a second longer than it has to be." Ivanka's voice got higher as she got angrier.

Faron took out his phone and took a picture. He sent it and a message to a few of the Zombie Church members.

The replies came back immediately. "On my way."

"Bringing razor blades and paint."

"Fuck that noise. Tell your mom we'll take care of it."

Faron was glad she wasn't there. The last thing she needed was to feel like she and her friends weren't safe. From the living.

"I'm going to go get started on prep." Fred dropped Ivanka's hand.

"We can't open today. This is threatening." Ivanka looked at Faron and then back to Fred, like Faron was going to tell Fred what to do.

Fred stepped over the broken glass and opened the door. "We open. They don't get to tell me where to live, and they sure as hell don't close us down, even for a day."

Vesna and Gregor nodded. Ivanka and Gregor followed Fred into the shop.

"You should go to class. We've got this." Vesna took Faron's hand.

"Are you going to call Mom?"

"Not yet. Her phone's turned off, anyway." She shrugged, but it was clear she was worried, too.

"She'll be pissed if you don't tell her."

"I will. When she gets back." She said it with finality.

He hiked his backpack up on his shoulder. "Call me if anything else happens."

She nodded.

As he turned to go, Goran stopped him. "It's none of my business, but you should be wary of Dušan Črnigad."

Faron nodded. "I know." He turned and walked through the arched doorway back out onto Zajčeva and headed toward class. No one needed to warn him about a man who had never bothered to show up before.

His mom had enough crap on her plate, but he really needed to talk to her. She couldn't stay up there forever, right? If she knew about the graffiti, she'd be back to town in a heartbeat. Fuckers. Fred had been in Slovenia since before Faron had been born.

His phone buzzed in his pocket.

"Are you still there?" Marko was on his way to the shop and would gather up some others from the Trans-Universal Zombie Church of the Blissful Ringing. They usually protested corruption in the government and were working on opening a pro bono clinic, but cleaning up racist garbage, especially for friends, was right up their alley.

"No, I've got class. Ivanka's there." Faron hiked his backpack up, redistributing the weight of the books and computer wedged in it.

"Picking up some paint brushes. Bastards."

He slipped his phone back into his pocket and walked into the Faculty of Arts building. It was going to be hard to focus on the history of the southern Slavs this morning. Maybe the lecture would be short and he could skip his lit class in the afternoon and go back to the teahouse.

———

Vesna wanted to call Jo, but her friend's phone was still going straight to voice message. Vesna called her uncle instead.

"Are you going to go or not?"

"Good morning to you, too, Vesna."

"Sorry. Can you come to the shop? I think we could use

some spiritual advice this morning." Her uncle's gentle reproach rankled against her ungentle mood.

"That doesn't sound like you. What happened?" His concern drifted through the connection, as diaphanous as his aura.

"You'll see when you get here." She tapped the screen to hang up. She had hoped he wouldn't answer because he was already on his way to see Jo.

Gregor knocked on the frame of the office door. "The police are here."

She nodded and shuffled some random papers together on the desk. The police weren't going to be able to do much, take some pictures and add it to the list of hateful graffiti she'd seen around town. Frédéric was hardly a threat to the hegemonic whiteness of Slovenia, as if that were even a good thing, but nationalism wasn't rational by nature. She followed Gregor out into the shop and grabbed her coat off the hook. Gregor held the door for her while she struggled into the sleeves.

Investigator Marta Klančnik stood with her hand on her hip, watching a uniformed officer take photos of the graffiti and the damage to the door and planters.

"I didn't expect to see you here." Gregor reached out to shake Marta's hand.

"Anything at this address gets forwarded to my desk." She grunted. "Is Lichtenberg around?"

"I haven't seen him this morning, but that isn't unusual." Vesna shook the investigator's hand. Marta had been lead on the investigation into Helena's death and the events that followed. That she was aware of the goings-on behind the Veil had come as a surprise to both Vesna and her Uncle Leo.

Marta nodded. "Do you have CCTV set up?"

Gregor shook his head. "Jo doesn't want it."

"She might change her mind after this." The investigator toed an uprooted rosemary plant on the cobbles.

Vesna laughed. "I doubt it. It's a bit too Big Brother for her."

"Where is she?" Marta looked up and glanced from Vesna to Gregor.

"Not here. Up in the mountains for a few weeks."

Marta smirked. "Must be nice to be able to take off for awhile."

Gregor arched his eyebrow at the investigator. "I doubt Jo sees it as nice. The rest of us saw it as necessary."

"Is she up there alone?"

Gregor and Vesna both nodded.

"You think it's a good idea?"

"I think it's what Jo needed, and she's an adult." Gregor bent over and righted one of the unbroken pots, spilling more dirt onto the cobbles.

Marta harrumphed at them. "I take it your chef has already seen this?"

Vesna nodded. "Fred's inside doing the prep."

"You aren't going to close today?" Marta looked both surprised and impressed.

"No. Fred says no. Gregor and I say no."

"I'm finished, Investigator Klančnik." The uniformed officer held out a small digital camera to Marta.

She took it. "Good. I'll take the statements. You can head back."

He looked at her with uncertainty. Vesna guessed it wasn't how things were usually done, but it was already clear most vandalism incidents didn't merit attention from the Homicide and Sexual Offense Division.

"It's okay. You can tell Primož to call me if he has a problem."

"Yes, ma'am." The officer nodded at them all and disappeared through the arched door onto *Zajčeva*.

Marta leveled her gaze at Gregor and Vesna. "Is there anything else going on I should know about?"

"No. I think it's asshole kids or something." Gregor didn't sound as certain as his words indicated.

"Maybe." Marta didn't look or sound reassuring. "We've got photos. You can clean up."

"I'll talk to Jo again about cameras." Vesna already knew how that conversation would go. She could see her friend's lowered "you're kidding, right?" gaze as clearly as if she were standing in front of her.

The investigator shook their hands and left.

Gregor looked at Vesna. "Do you think we need to be worried?"

"Not worried. But cautious."

"Aren't we always."

Gregor still didn't like knowing there was anything beyond

what he could touch and see. Vesna and Jo both attempted to shield him from what they could, but nationalist vandalism was beyond even her best efforts.

"Yes. But this is much more of-the-world. Are you going to hang out here for a few minutes? I need to run a quick errand." Vesna shoved her hands deep into her coat pockets.

"Of course. I think I could use a cup of Frédéric's tea."

She smiled. "It's definitely bracing."

Gregor went back inside, and she crossed the courtyard to Goran's. When she pushed the door open, a chime sounded in the recesses of the antique shop. Goran's salt-and-pepper head poked out from behind a partially opened door that lead to the private area of the store.

"Ah, Vesna, come on back. I was just getting set up."

"Set up for what?" She'd only come to ask if he had a charm or something for the shop.

She walked through the orderly tangle of furniture and home goods to the back of the store. The smell of beeswax from the wood polish and from freshly lit candles mingled at the threshold to the back room.

He closed the door behind her. The back of the shop was a completely different world. Heavy black drapery covered the walls and could be pulled over the door. Standing candelabra filled with long tapers whose flames licked at the darkness ringed the room. Goran's altar was centered inside a painted circle and pentagram on the floor.

"Would you like to join me? I'm going to do a stronger protection spell for the building. Jo's wards are pretty good for a novice, but they are only against malevolent spirits —

not malevolent people."

Vesna nodded. "Good idea. But I wouldn't know where to start. It's not my thing."

"I'll walk you through what you need to do. You live here, too, and adding your energy will strengthen the wards."

"I guess." It wasn't the strangest thing she'd been asked to do.

He fanned incense smoke over her and had her step inside the circle on the floor. He invited his ancestors and the elements of the cardinal directions to join and protect them as he lit candles clockwise around the circle at the points of the star. He chanted as he poured a thin line of Piran salt over the painted circle and took her hand when he finished.

"Here we go, dear. Nothing to worry about."

———

Vesna blinked against the dull winter light when she walked back into the courtyard. Her arms and face were still tingling from whatever energy Goran had called up in his circle. He followed her out onto the cobbles with a hooked stick and a string of brass bells on a red cord.

Ivanka and friends of hers and Faron's from the Zombie Church were using razor blades to scrape spray paint off the windows. Two other Tuesday night regulars, Marko and Aleš, were replanting what was left of the winter herbs that had been scattered on the cobbles into new pots.

She watched as Goran hung the bells over the arched doorway on an iron hook embedded in the stonework. She'd never noticed it there before.

He dusted his hands when he'd finished and whispered to her. "That should keep the bastards out."

"I hope you're right. Should Jo continue to do her thing for the bad spirits?"

"It can't hurt. The wards will only strengthen each other. You should eat something to ground you." Goran waved and disappeared back into his shop.

Vesna thanked the Zombie Church folks for helping and asked them in for tea and lunch when they finished what they could do. One of them had taken out the broken pane of glass in the front door and replaced it with a piece of plywood.

Leo was camped at a table with Gregor at the back of the teashop. She hung her coat on one of the hooks by the door and joined them.

Fred must've heard the bells strike the wood when she'd come in and stepped out of the kitchen. "Would you like some tea?"

"Thanks, I can get it myself." She stood back up and walked to the orderly tea station. Jo had been insistent on keeping it stocked and arranged in a way that made it easy to have multiple pots brewing and have access to all the teas, not only the brews for the day. Vesna's heart stung at how little she'd been able to help her friend arrange her life back into some orderly fashion. At least she'd introduced her to Leo, but maybe that was its own complication. She'd watched Jo's aura swirl out and back around her uncle when they spoke. It had been unlikely her friend would let herself fall for someone before, now it seemed impossible.

"Fred, do you need some help?" She watched as he stirred the day's soup. The smell of cumin and turmeric filled the small kitchen.

"Everything is in the oven or needs to be prepped closer to opening. Ivanka will finish the sandwiches when she's done out front." He wiped his hands on the towel he kept tucked into the top of his apron.

"I'm really sorry this happened."

He nodded. "But not surprised. I've seen the other graffiti. I am angry the shop got vandalized, though."

"That can be fixed. Goran put ... Goran said to let him know if you need anything."

"Is Faron coming back to wash dishes tonight?"

"As far as I know. Why?"

"Worried about him. Having your father show up unannounced ..." He pursed his lips.

"I think he has his head screwed on pretty straight. He's unlikely to be dazzled by Dušan after being ignored by him for his whole life."

"I hope you're right."

"Me, too." She poured the last of Fred's builders' special into a clean cup and walked back to the table.

Her uncle looked up at her. The turmoil in his aura was reflected in the dark circles under his eyes. He had fallen hard for Jo, just as she predicted he would. She wished she could be wrong about these things.

"So, I think we need to tell Fred what's going on with Jo and the neighborhood he works in. I nearly spilled the beans about Goran."

"Goran?" Gregor looked at her, his eyebrow arched.

"Yeah. About Goran." She flicked some lint off her pants. "He's a witch."

Gregor continued to look at her, both eyebrows now closer to his hairline. "Jesus, is there anything in this town that isn't supernatural?"

"A few things." Leo took a sip of his tea.

"Like white supremacists who trash shops because brown people work there?" She wasn't smiling.

"Yes. That is something to be concerned about." Gregor set his cup back on the saucer.

"Well, doubly so. The new girl starts Monday, and she's Romani. Goran put improved wards on the building. He said Jo's were only for ghosts, but his were for malevolent people." Vesna looked down into her tea but had no desire to see if it held any of their fortunes.

Gregor laughed. "Maybe that will keep Dušan out. I can't believe he was brave enough to show up here."

"You shouldn't be surprised. Dušan pretty much does whatever the hell he wants." Vesna had been witness to that from the beginning of his relationship with her friend.

Gregor sighed. "True."

Leo looked at both of them. "So who is going to tell Fred?"

"Tell Fred what?" Fred stood behind Gregor with a plate of scones. He set them on the table. "I thought you all might want something with your tea."

Leo took a scone and set it on the edge of his saucer. "You might want to go get your cup. This is going to be a long story."

Frédéric looked at all of them in astonishment and swore in French and then Arabic for good measure. "Is there a reason you waited this long to tell me? And did you honestly think I didn't know anything was going on?"

Vesna took a sip of tea. She'd never seen their Algerian friend so upset. "I knew you were observant, and Jo is a poor actress and a worse liar. She wasn't ready for everyone to know she was a 'freak.' Her word."

Fred laughed. "I work in a den of *alsahara*. It explains a lot." He stood up.

"Are you angry?" Vesna watched his face and the swirl of color around his crown to see if they matched.

"No. Hurt perhaps, if Jo and you felt you could not trust me."

"It wasn't about trust."

Fred nodded. "Since we are all sharing, you must know that Dušan Črnigad is also *sahira*." He walked back to the kitchen.

Vesna looked at Leo. "Did you know this?"

"I have never met the man." Her uncle looked uncomfortable at the mention of the name.

She put her head in her hands. "I've met him, several times. The first time was a million years ago at ŠKUC."

"Could you not tell anything about him from his aura?" There was an accusation in Leo's question. She had failed to protect Jo from Dušan, whatever he was.

"I was very drunk, and he and Jo were talking and standing so close together that their auras were all entwined. I thought it was just lust." Dušan's intellectual bad-boy routine had been like catnip for Jo.

Gregor patted her hand. "This is insane. You can't possibly blame yourself for Dušan, and without him, we wouldn't have Faron. And you." He turned to give Leo another of his perfectly arched eyebrow glares. "Surely you've figured out by now that Jo keeps her own counsel in that arena, and no amount of advice from Vesna or me would have changed anything she did then. Or now." The now was rather pointed.

Leo looked properly chastised. "I didn't mean to imply–"

"You did, but I understand. I have work to do, as does Gregor, I assume." Vesna stood and put her hand on Leo's shoulder. "You have a rental car to pick up."

CHAPTER 7

Jo was pissed. She had told Gregor and Vesna no one should come to the house. The black car was a rental, so it could be anyone, but she suspected Gregor, or maybe Leo. They had both clucked over her like hens the week before she left.

She opened the door expecting one of them to jump at her return. She was the one who jumped.

"Only milk, as I recall." Dušan stood in the small living area holding a cup of coffee out to her, looking almost exactly the same as when he'd walked away from her more than two decades before.

She took the cup and stared at him.

"I thought you would be surprised to see me, but not enough for you to be at a loss for words."

She took a deep breath. "How the fuck did you get here?"

"In the car outside, of course."

"Amusing. How did you know where I was?"

"Does it matter? I am here because we have much to discuss regarding our son."

"Now he's 'our son'? I thought he was just a line item on your monthly expenses." Being in a room with Dušan was like having a bucket of ice water poured down her back. She could barely breathe, but she was not about to give him the satisfaction of seeing how upset she was.

"You should drink that before it cools. Would you like to sit at the table or would you be more comfortable on the couch?"

His calm was infuriating and calculated. Dušan never did anything by half measures, not even being an asshole. He went in full-bore on that. "The table." She'd have a better angle for kicking him.

He started to take the cup from her. "Take your boots off. You'll track snow through the house."

She pulled her arm back and threw the cup at him. He put his hand up, and the cup and the coffee stopped in mid-arc on its way to his face. He turned his hand and flicked his palm toward him and the coffee went back into the cup. He plucked it from the air. "You're angry, but that was unnecessary."

"How dare you let yourself in and patronize me."

He laughed. "Jo, you have not changed. Anger still registers before surprise."

"There's little left to surprise me." At least his intentions had been revealed. He knew what she was. She kicked her boots off and shoved her feet into house shoes. Dušan's boots were lined up against the wall, immaculate next to her snow-caked ones.

"Sit. We do have much to discuss."

She sat and took a sip of the coffee. It was fresh and tasted better than the pot she'd made that morning.

"I brought my own."

She looked up at him over the edge of the mug then set it down. "It is good. Can you read minds, too?"

"Only faces, and yours was always and remains an open book to anyone who can see."

Was she so transparent? "Why are you here?"

"I am here because you and Faron have no idea what is coming for you."

"You mean it isn't sitting across from me smirking like a jackass?"

"I am the least of your troubles. Does that hideous hat actually work? Have you spoken with Helena since you have been here?"

"It isn't 'hideous,' and yes it works. Though–"

"I am not worried about your companion. I do not think he is involved or of much consequence."

"How could–"

"There were two mugs on the table, and there were breakfast dishes for two. You came in alone."

"Now you're Sherlock Holmes, too?" He'd washed the dishes. It was inconvenient when assholes did nice things.

"That does not require much in the way of deduction. You never did like to sleep alone. And clearly you have no problem playing with fire."

Why did she care what he thought? Her face and chest

flushed.

"And you still blush like a schoolgirl."

She kicked him in the shin, not that it did much damage in slippers.

"I hardly deserved that."

"You deserve more than that."

He ignored her pronouncement. "What do you know of Faron's abilities?"

The shock must have registered on her face.

"He has not told you. I thought he might call after we met."

"Wait. What? You saw Faron? You spoke with him?"

"Yes. And I got the distinct impression his next conversation was going to be with you."

"My phone's turned off and in a drawer. I didn't want to talk to anyone."

He laughed. "You seem to have found someone here to talk to."

"That's none of your business."

He grabbed her wrist. "Oh, but it is."

She tried to pull away, and he let go. "How I loved your fire. But I see your stubbornness still prevents you from seeing. Have you figured out what you can do for your ghost lover? Did you fuck him anyway?"

She stood up. "I think you should leave."

"I am not going anywhere until I am finished. Sit down and listen to me." His eyes, his irises, flashed dark.

Fear crept into the back of her throat. She backed away. "What are you?"

He looked up at her. His eyes were completely black with no edge to the space they contained, like looking into the sky on a starless night. "What I am matters not. That I can protect you from what others want from you and Faron is far more important."

She edged back to her seat and sat down farther away from the table. He blinked and looked at her again with familiar green-gold eyes.

"You do not need to fear me, but you need to do as I tell you."

"How am I supposed to trust you?" He had to be a demon. She'd fucked a demon, and Faron was a half-demon baby. What had she done?

"I am not evil, not a demon." He laughed. "Nothing as petty as that."

"Then what?"

"You are not going to let it go, are you?" He stood.

As he stretched to his full height, his clothes changed to a dark shroud cinched with a belt of human bones. His skin blackened and absorbed the light from the room. She looked up into his face; his eyes had gone dark again, but she could see through and into them to the stars beyond their own sky. Snow started to fall inside the house. The griddle plate on the woodstove hissed as each snowflake landed. The world fell out from beneath her. Dušan, or whatever he was, grabbed her hand before she disappeared into the nothingness that engulfed them.

When he touched her, her stomach lurched and bile rose in the back of her throat. She begged him to stop, but no words came out — or if they did, they were lost in the abyss they fell through.

After what felt like hours, they didn't land, but they stopped. He pulled her into him, and his cloak enclosed her so only her face was exposed to the blackness around them.

His voice echoed inside her head, its honeyed tones softer than the words he'd spit at her in the kitchen. "You asked. And I will show you."

The air around her lightened, like her eyes growing accustomed to a darkened room. The landscape was a charcoal sketch of wasteland. Shades, or what she assumed were shades, crowded against them, each touch filling her veins with ice.

"These are the dead who have not passed into the next existence. They faded from the world you know without crossing, because they could not accept death."

"They're being punished?"

"No. They are lost."

"Why are you showing me this?" The thought that souls could exist in nothingness forever brought on a new wave of nausea.

"Because you need to understand. This is how it works. There can be no paradise without a place of sorrow."

"Okay. But what does this have to do with me?"

His hand reached into the pit of her stomach and wrenched the center of her back up through the darkness. She landed back in the chair at the scrubbed table in the farmhouse and vomited into her hands.

Dušan, now dressed in black street clothes and with his perfectly human eyes, waved his hand to clean her up. "Faron can bring people back from the dead. Together, the two of you have a power even I do not possess as the god of darkness."

"Why would we do that? You just said it is against the natural order of things." God of darkness. Could she go back to when she thought she was a demon fucker?

"There are those who believe they are beyond the natural order of things, *Miška*."

"Don't call me that."

"You will always be *Miška* to me." He was standing in front of her and brushed her hair from her face.

Miška, the mouse, the easily cornered. The bile was rising again in her throat. She ran to the toilet and threw up again and again until there was nothing left inside her.

Dušan stood in the doorway and handed her a warm cloth to clean her face.

"I hate you." She stood up. "I loved you so much. Even after you left. Even after I knew you weren't ever coming back and you didn't give a shit about me or Faron. I still loved you, and I spent twenty fucking years trying to drown it." She looked in the mirror, like Henry had done. Had he hated what he saw there as much as she did in that moment? "You used me. You knew what my family was. You knew …" She leaned against the sink. "None of it meant anything to you."

"*Miška*, it meant everything."

"You are a terrible liar, O Lord of Darkness."

He touched her face to turn her to look at him. "I never lied to you. I never promised you anything."

"What is Faron? What did you give him?"

"Your son can raise the dead."

"Like zombies or like me?"

"No."

"No to what?"

"To both. Come, sit back down. Finish your coffee."

———

She barely had the energy to stand to walk him to the door. Every sentence he'd uttered was a new terrible revelation. She wanted him to leave. She wanted to sit alone to figure out what to do next. She'd have to send Henry away.

"*Miška.*" He put both of his warm hands on either side of her face and kissed her chastely, as a goodbye.

She flushed with the embarrassment of wanting more from him. Desire had come out of nowhere up through her chest with the barest touch of his lips against hers. Gods should not have that kind of power.

"There may be time for that later, but are you certain it is what you want?"

She shook her head to clear her thoughts.

"When I leave and your friend returns, do as he asks you, then go back to Ljubljana. You should be with Faron, but you have obligated yourself here."

He put his finger under her chin like he was going to turn her face up to kiss her again.

She stepped back and slapped him with all the force she could muster. "That's for Faron. And for leaving me, whether you lied or not."

He laughed, but his cheek was crimson where she'd struck him. "I probably did deserve that."

"And so much more." She closed the door on him and leaned back against it. The SUV tires crunched against the gravel on the drive. She stood there listening with her eyes closed until he was gone.

The air chilled around her, and she opened her eyes again. Henry stood in front of her. Why did everyone want something from her?

"Are you all right?"

"No. But that is what it is."

He reached out to her, but she put her hand up. "First you need to tell me what it is you want from me."

"I need you to let me go."

"I'm hardly keeping you here. I have no control over the comings and goings of shades."

"No. I need you to help me." The word *help* caught on his tongue like an epithet.

"Apparently that is my lot in this life." She sighed. "What do you need me to do?"

He explained his plan to her. She started to gather her things to go out onto the mountain and begin.

Henry stopped her. "It can wait until tomorrow."

"It can't. I need to go back to Ljubljana."

"You aren't going down the mountain tonight."

She sighed. She wanted to slide right down the door and sit on the cold flags in the entryway, but her butt would get wet.

"What did you have in mind?"

His eyes were heavy-lidded. He put his hands flat on the door on either side of her head and leaned in to kiss her. It was a hungry, open-mouthed kiss that pushed Dušan and his demands to the back of her mind, at least for the moment.

He led her to the small sitting room and sat on the couch, pulling her onto his lap. Her knees dug into the upholstery as she straddled him, and she shivered in the chill air surrounding him and with the cold trace of his hands on the bare skin of her back under her sweater.

"Thank you." He kissed the words into her hair.

She leaned back to look him in the face. "For what?"

"For these hours. For bringing me here."

"I didn't bring you. You showed up in the woods when my hat fell off."

He laughed. "I had seen you before, walking. You pulled me to that place."

She shrugged. "I'm glad you came." She leaned in to kiss him again, but he stopped her.

"That first time you saw me in the woods, you were burying something."

She waited for him to continue. Goran had given her the

spell to call a lost shade to her. The ritual hadn't worked, and telling Henry probably wouldn't break the spell, but dwelling on the whereabouts of a dead ex-lover would produce a very different end to the evening.

"What did you put in that hole?"

She shifted her weight against him. "This is more important at the moment."

He moaned and pulled her to him, covering her mouth with another kiss. "You do keep your secrets, Jo."

She leaned back again and looked at him. "Not so many as you, *Henry*." She stood and offered him her hand.

"Why not here, nearer the fire?"

"Because I'm about to have a couch spring embedded in my kneecap."

He laughed and took her hand. When he stood, face to face, she had to look up at him. He wasn't that much taller than she was, but so close, the few inches were noticeable. His eyes were still soft with hunger, but there was a sadness there, too.

He ran his fingertips over the hair at her temple. "I think I would have loved you."

"I wouldn't have let you."

CHAPTER 8

Picking up a rental car had to be up there with having dental work done and removing splinters on Leo's list of things he'd prefer not to do. He'd prefer not to drive at all, but there wasn't an easy way to get to Tolmin and Jo's remote location without a private car. The agent at the desk clearly hated his job and possibly all of his customers, as well.

"Sir, you have to get the insurance if you are taking the car off-road."

"I am not going off-road. I am going to Tolmin on official paved roads." Losing his cool in public and berating a clerk at a rental car company wouldn't be great PR for the church.

"In winter. You should get the insurance."

Leo sighed. "Where do I sign?"

The clerk pushed the paper back to him after circling a blank at the bottom and two places to initial to indicate that he had read whatever agreement he was offered and would not use the car for illegal purposes or to transport burnt offerings, or whatever nonsense was necessary to procure a vehicle for a mission he was less and less sure he should undertake.

"Thank you." The clerk handed him the keys and walked him out to an Opel estate car parked outside the door.

"Is this the best you have? Nothing with all-wheel drive?"

The man shrugged and handed him the keys.

Leo folded himself into the car and pushed the driver's seat back as far as it would go. His knees were even with the dashboard and wedged on either side of the steering column. The man returned to his counter inside the dusty office as Leo backed out and drove to the edge of the lot.

He sat for a minute at the lip of the street. He could go on to Tolmin and be there about eleven. Jo would be furious. That line between her eyebrows would deepen, and her eyes would darken to a stormier blue than usual as she glared at him. He and Gregor and Vesna had promised not to go to the farmhouse and not to ask when she would return. But too much had happened in the past few days not to make contact, and she hadn't answered her phone no matter how many messages Vesna left.

Lunch. He would stop at the market and put together an indoor picnic as a peace offering. She'd been up there for more than two weeks. Surely she was tired of whatever she'd brought with her. And wine. Maybe a couple of bottles. What if there was a reason for him to not drive back? Maybe it was best not to think on that either. Shakespeare had it so wrong. Frailty wasn't named Woman. It was the weak will of a lovesick man.

He turned left out of the parking lot when the street cleared and headed to the closest market. Wine, cheese, bread, fruit, and, he hoped, with it, forgiveness.

———

Faron didn't want to see Dušan again. The more he thought about his conversation with his father, the more he wished he hadn't told him anything. He should've talked to his mom first. Or to no one. He shouldn't have told Ivanka. If he'd kept his secret, he wouldn't be worried about what plans his father had for him or what danger he may have dragged his girlfriend into.

He stopped in front of Cacao. It was one of his mother's favorite places along the river. She liked to sit outside, even when it was cold, but the day was too wet for outside service. He opened the door to the smell of roasted coffee and burnt sugar. His father sat against the wall at a small table at the front of the shop. A few faces looked up at him but returned quickly to their conversations. A few more heads turned when he sat down with Dušan, and his father's name floated above a couple whispers. People pretended to casually glance at him but looked away when Faron caught them.

If this was what it was like to have a famous father, he was grateful for the anonymous upbringing his mom had given him with her last name. Being teased for being British or American was much easier.

Dušan shook his hand and motioned to the server at the counter.

"*Bela kava, prosim.*" Faron looked up at the server.

As soon as the man walked away, Dušan dug into the conversation. "Have you spoken with your mother?"

"No. I tried to call after I saw you and again when the shop got vandalized but–"

"The teahouse? What happened?"

"Some jerks spray-painted racist garbage on the front and broke the door and some pots." The thought of it made him angry again and worried for Fred. And for Ivanka.

"I would have thought your mother and that witch who owns the antique shop would have put up better protections against such things."

"What?" Goran was a witch?

"The good professor studies things much more interesting than European domestic arts." Dušan scratched his jaw where his beard shadowed the skin.

Since the night Faron had brought a dead mouse back to life at Helena's apartment, nothing was as he thought it had been. His mother was a Voice of the Dead. His girlfriend's parents had been murdered. Now his old neighbor was a witch and his father was whatever dark thing he was. Dealing with white supremacists seemed like the most normal thing he'd done all week.

"Your mother said there was not much left that could surprise her. You must feel the same." Dušan took a sip of his water.

"It's hard to be surprised by much after you find out you're a freak."

"You are not a 'freak,' as you say. What you are and what your mother is and even what I am, is part of nature. It is not a part available to everyone, and the Board has made certain of that for a very long time."

"People used to know about these things?"

"They had their ideas and superstitions. They asked cunning folk for assistance and left offerings for the house elves and whatever else they believed kept the fires burning and the milk from souring. That all changed, and we became fairy stories and legends. Who needs magic when you have industry and technology?"

"Everyone? Look at movies and TV and books. People seem to desperately want all those things to be real. Even the monsters. Even demons and devils."

"No. They want to escape their own boredom and the isolation of modernity. Do not kid yourself that anyone will welcome the weird back into this world with open arms. Even your girlfriend."

He was not going to discuss Ivanka with his father. She was none of his business.

"I saw your mother."

"You went to Tolmin? Jesus, I bet she was pissed." Faron took a sip of the coffee that had appeared at their table.

"Angry. Yes."

"Did you tell her?"

"It is the reason I went to see her."

She would be hurt. She had promised not to keep secrets from him the night they were all sitting out in the cold on lawn chairs at Gregor's. She'd barely been able to walk, she had been so badly beaten trying to save him, but she'd wanted to look at the stars. He had lied by omission then. He'd done the same thing he'd been angry at her for, because he thought he was protecting her, like she had thought she was protecting him. Families were really fucking complicated.

"She is not angry with you. Hurt perhaps, but your mother covers that well."

"She should be angry."

"I think now she is worried." Dušan finished his coffee and raised his hand again to signal the server. "Were you going to tell me about Helena?"

Faron's face flushed hot. "Did Mom tell you?"

"Only what she knew. I believe there is more."

His mother must have trusted Dušan enough to talk with him, and she trusted very few people lately. Maybe it would be better to have it all out in the open.

"She doesn't know about the mouse." He looked down at his hands in his lap and pulled the leather bracelet Ivanka had given him around his wrist.

"Tell me about the mouse." Dušan propped both forearms on the table in front of him and clasped his hands together.

"The last time I was at Helena's, before she was killed, before I stopped going over. Her cat trapped a mouse in the kitchen and gave it a mouse heart attack or something. It wasn't bleeding or anything, but Helena asked me if I'd take it out to the trash before I left. I picked it up by the tail with my bare hand." He looked down at his hands again. They didn't seem like his anymore. "On the way to the door I felt this spark between my fingers and the mouse. It squeaked and jerked out of my hand and ran toward the door."

"What did Helena say?" Dušan leaned in closer as he spoke.

"She laughed. She'd asked me if I'd always been able to wake the dead."

"That is all?"

"Yeah. I thought she was joking or flirting in her weird way. I figured the mouse was stunned or something."

"Did you see Helena after that?"

"No." Dreams didn't count, right? He had stopped going to Helena's when things had gotten more serious with Ivanka, but he couldn't control what his brain did when he was asleep.

"Have you seen her since she died?"

Faron's stomach tightened. "No. I can't do that thing Mom does." It unnerved him that his mother still hung out with Helena. He didn't want to be a topic of conversation between them.

Dušan leaned back against the wall. "You are a better liar than your mother, but not by much."

"I don't want to talk about it anymore."

"What you want factors very little into this. It is almost entirely about what Helena wants from you. I suggest you get over your distaste for me and start being honest. I cannot help you if you are not truthful."

"What are you talking about?"

His father turned the cup in his saucer until the handle faced away from him. He peered into the cappuccino foam rings then picked it up and looked into the bottom. His eyes darkened for a flash of second, and he smiled to himself.

"What did you see in that cup?" Faron's stomach turned

over when his father looked up at him, his eyes completely blackened, even to the edge of the whites.

"Nothing I had not already seen."

"What are you?" Running was probably the smartest thing to do, but giving his father the satisfaction of his fear wasn't going to happen.

"Your mother asked me the same question, and she did not like what I told her. I suggest you think about whether you are ready to know the answer yet or not."

The server approached and asked if they needed anything more. Dušan looked up at him with his usual eyes and shook his head.

Faron put his hand in his pocket to get his wallet, but his father stopped him. "Go. Look after the shop. I suspect your vandals will return."

CHAPTER 9

Jo shivered in the early-morning darkness. The sun took a long time to find its way over the snow-covered mountains and into the bowl of the high valley where she stood in another foot of fresh powder that had fallen the night before. Her breath billowed into a cloud in front of her face. She'd have icicles hanging off her nose if it didn't warm up a little when the sun came up.

Her companion didn't have a cloud of breath floating in front of him. He didn't even have a coat. He had an armful of blankets and a flask of milky coffee to get her through this. She had no idea how this was going to work. She needed to be more careful about the pillow-talk promises she made to shades. She needed to not be indulging in pillow talk with shades.

Henry had uncovered a camp chair in one of the closets at the farmhouse. He dusted off the spider carcasses and set it up for her. She sat down and draped herself with blankets. Still cold. Her feet were warm though. She'd stuck the chemical hand warmers Gregor had tucked in her coat pockets into the calves of her boots.

"Are you ready?" He looked terrified. He knew what was coming better than he'd let on.

She nodded and took off the tam she'd knitted, poorly, with her own hair and the silver thread Jackie had recommended twined into the yarn. She replaced it with a much warmer toboggan and waited. The mountains always hummed with a dull drone when she was outside. With her freak flag of an aura let fly, the drone quickened and pulsed. The souls of thousands of days of war headed her way.

The first shade who appeared fell into the snow ten feet from her chair. Henry opened his notebook and folded it over to expose a clean page. He was going to record the names for her to leave with the museum in town. She was pretty sure the curators would think she was crazy, but she'd promised.

The shade, a teenager by his round, beardless face, stood and stumbled his way to her. His eyes were wide, and his hair was matted to the side of his skull with blood and tissue. He reached out to touch her. It took everything she could muster not to flinch when his dirty fingers gripped her arm.

"*Puoi vedermi.*" His astonishment would have made her smile if the situation had been different.

He'd spoken Italian, but she had no idea what he said.

Henry put his hand on her shoulder. "He says, 'You can see me.'"

She nodded at the young man. "*Come ti chiami?*" Henry taught her the simple Italian for "what's your name?" She knew how to ask in German and Slovene.

"Arturo. Arturo Ballarin."

"Arturo." She touched his face. He wasn't as old as Faron, or he hadn't been when he had died. He'd probably been born before her grandfather. Tears froze in her eyelashes but came anyway.

She felt a door open behind her. She was afraid to turn to look in case it disappeared, but she could see the relief in Arturo's eyes. He looked at her one more time and whispered, "*Grazie.*" He stumbled past her in the deep snow.

The pale light of dawn pulled the snow-topped, blue-gray mountains around them into sharp relief and revealed an international army of mangled and frozen soldiers making their way to her perch on the camp chair. The beauty of the place and the horrors that had been visited on the soldiers were completely incongruous.

Each one needed to touch her to reassure themselves she was real. Some touched her arm, others picked up her hand, a few caressed her face with their frozen fingertips. One older man burdened with a medic's bag kissed either side of her face. She asked their names, and Henry wrote them down. She didn't tell them they could leave, but they knew the way was open for them as soon as she repeated each name — even when she tripped up on the harder Italian ones.

Her cheeks were chapped with wind and the tears that came and went. The bodies of the soldiers as they became corporeal made the air around her even colder. The sun was bright and clear but did little to warm the thin mountain air. She looked into each face, some torn or frostbitten beyond recognition as faces, until the sun made its way across the sky and began to tuck into the western peaks where it met more snow clouds. They would get another storm tonight.

There were many more men making their way to where she sat with Henry as her sentinel. This would take far more time than she had imagined.

"John Wiley." His English was clipped and surprising. He must have come to this place like Henry had, a volunteer in a war that wasn't exactly his.

"John, my name is also Wiley."

"From Hanging Langford. But you're a Yank." His eyes were the same shade of blue as hers and looked out from a gray face ravaged by frostbite.

She nodded. "My people are from Wiltshire, as far as I know."

"Well, thank you, dear cousin. This was more adventure than I'd bargained for." He shook her hand and walked behind her.

She craned her neck up at Henry. "I have to stop. I'm frozen, and I don't think I can take any more today."

He nodded and found her hat so she could switch.

The next man also spoke English, with a heavy Austrian accent. "Are you coming back?"

"Yes. Tomorrow." She'd already promised Henry she would.

"I have waited this long. What is another day?"

She looked up into the shade's long face. "What's your name?"

"It can wait. I will tell the others."

She nodded and put her tam back on. The hum of white noise pitched higher then subsided. Whoever the soldier had been, he'd kept his end of the bargain.

Her knees were stiff. Henry helped her stand and looked down into her face.

"You look exhausted." His broad American accent after all the Italian and German speakers was oddly comforting.

"Thanks."

"And beautiful. I've never seen a face I had so much respect for."

Her words caught in her throat. This thing she could do came with responsibilities. As soon as he'd asked her to help him mourn the lost souls on the mountain, she'd known she had to. Souls didn't disappear into nothing after they'd been here too long, as Leo believed. They went to the horrible place Dušan had dragged her to. He'd said those had been the souls of people who couldn't accept death. If they accepted death, could they leave and move on? Henry cared for these shades of the unmourned in the mountains. She would mourn every one of them if it meant they wouldn't have to meet Dušan.

———

Jo kept one of the blankets and wrapped it around her on the way back to the farmhouse. The wind increased with the advancing storm and whipped up the previous night's accumulation. Henry carried the camp chair, other blankets, and the empty flask. There were advantages to being able to make a shade real; she didn't have to transport all the stuff.

They crested the last small ridge that looked over the farmhouse to find another car marring the drifted snow on the drive. Clearly people had no idea what it meant to leave her alone. Henry walked to the door with her and handed her the gear. He gave her a half-hearted salute.

"I'll see you in the morning. Not as early. It looks like we'll get more snow tonight." What was left of the sunlight had been hidden by heavy storm clouds. He disappeared off to wherever it was he went.

She pushed open the door and stamped her boots on the mat outside, and stamped them again on the mat inside the door. She was caked with snow to her knees. She looked up into Leo's worried face as she unzipped her footgear.

"Where have you been?" He, like his niece, gave good mom face.

But Jo wasn't having it. "'Why are you here?' is a much better question." She finished removing her boots and slid her feet into the fleece slippers that waited beyond the runoff from the melting snow. She hung the blanket on a peg next to her sodden coat.

"Vesna sent me." He watched every move Jo made like she might jump at him.

"She doesn't need to be worried. As you can see, I'm fine."

"You're frozen." He took one of her hands in his and rubbed it between his palms. "Your hands are like ice."

She'd become a shade, if momentarily, or as cold as one. She pulled her hand away. He wasn't going to get off the hook that easily. "Why are you really here? Even Vesna would have difficulty convincing someone to drive up here in this weather."

He stepped back. "I was worried, too."

"I'm still fine." Her words came out more annoyed than angry. There had to be a reason he'd braved the shitty roads in a crappy rental car to get to her. It was shocking he'd made it, even with chains.

"There's news. Dušan–"

"I know. He's been here already." She walked past him into the sitting room. He must have fed the fire because it was warm.

He shut the door to the entry room and followed her. "How did he know where to find you?"

"He's got resources, apparently." She put the kettle on the griddle plate to boil water for tea. She needed something to warm her hands and insides.

Leo nodded. He looked lost as to where to take his story from there. "He talked to Faron."

"I know." What she didn't know was how Faron had taken it all. The faster she completed her task here, the faster she could get to him.

"And the shop. Did he tell you about that?"

She reeled around on him. "What about the shop?"

"Vandals spray-painted racist nonsense on the windows and bashed the planters in."

"Why didn't you call me?" The words sounded stupid as soon as she let them leave her lips.

He glared at her.

"Duly chastened. I'm sorry. Is Fred okay? Has Reka started?"

"Fred's fine. Reka should be there sometime this week, according to Vesna." He sat at the kitchen table; it looked like doll's furniture next to his lanky frame.

She pulled two mugs from the cupboard and plonked a tea bag in each.

"Tea bags? I'm shocked."

"Hey, it's like camping up here." She went to the sitting room and brought the lamp he'd lit to the table. "I guess you figured out pretty quickly the power's out?"

"Yes. The light switch didn't work. That's when I started to worry."

"Wood fire for heat and cooking," she motioned to the cook stove, "and a whole lot of blankets."

"Why were you out in the snow?"

"It's a long story I'm not quite ready to tell." She picked up the whistling kettle and poured boiling water into both cups. "I'm out of milk, but I have brandy or whiskey."

"Whiskey."

She set the bottle on the table and carried the two mugs over. "You know you can't drive back to Ljubljana tonight."

He nodded. "I hadn't anticipated it taking so long to get here."

"You must have been determined."

"And slightly terrified. There were a few moments when I thought I might be going back down the mountain the hard way."

"I'm glad you're safe, even though it was absolutely idiotic for you to drive up here in a fucking Opel."

"Needs must."

She shook her head. "You are full of shit. You've delivered your news, and I still find it hard to believe either of those things warranted you taking your life into your hands."

He pulled the tea bag out and set it on a spoon on the table. "I wanted to see you."

"That couldn't wait a few days?"

"I wanted to see you, alone."

Alone could be problematic. She waited for him to continue.

"I don't know where to start or …" He looked at her again, like he would find direction in her face. "What do you think of me, Jo?"

Now she had an idea where this was headed. "You're my friend, and I trust you." It was true. There was more, but she'd drawn a firm line, even if it was in sand, between her friendship with Leo and any other feelings she had for him. However much she trusted him, however attracted to him she was, he was off-limits.

"Is that all?"

"Isn't it all there can be?" Her tea was suddenly fascinating and a reason not to look up at him again.

"I don't know."

She stood up. "Please don't say anything else. Not right now."

He sank back against the chair.

She didn't want to hurt him. "I need you to be my friend. I need you for my sanity. You know me. I don't do … I can't …"

He nodded. There was a look of defeat about him.

"I am attracted to you. I have been since our conversation at the rectory. But, I'm … and you're–"

"Not supposed to want that? Is that what you were going to say?" There was sarcasm in his voice, but it was wrapped in a deep sadness.

"You said this dead whisperer thing was a duty. Don't you have one, as well?"

"I do. And I have thought of that. But I also–"

"Think of me." There was no judgement in it. The heart wants what it wants and will take the long way 'round if necessary. She'd found that out the hard way. She could stuff her feelings down all she wanted and bury them under strings of one-night stands, but she'd made her own rule about letting her thoughts linger too long on Leo.

"Yes."

She sat back down. "I cannot actively encourage you to leave the church, even if I don't believe like you. I also can't promise you anything if you do. If you leave, it can't be for me."

"And there can be no you unless I leave."

She sighed. Sorry was the wrong thing to say. There was nothing that was the right thing to say.

"So that's why I came. And now you know. And now I can't leave in a sweeping gesture of romantic folly."

"I wouldn't let you leave. Folly is putting it mildly. It would be suicide tonight."

"Would you like to eat, then? I'm starving."

They both laughed, if nervously.

"I have dahl and bread. Afraid I've finished off the rice."

"I brought dinner, though I had planned for it to be lunch." He stood and retrieved a basket from the entryway.

She had planned to spend the evening and night with Henry. She assumed it would be their last. Instead, she and Henry and Leo would all sleep alone.

CHAPTER 10

Goran handed Vesna a small bundle of stained muslin and climbed down from the stepladder. She started to peel back the layers.

"Stop. Don't open that here. We don't know what's in it." Goran took the bundle from her and placed it in a black bag he produced from his pocket. "Let's go downstairs."

She had seen the thing peeking out of the gap above Jo's door where the old transom had been boarded up. It had given her pause, and Goran had pronounced it a hex as soon as he'd seen it.

She followed him down the stairs and into his shop. He headed straight for the back where he had his less-mundane workshop.

"Goran, what do your customers come to you for?"

He turned to look at her as he opened the door at the back of the shop. "What do you think my customers buy?"

"Not antique end tables." She laughed.

"You'd be correct." He pushed the door open. It was brighter than it had been when she had been in last for an impromptu, at least on her part, ritual. Electric lights recessed into the plaster ceiling cast cooler light over the space, and it lost some of the otherworldly feel it had in golden candlelight. Goran walked to the back of the room and opened a door into another space that must have been behind the always-closed accountant's office next door.

"Do you rent the accountant's office, too?"

"No. My storage room is behind it."

She nodded as she followed him in. There was a single bare bulb dangling from the ceiling. It illuminated shelves stuffed with jars and boxes of herbs and stones and things she would rather not know about. A battered work table was crammed into the far corner. Candles lined the wall at the back of it, and a circle was carved into the top.

"If this spell has a spirit attached to it, I'd rather not let it out into the world until I know what it is."

"You can do that? Trap a spirit in a spell?"

"Some witches can. I think it's barbaric to imprison something against its will."

She held her breath. Surely he didn't think it was wrong to imprison demons.

He must have sensed her concern. "Unless it's dangerous. Some things don't belong in this world."

She nodded again.

He placed the bundle in the center of the carved circle and lit the candles with a long match as he mumbled in Latin. He took down a jar from the nearest shelf and scooped out a handful of small black crystals.

"Black salt." He filled the groove of the carved circle with it, ending where he began. "It'll keep whatever is in there inside the circle until I release or destroy it."

She shivered. Who would shove such a dark thing above Jo's door?

He started to unwrap the muslin. Inside was a more tightly bundled package bound with black velvet ribbon. Goran unwound it and laid it next to the muslin inside the circle. The inner package opened under his deliberate movements to reveal a blindfolded, dead sparrow. Under the sparrow, "*kurba,*" which translated to bitch, was printed in neat, square letters in what looked like red lipstick. Goran brushed his fingertips over the sparrow's face, and a glowing ball no bigger than a spark from a fire hovered above the workbench and bounced around inside the circle. Goran waved his hand below it, and the ember flew through the door into the back room.

Vesna gasped.

"Sparrows have such small souls." He prodded the fabric the bird had been wrapped in and ran the ribbon between his fingers as if he could read the intention of the spell like Braille in the warp and weft of the velvet.

"What does this do?" It couldn't be anything good. That someone would try to hurt her friend, and kill an innocent bird to do it, was unforgivable.

"It's a complicated curse, and not one I've seen before or heard of. At least not in this way." He bent over the bird and wrappings and sniffed. "Flowers, more than one." He ran his fingers through his short-cropped, salt-and-pepper hair. "Would you hand me that book on the bottom shelf next to you? The green one?" She bent to find the book among a shelf of battered, leather-bound volumes and a few random paperbacks.

He opened it to a page filled with illustrations of southern European birds. A little, brown sparrow like the one on the bench, like the ones as common as leaves along the river, was drawn in careful pen and ink in the right-hand corner of the page. There were markings underneath that looked like words, but not in any alphabet she knew.

He closed the book. "What do you know about sparrows?"

"Not much. I mean they're everywhere here, and Jo has a tattoo of one inside her left wrist."

He looked taken aback. "Do you know why she has it?" "She mentioned one time it was to remind her that if it hadn't been for Gregor she would have been a sparrow. I assumed she meant begging for food along the river like the little birds at cafés."

"Maybe. Prostitutes were once referred to as sparrows. French prostitutes in the 19th century wore black ribbons around their necks."

"Why would someone go to so much trouble to call Jo a whore?"

"She wasn't intended to see this. Whoever put this spell together wasn't calling Jo a whore. They were trying to make her one, or, at the very least, make her careless about who she brought to bed." He pulled two long hairs from around the sparrow's stiff legs. They were dark blonde like Jo's.

"You can't make someone a sex worker. That's not how it works."

"I don't think that was the intent exactly. This wouldn't compel her to do anything, but it would definitely cloud her judgement." He looked concerned.

"Who would do such a thing?"

"Good question. Someone who knows her well enough to procure her hair and unprincipled enough to wrap up and suffocate a live bird." It sounded like he had an idea, but he didn't share. He scooped up the bird and all the fabric and tucked it back into the black muslin bag he had carried it down in. "And familiar enough to be here without raising suspicion."

That was definitely not good. Dušan wasn't the likely hexer. He hadn't seen Jo to get any of her hair. Had her friend broken the heart of one of those idiots she picked up at Niko's? How many witches were in Ljubljana?

"They shouldn't be able to get back in with the new wards in place." He dusted his hands in the air and snuffed out the candles.

"I wish I were more relieved by that thought." She looked at the bag on the table. "What are you going to do with that?"

"Throw it in the river. Running water will dissipate any lingering magic." He pushed the bag into the pocket of his coat. "Are you going to turn me in to your witchfinder uncle?"

"No. He knows you're a witch. He couldn't care less. You aren't slinging curses and sacrificing goats. You're not, right? Sacrificing goats, I mean?"

He stared at her. "You aren't serious?"

A self-conscious laugh escaped with her hasty "no."

The bird and all the things it may have set in motion swarmed Vesna's mind as she walked back up to her flat. There was no way Leo was going to make it back tonight. Snow falling in town meant it would be snowing harder in the mountains. How long did magic last? Would Jo do something she'd regret while he was there? Did it even matter? Maybe they needed to get it over with and out of their systems.

Vesna dragged her stepladder from where she and Goran had left it at Jo's door. She parked it in front of her own door and thoroughly inspected the recesses around the top of the frame and then down each side. She picked up the doormat and shook it out. Something silver flashed and skittered across the flags. She put her foot on it before it went over the edge of the balcony and down into the courtyard.

It was a charm from a child's bracelet, a broken heart with a jagged line down the center. She turned it over. A "V" and an "I" had been scratched into either side and then scratched through with rough Xs. The broken line on the back had red wax caught in the shallow groove. Someone was hell-bent on causing as much commotion in their corner of the city as possible. Maybe the white nationalist crap on the shop was part of the same.

She pulled the stepladder inside and locked the door behind her. She walked straight to the bathroom and flushed the charm down the toilet. She'd fallen too hard for Igor to let some shitty *čarovnica* interfere with her relationship or mess with her friend's head any longer. She looked up at her reflection in the mirror. As much as she distrusted

Lichtenberg and all he stood for, he should know what was going on under his nose. All that power he and the Observers wielded should be good for something. He could at least give her a list of names.

CHAPTER 11

Jo was standing in a field surrounded by green, rolling hills as far as the eye could see. Stone fences ran in meandering lines, slicing the countryside into clean pieces of emerald-iced sheet cake. The field around her was less idyllic. The bodies of men and horses, torn and run through, lay bleeding at her feet. The stench of death with its fetid bouquet of piss and shit and gore burned her nostrils with each breath. The cheeriness of a bright sun and a blue sky mocked the slaughter around her. She pulled her tam from her head, and the air thrummed like bees in clover. The shock of the dead registered like no other sound. Their cries and moaning resonated in her bones.

The shades of the dead closed in on her, but there was no fear. They came for a kind of absolution. They called their names to her and she echoed them, her voice carrying across the field. The doors opened behind her, one for each broken man. She couldn't see them, but there was a pull in her breastbone — like her heart wanted to follow the bloodied men into whatever lay beyond the door. She knew, as she always did, if she turned to see the opening provided for them, it would disappear. It wasn't meant for her, at least not yet. She wasn't comforted by knowledge of the beyond. Before coming into her abilities, she would never have believed that *knowing* there was life beyond death would be more unsettling than not knowing.

The shades came, some touching her hair or clothes without leaving traces of the blood and viscera that covered them. She was no longer sickened by the sight of them, but she was unable to forget what swords and daggers could do to human flesh. The last man came to her still clutching his sword. He didn't speak. She looked into his face to ask his name. His eyes were black and filled with the faraway stars of a moonless night. The pull inside her chest turned to fear in the pit of her stomach for the first time.

"What is your name, sir?" The words fell out of her mouth and disappeared into the space between them.

"Winifred Wiley."

"That is my name." And she knew he had not come to be mourned.

He raised the sword above her and brought it down where her neck met her shoulder.

———

Jo gasped awake. Her neck was stiff, and her mouth felt like the Russian army had marched through it in stocking feet. Her head was in Leo's lap, and he was sprawled over the end of the couch. His legs splayed out into the living room, and his head lay at an uncomfortable angle on the back of the couch. Two empty bottles sat on the table in front of her with two wine glasses stained red at the very bottom of each bowl. At least they hadn't done anything stupid or irreversible. Her head had been a little clearer since her conversation with Dušan. She wouldn't have trusted herself with Leo and two bottles of wine even a week before.

She sat up, hoping not to disturb her guest. He stirred and shifted, but his eyes didn't open. Maybe he was used to sleeping in uncomfortable places.

She wiped her hand over her face and adjusted the tam, thankful it hadn't fallen off. She needed to get back out with Henry and take advantage of Leo's car to head home. It was still dark outside, but the black of night was already losing to the deep blue of pre-dawn. She stood, knees and ankles popping, and headed to the bedroom to put on cleanish clothes to brave the cold and the ravaged faces of the soldiers up on the mountain.

Henry was sitting on the bed when she got there. "I was trying to figure out how to wake you without waking your guest."

"Thanks for not trying. I'm not ready to explain all this to anyone, especially Leo."

"You lead an interesting life, Jo."

"Interesting is a word." She swapped the previous day's clothes for clean silk long johns and fleece-lined pants. The last image of the dream came back to her. Was Henry the knight sent to take her through the door? "Let's go do this. I have to go home today."

"We aren't going to finish."

"I know." She zipped her sweater up and looked up at him.

He wanted to ask her if she would come back. It was as clear in his face as if he'd said it, but he wouldn't.

"I'll come back as soon as things are settled there." She had to. She had a duty and a purpose now. There was a real reason for this "gift" she'd been given.

He laughed. "I don't think 'settled' will ever apply to you."

"Probably not. But I will come back. I promised you, and I promised those people out there."

He nodded and stood. "Let's go."

There was a light knock at the bedroom door. Leo was awake. She motioned for Henry to go and mouthed, "I'll meet you there," before opening the door.

"Are you okay? I heard you talking to someone."

She nodded. "I'm fine."

"Is Helena here?" He looked past her into the empty room as if he would be able to see her guide.

She shook her head. "I need to go do something, then I'd like to go back to Ljubljana with you."

"What could you possibly need to do up here?"

"Can we talk about it on the way back?" She picked her scarf up off the bed and walked past him to the living room.

"You're going to go out there now? It's freezing."

"I know. I've gotten fairly used to the cold." She didn't tell him why.

"Is that where you were yesterday?"

She nodded and wound the scarf around her head. She crammed the toboggan she'd worn the day before into her coat pocket. She looked at his skeptical face. "Can you trust me on this one thing? I'm not in any danger, I promise."

She had always been a bad liar. That she had become more comfortable with bending the truth wasn't a source of pride. Her aunt told her it was part of the package: You can't lie to your guide, but no one wanted to know everything a Voice knew.

He flung himself on the couch. "I guess. But we'll need all the daylight available to get back to the city."

"I'll be back as soon as I can. I just need to grab a few things when I get back and we can go." She slung the camp chair over her shoulder and grabbed the pile of blankets on the bench and went out before he could say anything else.

Henry stood on the snowy drive. The sky was royal blue behind him with the first traces of pink gold showing between the peaks. He had the strangest look on his face.

"Go to your son. Go do whatever it is you need to do, and then come back when you can."

"But, I promised. I–"

He took her free hand. Every word looked like it hurt him to say it. "The needs of the living are more important than the needs of the dead. We will all be here when you come back."

She shook her head. "You, they … you've all waited so long." What if some of them faded and ended up in that place with Dušan while she was gone?

"And we can wait longer." His face didn't match his words.

"I don't believe you. You aren't hiding the pain on your face."

He closed the distance between them and put his cold

hands on either side of her neck. "I thought I would always wait. I thought the side of that mountain was a hell I built for myself. And now I know it is not. I can wait. You will never forgive me, or yourself, if you don't go now."

She nodded. Maybe Henry wasn't the shade sent to slay her. He ran his hand down her hair, rubbing the strands between his fingers. "Go."

He was gone. Like Helena, like her father, there was no evidence of his departure or that he had been there at all, except that her hair settled back onto her coat. The air wasn't even troubled by his presence, or the sudden lack of it.

She turned to go back inside and gather the few things she needed. Leo stood watching from the window.

———

Leo walked to the window after she closed the door. He couldn't believe she was going to walk off into the snow by herself, for any reason, or that he was going to let her. But she was determined, and he knew her well enough to know arguing was pointless. He debated following her, but a man more than two meters tall in a black cassock didn't blend well into a white landscape.

She stopped near the car. He couldn't hear anything, but it looked as if she'd stopped to talk to someone.

Maybe Helena was there. Or had another spirit joined her at the farmhouse? Her posture changed. She leaned her head back for a moment and then dropped her chin before turning around abruptly and looking into his face.

Jealousy was the first emotion that washed over him, though he had no idea if it was Helena or another spirit. It shamed him more than his aborted attempt to woo her the previous night had. She had told him she was attracted to him, and he had been too much of a coward to act or to say all he truly felt. He was afraid to step out onto the ledge until he knew it was completely safe, but he knew there were never any guarantees in life, not when other people were involved and certainly not with love.

It had been easier to keep his emotions at bay when he had convinced himself it was only lust he felt for her. But they had spent too much time together and shared too much for him to continue pretending. His niece's observations had also pierced his charade.

Jo opened the door. "I'm sorry." Her eyes were wet. "What did you see?"

"Only you. But you were talking with someone, weren't you?"

She nodded. "I'll explain everything on the way back to Ljubljana. Let me get my things, and we can go." She rushed past him, not even taking her snowy boots off.

He'd seen last night that she was different. She was surer than she had been since the night she and her son had almost died. She was more the Jo he had met at the cathedral. The memory of carrying her, injured and unconscious, out to the waiting ambulance haunted him. He sometimes wanted to touch her chest where the horrible burn had been, to see if it had healed. She told him she had gotten a tattoo over the scar, but not of what.

He had a decision to make. If he renounced his vows and left the church, he might have some time with Jo out on the ledge for however long it held their weight. If he was willing to leave for a long shot, he needed to accept he was ready to leave full stop. Though that was a big decision, it wasn't necessarily a soul-shattering one. He had not made his initial decision to join the church with a clear head, and the weight of it had never settled into a comfortable reality. He could continue his work without the church, and his niece would be happier if he gave up the trappings of what she labeled "medieval thinking."

Jo returned. She had a leather bag slung over her shoulder and a flask in her hand. "Let's go." She held the flask up. "Coffee. With a kick. At least one of us is going to need it to get out of here."

He laughed. "I think I'm going to need to be as sharp as possible."

They climbed into the car together and shut their doors in tandem. She pushed her bag onto the seat behind him. "Are you comfortable?"

The seat was back as far as it would go, and his knees were still folded up on either side of the steering wheel. "Not exactly, but I have yet to drive a car that was."

She nodded but didn't say anything as he backed the car into the edge of a drift before getting them pointed in the right direction.

He put both of his gloved hands on the bottom of the wheel and looked down the road. It was only discernible as a flat ribbon of snow between the bumpy snow on either side covering undergrowth and post boxes. "So, tell me about the shade you spoke to outside."

CHAPTER 12

Veronika had begged off going to the teahouse again. She missed her friends but not the smell or sound of the place. Her sister working there with that woman was unforgivable. She pulled her hair into a ponytail on top of her head and wound it into a tight bun. She wanted to get to Avgusta's before the weather got too bad. The rain outside was turning to sleet.

Coat, scarf, and boots and she was out the door onto the quiet street. It looked so much like their old neighborhood, but the differences annoyed her. Her aunt's house was stifling and filled with her stuff for work. It made her resent Ivanka more for choosing to live away from them. Her little sister, Ana, acted unaffected by everything and went on about her life. It wasn't fair. Everything had changed, and she was the only one who seemed to care.

It would take too long to catch the bus to Avgusta's, but she'd have to walk fast to stay warm. The heel had worn down on her left boot, and the plastic popped on the concrete with every step. The wind picked up as she went, and she pulled the collar of her coat up to protect her ears. She wished for a long coat that would cover her butt and more of her legs, but she'd chosen the short one when Olga had taken her shopping. She thought it was more stylish, and her aunt hadn't insisted.

The sky would've matched her mood a month or two ago. Now she was too angry to be sad. Her emotions were more like the tiny ice chips smacking against her face in the wind. She had a plan now. She could make that woman pay for her parents' deaths. If she and Ivanka hadn't started going to that place, if they hadn't met Faron, none of this would have ever happened. If her father and her aunt hadn't known Jo and Gregor, her parents would still be alive, and she wouldn't be wedged into her aunt's life where she didn't belong.

Whatever bad luck that clung to Jo and Faron Wiley had spilled all over Veronika's family and ruined her life. She was grateful Avgusta had helped her see things more clearly and given her the skills to settle the score. Their mutual hatred for Jo Wiley had been a bonding point, though Avgusta's feelings came from an even darker place than hers. Avgusta would barely speak the woman's name. Veronika was grateful for whatever luck led her to the job posting. It had started as a reason to get out of the house more after school, but it had become the thing that had given her anger purpose and direction.

She walked through the courtyard of Avgusta's block of flats. The sleet turned to snow before she made it to the door, which was even with the sidewalk. Avgusta was lucky to have found the apartment; much of Ljubljana wasn't accessible to someone who used a wheelchair. It was why she'd hired Veronika, to run errands and take care of things she couldn't manage.

The errands had taken her into stranger locations and sometimes to places she didn't exactly feel safe. Avgusta had told her not to worry. The people she did business with would never bother someone who worked for her. Veronika didn't doubt her. Avgusta was the kind of person you believed whether you wanted to or not. After Avgusta had sent her to Plave for some herb concoction that smelled of grass clippings and paint stripper, she'd gotten brave enough to ask why she needed all these weird things.

Avgusta had looked at her hard and long enough to make her feel like it had been a mistake to ask. Without a word she'd beckoned Veronika to follow her into the one room in the tidy apartment she'd never been in. When Avgusta opened the door, the smell of snuffed candles and lilies nearly knocked Veronika flat. The wall of scent was more oppressive inside the airless room. Avgusta lit a few candles, revealing walls hung with representations of horned gods and dark-eyed goddesses. A table, she'd learned it was the altar, made from a felled tree was pushed into the center and covered with statues and beeswax candles that had dripped down onto the bases of the silver candle holders like stalactites and stalagmites in Postojna cave.

Avgusta had turned around in her chair, the gold flecks in her eyes glinting in the flickering light. She'd said: "I am a witch, Veronika. Are you going to be able to handle that?" Veronika could recall the sound and steel of Avgusta's voice as if she had just said it to her. It had made the blood in her veins turn to ice with the memory of what happened to her father–

She didn't go back there, not if she could stop herself. Occasionally when she looked in the bathroom mirror, she could see the spots of her father's blood on her face like she'd never tried to scrub them off. She'd backed away from Avgusta and turned to run when the door slammed in her face. Now she was grateful Avgusta had forced her to stay, but that day, that moment, had almost been too much.

———

Veronika knocked on the door, three hard raps, to let Avgusta know it was her before letting herself in with the key she wore around her neck on a leather cord. The front room was dark, but the kitchen light was on and the smell of stew greeted her. Veronika took her boots off at the door and set them on the rack to dry. Avgusta had her clean the tray out regularly. She hated for anyone to bring in dirt from outside; she said it stuck to the rubber on the wheels of her chair and marred the floor.

Veronika stood in the doorway of the kitchen. It was surprisingly large for an apartment, but Avgusta needed the room to maneuver. The counters had been lowered to accommodate her. She'd told Veronika once that her son worked in construction and had customized everything. Veronika had wondered if he'd set up her "work" room, too, but she doubted it. She'd let it slip once that she'd only had to hire someone after her daughter had been killed. It had made Veronika trust her more because Avgusta knew what it meant to have someone ripped away.

"You're late." Avgusta stirred the stew and didn't turn to look at her.

"It's snowing."

"Then you should have left earlier."

Veronika nodded.

"I can't hear you nod." Avgusta turned in her chair and looked at Veronika for the first time.

"I'm sor– Yes. I should have. It won't happen again." Avgusta hated it when she apologized for every mistake and screw-up. She said it made her look weak.

"Good." She wheeled over to the fridge and pulled out a bottle of wine. "Get some bowls. We'll eat first."

Veronika wasn't sure what the plan was. She'd been grateful Avgusta had called to give her a genuine excuse not to go to the teahouse. It was getting harder to stomach being there, and as much as it pissed her off to admit it, it was getting harder to hide things from Ivanka. Avgusta took down two flat bowls and ladled the soup into them. Fat dumplings with soft carrots and pork floated in a rich broth. Veronika's grandmother had made the same soup, and she missed it. She carried the bowls to the table, already set with white napkins and Avgusta's heavy silver flatware. Veronika imagined the older woman living in a grand house before whatever had happened to her.

Veronika poured the wine and waited for Avgusta to start eating before she picked up the hefty spoon and took the first bite.

"The soup is very good. Thank you."

"You'll need the sustenance."

The last time Avgusta had fed her before they worked it had been for the spell with the bird. Veronika's stomach had turned as she'd watched it struggle against its wrappings and then die. She'd thrown up in the street and showered immediately when she'd gotten home to get the smell of incense and death out of her hair. "What are we working on tonight?"

"A summoning. I need to speak with my daughter."

Veronika almost choked on her soup. "You can do that?" Why had she not offered to summon Veronika's mother or father?

The woman nodded and took another sip of wine as if the thing she'd said hadn't opened a hole in the floor beneath Veronika.

She took a deep breath. Avgusta hated it when she was overly emotional. "I didn't know you could do that. Can you call up anyone who's died?"

"Of course not." She didn't even glance up from her soup.

Veronika knew that was the only answer she would get.

"If you need ingredients for workings, you can ask me or you can purchase them yourself."

Veronika's face burned. She hadn't been as careful as she'd imagined.

"Petty charms are beneath your abilities. There is a book with more appropriate workings marked for you by the door."

Veronika nodded and started to get up to retrieve the book.

"Finish eating. You can collect it when you leave."

When they'd finished the meal, she got up to clear the dishes.

"Leave it. You can do that while I speak with my daughter." She turned her chair and rolled toward the workroom.

Veronika followed her, a little resentful she wasn't going to be allowed to meet this ghost or whatever it was. She'd started to buy books with more information than Avgusta seemed willing to share. But Avgusta's attitude seemed to have changed. Still, she'd have to look up summoning the dead when she got back to her stash.

———

"Hey, where's your sister?" Marko looked up into Ivanka's face.

She still had her apron on, and Faron could see the pulse in her neck. She had gotten so thin, even more so in the last few weeks. He wanted to protect her. Maybe the only way to do that was to let her go. Tell her to run.

"Being Veronika and sulking somewhere." She picked up Marko's empty soup bowl. She didn't usually wait tables, but with his mom gone there wasn't anyone else to pick up the slack.

Aleš and Marko laughed, but it was hollow. The story they knew of the Novaks' deaths was a lie the police and Gustaf Lichtenberg had cooked up to hide the truth. It painted them as thieves and worse, and it left Ivanka and her sisters with a legacy that indicated their parents had deserved what had happened to them.

If Veronika was sulky, she had a reason to be. Her life had been turned upside down in the span of one night. Ivanka had a job and another place to live, but Veronika had no choice but to go with their little sister to live with their aunt. He caught Veronika looking at him sometimes. There was something in her gaze that disturbed him, but he couldn't explain it exactly. She avoided him now, avoided all of them.

Ivanka shrugged and walked back to the kitchen, maneuvering between the tables with her arms full of dirty dishes.

Marko bent his head to whisper. "Is Ivanka doing okay?" He'd had a crush on her before she and Faron got together, and Faron was pretty sure he had a thing for Veronika now.

Faron nodded. "As okay as you would expect. A lot happened to her family." A lot had happened to his family, too.

Marko and Aleš both nodded and went back to drinking their tea. Faron stared into his cup. They should get Veronika to come back to the teahouse on Tuesdays. He personally shouldn't be the one, but maybe Marko would be able to convince her. It wasn't good for her to be alone so much, not if her thoughts looked anything like his.

CHAPTER 13

"Would music make this any easier?" Jo turned in her seat to look at Leo when she spoke.

"Maybe. Do you have something on your phone? I think the car has a port somewhere." He wanted her to talk, but she wouldn't until she was ready. He hadn't loosened his grip on the steering wheel since they'd left the farmhouse. There had been a few moments when he'd been certain only his will, or God's, was keeping the car on the road. Jo sipped her doctored coffee and watched the snow-covered landscape's slow parade past their windows. At this rate, they would make it back to Ljubljana sometime next week. Maybe he should have asked her to drive, though he wasn't entirely sure she had a license or even knew how.

She pulled her bag from the back seat and rooted around until she produced a cable. She plugged in her phone and fiddled with the console. He recognized the song but not the singer.

"It's a cover. Nick Cave singing Leonard Cohen." She turned the volume low and settled back in the seat, still watching him.

When he got to the next intersection, the back end of the car fishtailed as he braked. He kept it on the road, or what he thought was the road, but the engine died. The crossroad was more travelled, and snow had been pushed into a mound where the road they were on met it. A snow-covered shrine to the Madonna stood in the corner of the crossroads where they stopped. The faded blue of her dress was the only point of color in the black-and-white landscape. He didn't remember there ever being a shrine to Mary there.

"The lady of the various sorrows." Jo's voice was quiet.

"What?" He turned to look at her.

"It's from a song." She tapped the screen on her phone, skipping ahead through the playlist.

A steady low beat on a cymbal opened into ambient guitar and incessant piano. He reached over and turned the music off when Cave and his backing band wailed the title lyric, "Do you love me?"

Her expression was difficult to parse. He would've given almost anything to have his niece's gift in that moment. Instead he had to go with his gut, and there was no way to know where it would lead.

Everything he wanted to say to her compressed into one syllable. "Yes."

He took off his seat belt and opened the door. His pulse hammered in his ears on the walk around the front of the car. He pulled her up out of her seat and into him. She'd never cried in front of him before.

She leaned away and he expected a joke to cover the embarrassment at her tears. Instead she looked like she was waiting.

The scent of vanilla came off her skin and hair even in the cold. She kissed back but not the hungry, open-mouthed kiss he wanted. Her hand moved up his chest to his neck. She stopped at his collar and pulled away.

She glanced down at the sliver of empty space between their bodies. When she looked back up at him, her expression was open, though her eyes were still wet. "Do you really want this?" It wasn't incredulous so much as cautious.

"Yes." He paused.

"But you're still uncertain." She stepped backward and wrapped her arms around herself. It was freezing, and he'd dragged them out of the warm car.

"Not uncertain. Maybe afraid." He motioned for her to get back into the car.

He closed the door and walked back around the front, trying to collect his thoughts, to tamp down the emotion threatening to override his better judgment.

When he sat down again in the car and arranged his legs the best he could, he looked out the window past her. The sunlight barely made it through the low wisps of cloud. It would be dark by the time they got back. The Madonna had watched them, a woman who could speak with the dead and a priest breaking his vows. She held a crowned heart in her hands, unchanged under the snowy eaves of her shrine. Or had her eyes been closed before?

The engine protested its way back to life when he turned the key in the ignition. The Opel made it through the pile of slush and debris with some difficulty but got them onto the clearer road. They'd be on the highway soon. He loosened his grip on the steering wheel and turned the music back on but with the volume down. He could still hear the lyrics, a man who had found his god and all the devils inside the woman he loved.

"Do you still want to tell me what you were doing up there on the mountain?" It wasn't exactly the smoothest change of topic, but it would have to do.

"Finding my purpose." She was looking out the window again but not at the landscape of snow-covered evergreens lining their path. She simply looked away from him. "Or, being found." She pulled her coat tighter around herself. "It found me."

"And what is this purpose?" He wanted to stop again. This wasn't a conversation he wanted to have watching the road instead of her face.

"What did your father know of Voices?"

"Enough to believe they were in league with the devil and needed to be put to death. It isn't something I'm particularly proud of, but my father and my brother were both rather medieval in their ideology." He gripped the steering wheel again, not in fear of the road but in anger at what his family had been responsible for.

"I think even in the Middle Ages they would have been wrong. We were something like professional mourners or maybe reapers. I've been up on the mountain naming the dead. The door to the Next opens for them, but I can never see it. I think we do this until we are called to join the dead ourselves." She leaned back into the seat and wrapped her arms around her chest again as if she were freezing. The car was smotheringly warm.

"What dead?"

"Soldiers mostly. World War I and II. Some others. Henry said they are the unmourned."

"Who's Henry?" So much for her being alone up on that mountain.

"A shade I met. I promised I'd come back to finish when this situation with Dušan is resolved."

There was more. He could imagine a story she wasn't sharing spinning out from the few words she had said. She didn't respond to prying, so the rest would have to come on her time.

"I'm glad."

"Glad of what?" She turned to look at him for the first time since they'd gotten back into the car.

"Glad you see there is a purpose and this isn't just a burden God set upon you."

She laughed. "I haven't blamed your god. I've mostly blamed my mother and aunt. Perhaps I should unburden them of my grievances and have a bitchfest with Jesus instead."

"He's probably better equipped to deal with your anger."

"I wouldn't be so certain of that." She turned to the window again. It started to snow.

"I'm not sure what the future holds for me, but I do believe there is something bigger than us." Bigger, yes. Did he still believe it was better?

"You were wrong, you know. About shades who take too

long to cross."

"What?" She wasn't very good at changing the subject either.

"They don't fade into nothingness. They go to some in-between place where they are separated …" Her voice trailed off.

"Separated from what?"

"Sunlight. Hope. Everything."

He pulled over into the slush at the side of the road and put the hazard lights on. "How do you know this?"

"Dušan showed me." She was angry now. At him?

"Faron's father? I don't understand."

"Dušan Črnigad, world-famous photographer, Faron's father, is the dark god of your Slavic myths." Her eyes bored into him.

"That's impossible." Of course it wasn't. He knew better.

She laughed, but it was a sarcastic, harsh laugh. "And apparently that was my other purpose. To bear the son of the lord of the fucking underworld."

"And Faron?"

"He has inherited a mixture of my gift and Dušan's power. Your family probably would have stoked the fire for him, too." She was angry at him, at least by proxy.

"That isn't going to happen, Jo. You know I would never let that happen to you, or to Faron."

"It doesn't matter. There are bigger problems." He watched the weight of whatever those problems were settle back onto her shoulders.

———

Avgusta wheeled into the center of the room. Veronika poured a circle of salt around her as she chanted in Latin. Slovenian seemed like a perfectly good language to do magic in, but Avgusta had assured her that was not how it was done. Veronika made sure to stay on the outside of the line as she poured; she wasn't going to get to stay for this.

When she met the beginning of the line she felt the air wobble, like the air inside the circle bounced against the air outside the circle. At least she'd gotten that right.

Avgusta nodded at her. She rolled the top down on the muslin bag filled with salt from the Piran saltworks and placed it back on the work table in the corner by the door. The slogan on the bag always made her wish she lived at the seaside, "Salt is the sea that could not return to the sky." She put her hand on the knob to go back out to do the dishes and other light cleaning Avgusta paid her to do, but the woman stopped her.

"Stay for a moment. I want you to see that this magic works, then you can tend to the dishes." Avgusta turned back to the altar in the center of the circle and sprinkled a handful of dried herbs into the wide black basin filled with water in front of her.

Veronika stepped closer.

"Stay outside the circle." It was more a hiss than a stream of words.

Veronika stepped back.

Avgusta chanted again in Latin, but Veronika understood the name *Helena*. Wisps of pale blue and white smoke spun up from the basin and wove themselves into a shape above the bowl.

A woman's face, the eyes smudged and sunken under a severe line of dark bangs, peered through the smoke. They flashed with surprise, then narrowed in anger.

"Mother." It was an insult not a greeting.

"Veronika, leave. Finish your tasks and collect the book. Contact me immediately if you have any questions."

She backed up to the door and opened it, slinking out without taking her eyes off the shifting face. It locked eyes with her before she closed the door. A cold, dark shard of hate twisted in Veronika's gut.

The air in the flat was cooler and less cloying than the workroom but still overly warm. She wiped her sweaty palms on her jeans and walked to the table to collect the dinner dishes. Everything had to be done a certain way. She washed the dishes in boiling-hot water perfumed with lemon and some sickeningly sweet flower she hadn't been able to name yet. The dishes had to air dry and then be put back into the cabinet and drawers lined up exactly like in a magazine.

She finished her other work: wiping the counters, sweeping, laying out Avgusta's nightclothes and toiletries on the table in the bedroom. She let herself out of the apartment, locking the door behind her. The transition to the cold night air shocked her into alertness after the torpor-inducing warmth and smells she had been wrapped in all evening.

What did it mean that some of the dead could be called

back to speak with and some could not? Avgusta had to know she wanted to speak with her parents. It would be like her to hold something precious out of reach to keep Veronika working and doing whatever she asked her to do. But there was the book.

Veronika skimmed over its pages before shoving it into her backpack. These were darker workings than she'd seen in the books she'd picked up here and there. Avgusta had marked a slim chapter on vengeance. Veronika knew exactly where to start.

CHAPTER 14

Vesna heard the footsteps on the wooden stairs echo up and bounce around in the funnel of sound the courtyard produced. She pulled a sweater on over the pajamas she'd changed into immediately upon getting home; she'd left Ivanka to close the shop. Vesna opened the door to peek out onto the walkway connecting all the first-floor flats.

Jo was scraping her key into the lock, and Leo stood to the side, hands deep in the pockets of his cassock. His aura swirled out around him, red and orange tendrils weaving in and out of the purple halo of her friend's aura. Jo was in love with him, too. It surprised her. The two of them had formed a bond even someone as walled off as Jo couldn't ignore, but whether Jo would act on it was another thing entirely.

Vesna stepped out onto the cold flags and spoke a quiet hello.

Jo turned to her and smiled ruefully. Vesna tried to restrain herself from rushing in and hugging her friend like she had expected to never see her again. She failed.

She let go of Jo and looked up into her uncle's face. His eyes were less haunted. Vesna suspected he'd said his piece, and that it hadn't been a disaster since Jo had agreed to come back to town with him. "Have you all eaten?"

"I'm not hungry, but I could use a warm drink." Jo looked up at the sky visible between the terra cotta rooflines. It had started to snow earlier, but it had gotten much more serious about it in the last hour. "You might need to feed Leo though. He's not eaten since breakfast."

"Put your stuff away, and I'll go put some water on." Vesna looked up into Leo's face. "Will you stay? I've got stuff for sandwiches. You can sleep on the couch."

He nodded, and she walked back to the apartment, the cold from the stone flags seeping through her slippers.

———

Jo got the door open and flicked on the light inside her apartment. It smelled stale from being closed up — even for what had been a shorter trip than she'd expected. She put her bag on the futon and knelt into the cushion to crank the window open a crack to let in a stream of cold, fresh air.

When she pushed herself up off the futon, Leo was still standing in the doorway. He looked a little lost, or sad. Maybe both.

"I've never seen your flat before." She had made a point of that.

Jo flung her hand out. "You have now seen everything except the bedroom." Awkward pause. That was probably not the thing to say. "It's just that small."

"You and Faron lived here together? How?"

"I slept on the futon, and he slept in the bedroom so I could put him to bed at night and have the rest of the shoebox to myself."

He nodded. "It's very … white."

It was a little stark, but she liked it that way. Order on the outside helped her keep a sense of order inside her head. "Vesna calls it monastic."

"She would." His gaze rested on the framed photograph of Rok and Faron at the top of Triglav. Their dark heads were tilted toward each other, both their faces a little sunburned and chapped.

Rok's half-smile made Jo miss him, and it stung. One of the tethers she had in this world had abandoned her when she'd needed him most. The only thing she'd heard from him was a request he'd sent to Gregor asking if he would arrange to have his flat packed up and his things put into storage. Well, that wasn't entirely true. He'd sent a package for her at the New Year, a kimono-style robe made of blue sari cloth. She wasn't sure if that meant he'd left Nepal and was now in Japan or back in India. There hadn't been a note.

"Jo." Leo's voice brought her back to the moment. "Where did you go?"

"Nowhere good." She ran her hands through her hair. "Let's get you some food."

He didn't move. He had something to say but looked to be struggling to get it out.

She tried to help. "I didn't mean to hurt you earlier. At the car …" She hadn't meant to but was somehow certain she had. How had they gotten to this place? And where the hell did they go from here?

"You didn't. You did make me see there's more than one decision to be made, and not only by me." He started to bury his hands back into his pockets.

She stopped him and took both of his hands in hers. "You don't need my permission. You don't need a place to land. Whatever decisions you make have to be for you. I'm not going anywhere." She hadn't realized until the words were out of her mouth how much she meant them, and that had been the other decision that needed to be made. She felt more than she'd let herself accept. She didn't need to protect him from her gift. He wasn't in any more danger than he would have been with or without her presence. No. She felt the need to protect him from her.

Sorting it out would have to wait. Nothing could happen now. Not until he had officially left the church, and not until Faron was safe.

He nodded. "Let's go drink Vesna's tea. I think we need to debrief all the way around." He dropped her hands and turned, a wall of black cloth with the briefest hint of red and orange smoke turning with it.

———

Ivanka tucked her hand inside Faron's. Snow was landing on her hair. A few flakes melted, leaving tiny droplets of water to reflect the street lamps. She was achingly beautiful sometimes. She was always Ivanka, with blotchy skin or messy hair or reeking of restaurant, but there were moments when she was more alive, less distracted and distorted by all that had happened, and Faron's heart stopped when he looked at her.

That tonight held one of those moments was incredibly unfair. He had intended to tell her to spend the night at Olga's with her sisters. He needed time or space to figure this stuff out with his father. Instead he could only think of getting to the room they shared and getting her out of her work clothes as quickly as possible.

She squeezed his hand and bent her head down to avoid a snowflake to the eye. They gathered on her lashes instead, like glitter. He really was hopeless, and his hopelessness probably kept her in danger.

"Marko asked if we wanted to go get beers and listen to this Croatian jazz band." Distraction.

"Go on and meet him. I'm exhausted." She punctuated her sentence with a yawn. "I'll see you guys back at the flat."

"Are you sure?" She'd walk home on the street if she went on without him. She only took the shortcut through the park if he was with her, so he didn't need to worry about that. What he needed was a distraction from her, long enough to sort out what to do next. He didn't want to be an ass about it, though.

"I'm sure." She walked away from him, waving as she went.

———

Faron unlocked the heavy metal door to their building. He'd ditched out of the bar early, unable to stop thinking about Ivanka and her sleepy yawn. The stairwell was dark, and the light switch didn't work. He tapped the flashlight app on his phone and walked up to the second-floor apartment his Uncle Rok had left for him and Ivanka to use. They'd needed a roommate to cover expenses, and Marko had needed a place to live in town.

When he put his key in the lock to the door of their flat, the door opened with his effort. Weird. Ivanka usually kept the door locked when she was home alone. The entryway always smelled of incense and curry. He figured molecules of turmeric and nag champa must have fused with the yellow linoleum over the time Rok lived there. The apartment smelled like something else, though. The scent was thick on the air and made his mouth taste like metal.

Faron walked down the short hall and tapped the kitchen light switch to his right. It worked. Too well.

Ivanka was crumpled on the floor next to the fridge. A large, bloody organ, a heart maybe, lay in the center of the floor, a circle of still-shiny blood drawn around it. Faron ran to Ivanka to see if she was breathing. She was warm and alive but unresponsive. It was probably the wrong thing to move her, but he wanted to get her away from that thing as quickly as possible. He pulled her into the hallway.

He quickly checked to see if the other rooms were disturbed, then tried to wake Ivanka. There had been a moment when he'd thought it was her heart bleeding on the kitchen floor, and his had gone cold in his chest. She finally came to, groggy and staring. He helped her stand and pulled her out of the apartment and onto the landing.

Faron closed the door and thumbed through his phone for Vesna's number. Ivanka's face was white, and she hadn't spoken a word.

———

Of course Jo's first night back in town wouldn't be quiet.

They'd filled Vesna in and listened to her description of the hex she and Goran had pulled from her doorway. Leo kept looking at her like he was waiting for her to reveal what she'd done under the influence of the spell, but that wasn't information he needed.

Vesna's mobile rang and threw them all into action. They collected a sleepy Goran from upstairs and trekked through the snow shower to Šiška. Jo hadn't been back to Rok's apartment since the night he left.

The familiar smells of curry and incense greeted her, but she immediately recognized the other coppery smell and the taste of blood in the air. She stood rooted in the hallway; the memory of gore dripping down the cabinets in a showroom kitchen was too easily recalled. The tang of old pennies in her mouth pulled it up like a highlight reel. In a bid to save her sanity, her gallows humor bubbled to the surface, and she could almost hear Marlin Perkins narrating the next few moments like a segment of Mutual of Omaha's *Wild Kingdom*.

She took a breath and looked into the kitchen. A heart, too big to be human — maybe from a cow? — lay in a small puddle of blood inside a smeared circle of blood. There weren't distinct fingerprints, but it definitely had the look of fingerpainting. Bile rose in the back of her throat, but not because she needed to puke. It was anger. White-hot, pissed-off, how-dare-you-fuck-with-my-kid anger.

Goran tried to talk to Ivanka, but she insisted she was fine and waved him away. Jo recognized the frustration on her son's face. She felt the same when he'd brushed off her assistance on many occasions. Goran stepped by the three of them into the kitchen and knelt close to the outside strokes of the circle. He sniffed the air and touched the blood pooling under the heart. He stood up and wiped his fingers on a handkerchief he'd pulled from his front pocket.

"It's human work, not demonic. Also very fresh, within the last hour. The blood around it isn't even tacky in the middle." He looked up at her and waited for her to say something.

"It isn't human though, right? I'm pretty sure that's a cow heart." She looked past him to the mess on the floor. Standing closer to it, there was a hint of an old-fashioned floral scent.

"I don't think it's human. I'm sure the police will check, though."

"That's something." She ran her hand through her hair, her fingers caught in the tangles. "What does it mean, though? And why does it smell like tea roses in here?"

"It's the work of a witch, the scent of tea roses. I don't know exactly, but it looks like a warning." Goran folded the handkerchief and put it back into his pocket. "I think it is the same person who left the sparrow. Or at least one of the same people."

"Pretty fucking effective warning." They walked back out to the landing where Leo stood with Ivanka, Faron, and Vesna. As she left the kitchen, she caught a confusion of scents underneath everything. Something out of place, old leather and orange blossoms.

The neighbors were poking their faces out of cracked-open doors. None of them were going to get much sleep.

"I called the police." Leo tucked his phone back into the recesses of his cassock. How many pockets did that thing have?

"Did you ask for Marta?" Jo wrapped her hair into a bun at the nape of her neck and wound an elastic around it.

"As soon as I gave the address, the operator asked me to hold."

Apparently *Zajčeva ulica 2* wasn't the only address on Investigator Klančnik's special attention list.

———

Marta arrived with Gustaf and the same uniformed officer who'd photographed the graffiti at the shop. Gustaf didn't look too pleased to be beaten to the scene by Leo, but he hid it well except for the little dark cloud hovering over his head. He was immaculately, if predictably, dressed. Gray pants, gray sweater, charcoal overcoat with a few snowflakes melting on the shoulders. His clothes matched his eyes and hair; even his skin had a gray cast. He looked faded standing next to Leo in his black wool cassock, his hair still mostly dark. These were her supposed protectors, a tiny gray man and a literal giant of the Church. There was a comedy sketch in there somewhere, but not tonight.

Marta shooed most of them to the entranceway downstairs. It was getting crowded on the landing. She went inside with Faron and the officer, then called Gustaf in after a string of swears sifted down the stairwell to them.

Jo went back up and leaned against the door jamb listening to Marta instruct the officer to take photos of everything in the kitchen. Faron and Gustaf stood in the hallway, though they hadn't noticed she'd returned. She reached her hand out to the opposite jamb on the side where the door closed and met the lock, then pulled it away with a start.

She'd seen Rok, opening the door, keys in hand, over and over again and then a flash of Matjaž standing in the door, his hand on the jamb where hers had been. Where the fuck had that come from? When had Matjaž ever been to that apartment? Maybe she had brought a vestige of him the night she'd pounced on Rok after she and Matjaž had had their moment in Tivoli? She definitely needed a further debriefing with Gustaf. He needed to come clean on all the shit Voices were capable of, because this piecemeal crap wasn't working.

Gustaf turned, saw her in the doorway and joined her on the landing. "This is not good."

"No shit." She hadn't even processed how angry she was at him for leaving out the dangers of being a door for shades to fuck their way back into the world.

"Faron and Ivanka cannot stay here until it is determined who left this grisly calling card for them."

"That thought had already occurred to me." Ivanka could go back to her aunt's with her sisters, and Faron could stay with her. But she doubted that's how it would pan out. Faron wasn't going to like the idea of being separated from his girlfriend, not after this. "We'll figure something out."

Gustaf stepped closer to her and lowered his voice. "I do not think it is a coincidence these things — here, the teashop vandals — have occurred now that Dušan Črnigad is in Ljubljana."

Jo had not connected the two. This wasn't Dušan's work. She was sure about that, but she would have been hard-pressed to come up with a concrete reason for believing he wasn't involved. Dušan, even with her new information about him, was always at arm's length. This was visceral and personal in a way he didn't seem capable of, at least not outside of the affair that had produced their son.

Their son.

When was the last time she'd even thought those words together? Faron had always felt like hers alone.

"I don't think it's Dušan. Something else is going on here."

"Perhaps." Gustaf looked dubious of her pronouncement.

"Look, Dušan came to warn me Faron might be in danger." This wasn't exactly what she'd imagined that danger would look like.

Gustaf looked up at her, startled. "You've seen him? I thought you only returned this evening?"

"He came to Tolmin."

"That is interesting. What else did he tell you?" He looked expectant. She had no intention of telling him everything, not until she got what she needed out of him.

"Maybe we should meet with Dušan, and he can fill you in?"

He stepped back. "Perhaps. Yes, that would be best."

Marta joined them on the landing. "Ms. Wiley, you seem to be unable to stay out of trouble." Her expression was hard to read but registered somewhere between darkly amused and exasperated.

"It would seem." She'd love nothing more than to stay out of trouble, especially the kind of trouble that spilled over onto the people she cared about.

"I'll leave Officer Kovač here until your son's roommate returns. The rest of you can clear out." She turned to go back into the flat and stopped. "Any idea who would leave this kind of thing for your kid or his girlfriend?"

Jo shook her head. "I'd like to know, though." This was way beyond kicking someone in the shins.

———

Jo had been right about separating Faron and Ivanka. Vesna offered her flat to them. She could sleep on Jo's futon. She watched as Faron and Ivanka had walked back to *Zajčeva* ahead of her and the others. Faron held his girlfriend's hand, and Jo sensed a glow between them, a soft pink light that bounced back and forth at their shoulders. She really needed some sleep, in her own bed. Alone.

Gustaf waved goodnight and took the stairs up to his flat. Leo waited with her outside her apartment while Vesna got Faron and Ivanka settled and grabbed her things for an overnight.

Leo took her hand once they were alone. "Your hands are like ice."

"I'm always cold. It started the night Helena died and hasn't gone away. I asked Aunt Jackie about it, but it seems, like too many other things, to be unique to me. Even Gustaf didn't have an answer." She'd gotten used to it, but it was yet another thing that marked her as changed.

He put his other hand up to touch her face but hesitated. "May I?"

She closed her eyes and nodded almost imperceptibly.

He cupped her jaw in his hand. "May I offer you a blessing, Jo? It may be one of my last as a man of the cloth."

She nodded again. She wasn't ready to talk about what his decision might mean, for him or for her.

He bowed his head and spoke in Latin, ending again with an amen.

"And what did you say this time?" She had to look up at him, way up.

"I asked God to keep his guardians close to you and Faron." He moved his hand to the back of her neck, almost cradling her head in his palm.

"There was more than that."

"There was. I also asked Him to protect you even if He withdrew His favor from me as I break my vows to the church."

"Do you think your god is as petty as that?"

"I don't want to believe that is true, but my experience of Him has been less, shall we say, immediate than my experience of other gods of late. And their actions are indeed petty."

She didn't think Dušan or even Achelous, with whom she had a tenuous relationship, were petty. Vain, maybe, but not petty. She hoped that held for Leo's god, as well.

"I never thought I'd be the one who had more faith in gods than you."

He laughed. "I never thought I'd hear you use the word 'faith' in that context."

"I'm not a worshipper, but you were right when you said I

did believe in something, even if I couldn't name it."

He leaned down and kissed her. It was warm but chaste, and it wrapped her in the scent of beeswax and brazier smoke. Would he lose that when he no longer belonged to the church?

They separated, almost guiltily, when Vesna came out of her apartment with a robe thrown over her shoulder and a bag in hand.

She rolled her eyes at both of them. "You do realize there isn't much you can hide from me? Your faces give you away more than your auras ever could."

CHAPTER 15

Matjaž sat up, awakened by the bedside light when he'd rolled over. He was on top of the duvet, still in his clothes from the day. A fog started to clear from his senses. When did he get home? The last thing he remembered was leaving the National Library and walking to his car.

He sat up on the edge of the bed, his limbs heavy and uncooperative. Where were his car and the notes he'd taken in the reading room?

Standing in front of the mirror in his bathroom, he looked into a tired face. His hair was down, and he noticed the gray that had started at his temples had spread into his crown. He was sure he'd aged five years in the few months since his sister's death. Every time he remembered her, it was an image of her body on the mosaic floor at the Emona house, her eyes wide and empty, that came to mind. He hoped eventually it would be images of their childhood or when he was at university and she had followed him like a puppy and flirted with his friends.

He took a piss and came back to the sink to wash his hands. Dried blood ringed his cuticles. Had he scratched himself in his sleep? A tear-shaped drop of blood marred the left leg of his jeans, but there was nothing else. He balled his clothes up and threw them in the basket.

The clock over the sink in the kitchen said it was almost midnight. He'd left the library at 7 p.m. at the latest. How had he lost five hours? The possibilities weren't particularly comforting. Coming from a family like his, those possibilities were narrow and always pointed to something dark. He thought he'd done a better job of separating himself, but his recent avenue of research may have brushed him up against those things he'd prefer to forget.

————

*Give in…give in…give in…*drifted through Jo's thoughts. Leo had gone to spend the night at the rectory. She knew Helena would come as soon as she was back in town and alone. She'd counted on it. Now she wasn't sure what to think. Why had Dušan asked her not to mention what was going on with Faron to Helena? Jo was really tired of feeling like everyone knew what was going on but her.

"You're far away." Helena sat on the edge of the bed next to her so they both faced the window overlooking the courtyard. The blind was up, and light shining out of her window and the other flats where people were still awake cast harsh shadows on the walkway and railings.

"Not so far. A lot has happened since I left. Shit, a lot has happened since I got back." Jo stood and leaned against the window sill, face to face with Helena.

"Care to share?" Helena ran her hand over the duvet, smoothing it over the edge of the mattress.

"How much do you know? I have no idea where you hang out and what you see when I'm not around."

"Not much. I know your shop got vandalized."

"Did you see them?"

"No, only the damage the next day."

"I still can't figure out how no one heard them. You can't even walk across the courtyard at night without everyone in the building knowing it."

"Magic?" Helena laughed.

"You might be on to something."

Helena cocked her head. "Jo, not everything that happens in this town, or even to you, has 'darker' meaning."

Jo shrugged.

"Now, tell me about your retreat into the snowy mountains. Did you accomplish whatever you thought you went up there to do?"

There was a long answer to that question, which would reveal more than she was ready to share with Helena or anyone else quite yet, and a short answer that would invite more questions. "For the most part. I can at least see things more clearly now."

"And what does that mean, my cryptic friend?"

"I don't know that I feel better, but I have a renewed sense of the order of things."

Helena laughed again. "For someone who prides herself on siding with anarchist rebels, you have an uncharacteristic aversion to chaos."

Now she knew what real chaos meant. Sexual politics and governmental corruption were nothing in the face of demons bent on destruction and gods who meddled in human lives. "You can't have one without the other."

There's no paradise without a place of suffering is what Dušan had said to her. She wanted to believe there was good and there was evil, but Dušan's true self muddied everything to gray. He was neither goodness nor evil. He simply was.

"Maybe. Anyway. I'm glad you got something out of it. It was frightfully dull here without you."

"I doubt that." Nothing about Helena's life, or afterlife, was remotely dull.

"Now, there is a matter of a promise you made me before you banished me for your communing with nature or whatever you did up there."

"I will call him tomorrow. I did promise, and I will keep my word." Reluctantly.

"I think you should call him now."

"Helena, it's midnight."

"Matjaž is a night owl. I'm sure he'll still be awake. You did promise."

"I didn't think it meant the moment I landed." Helena's motives were always her own, but the rush to reconnect to her brother was especially puzzling.

"Well, it's been hours since you got back."

"Jesus. Okay. But you need to take off. I can handle this on my own."

Helena waved like the Queen of England and disappeared

without so much as a rustled curtain in her wake.

Jo pulled her phone out of her sweater pocket and stared at the screen when she opened it. She'd replaced the picture of Faron and Rok mugging for the camera with a stock photo of a young Nick Cave looking balefully into the lens. It was meant to make her less angry at Rok when she looked at her phone, but the new picture reminded her every time that it was new and Rok was somewhere out in the world, location: unknown, return date: unknown.

Age unknown. Motive unknown. He was family, as much to Faron as to her. And he left them the same day everything had absolutely gone to shit. *Tread lightly.* That was the last thing he'd said to her. She still didn't know what it meant any more than she had the morning he said it. It was a sore spot that she cared about him too much to write him off. Their lives had been intertwined too long. Maybe for him it wasn't so long, and it was easy to move on to whatever new person he pretended to be to hide what he was. Whatever that was. Even Gustaf didn't know if he was an immortal or a Long-Lived. How did one even know the difference?

Fuck it. She scrolled through her contacts and tapped Matjaž's number.

"Matjaž, hi, it's Jo. I know it's late–"

"I was up. Are you okay?" He must have been asleep or distracted. Shit, he was probably in bed with someone and she'd called in the middle of all that. Though he didn't seem the type to answer the phone if it was going to be awkward for any party involved.

"Oh. I'm fine. You were just on my mind and, well, I guess I've owed you an explanation for a long time."

"I don't know that you owe me anything, but I will listen to an explanation. Are you free tomorrow?"

"I just got back into town and have a few things I need to catch up on. Tomorrow night?" She could help out with prep and disappear for service. They'd been managing without her for a couple weeks, one more night probably wasn't the end of the world.

CHAPTER 16

Jo stood at the edge of a field, the woods thick and dark behind her. A half moon hung low in the sky, a sliver above the tree line. The sickly sweet smell of the dead lay like fog over the land. The living armies had quieted the roar of battle, though stretcher-bearers and a few scavengers could be heard in the darkness, rifling pockets. She gathered her shawl against the chill of the late September night and waited.

The first soldier rose and walked to her. His body was torn by shrapnel or ball; both were gruesome deaths. Ancient eyes bored into her from a weary, beardless face.

"What is your name, soldier?"

"Am I dead? Are you the angel come to take me home?" He reached out to touch her and pulled his hand back as if he'd suddenly remembered some injunction about touching creatures of heaven.

"I am no angel, soldier. I am sent to remember you and open the way for those without mourners."

"Wilcox ... John Wilcox." He already struggled to

remember who he was in life. It wasn't unusual for the long-deceased she encountered, but these were newly dead men. Perhaps the many days and months of war erased a man's name, just as wandering in the In-Between did.

"John Wilcox." A door opened behind her, and the young soldier brushed against her as he passed, moving as best a broken body could.

The others came then. Blue uniforms and gray ones. So many gray ones, and yet they had won this battle. Whatever that meant, to win at slaughter. The last man of no mourners came to her, musket in hand. His eyes glowed green but illuminated nothing.

"And what is your name, soldier?"

"Rebecca Wiley."

"That is my name." And she knew it was her end. Her mother had told her many a Voice met her death at the end of a hard battle. A door opened behind the soldier sent to ferry her from life. It had to be hers, as she'd never seen another's door. It was not the way.

The green-eyed man leveled his musket to take aim. She ran toward him through the beckoning door before his musket ball could pierce her flesh. The retort rang through the trees as she slipped into the blackness beyond the threshold. There was nothing then but the sound of the wind in her ears as she fell through the void.

———

Dušan was waiting for Jo at the teahouse the next morning. Snow had drifted against the walls in the courtyard and covered the new planters in front of the shop. He was dressed, as always, in black with a slice of crisp, white shirt visible behind the turned-up lapels of his peacoat. Looking at him in his everyday form, with his human skin and musculature, it was difficult to believe he could be anything else. He was the man she had been naked with in the gloaming in the apple orchard the night Faron was conceived. That other being had to be a fever dream.

He nodded a good morning. "I know you have work to do, but we need to talk."

"I don't know that I do have work this morning. Fred and Ivanka didn't expect me back, so I'll probably just be in the way. Where do you want to go?" She needed to get out of the flat and away from the lingering scent of the dream. She didn't know as much as she would like to about all this supernatural stuff, but she knew enough to realize there was more to the dreams than reminiscing about her ancestors. Winifred and Rebecca were sending a warning. Who was the soldier bent on taking her out? Henry wasn't a good candidate, though she didn't have any valid reasons for ruling him out. There were hundreds of shades trapped up in those mountains. Any one of them could be waiting for her to return.

Dušan walked past her toward the courtyard entrance onto *Zajčeva* without speaking and without motioning her to follow. His assumption that she would pad along behind him without knowing where they were headed irritated the shit out of her, but her worry for Faron overrode her need to tell him so. She walked in his footsteps on the six or so inches of snow accumulated overnight. He led her to a café under the Triple Bridge, down a set of icy stairs. Sliding into the river on her ass wouldn't be the best way to start the day, so she kept a death grip on the iron railing as they descended below street level. Of course he would prefer a damn-near chthonic bar to a brightly lit coffee house.

He nodded at the bartender and raised two fingers when the man looked up from drying glasses behind an expanse of black marble and polished chrome. Dušan sat at a table near a window looking out over the river. She sat across from him facing downriver toward the market. She was still wary of the water, but it was less terrifying now that she knew there were gods of much darker realms.

The bartender brought two cappuccinos on metal trays with tall skinny glasses of water and a ceramic ramekin filled with sugar straws. Neither of them had spoken on the walk over or since they'd entered the bar, and she was not going to be the one to break the silence. He called the meeting; she was willing to wait for him to lay out his agenda.

He ripped the tops off three straws as she watched over the rim of her cup. He stirred and set the spoon down and finally looked up at her.

"Tell me what happened at Faron's apartment last night."

"I assume you know or we wouldn't be here." She took another sip of her coffee, trying to become her own calm river, glassy water hiding the angry turbulence below.

"Lichtenberg called me late last night after he got back to his apartment."

"And what did our little gray man tell you?" She set her cup on the saucer and waited.

"A bloody heart in the kitchen seems like overkill. Do you think it was for Faron or for his girlfriend?"

She jerked back. "Why the hell would anyone leave something like that for Ivanka?"

"Why would they leave it for Faron?" He took another sip of his coffee syrup and kept his gaze leveled at her.

She had the overwhelming need to look away but refused to give him that. At least his eyes were still bottle-green and amber and not the cavernous, star-filled ones he had revealed at the farmhouse.

"I don't know." She had no clue beyond the handful of people who were "in" on her secret. Who else could possibly know what she and her son were capable of? There were probably more people like Vesna who could see auras. The dead, gods, and demons could also see her coming a mile away. Maybe it was the same with Faron.

"I think you need to send Helena away." He continued to look at her. It was a game now between them. She wouldn't be the first to flinch.

"I don't see how Helena could've possibly done that. Without me, she's not even vapor."

"That is not the whole story of what Helena can do." He glanced away at a man opening the door to the bar and peeking in to see if they were open. Jo had won their staredown, but only on a technicality.

"What do you mean? Like she can be solid when she isn't with a Voice?" If that were true, then what was the purpose of being burdened with this particular set of talents?

"No. I am certain Helena can possess people. Either on her own or with the assistance of her mother's witchery." He looked down at the rings the milk foam left as he finished his coffee.

"Fuck." Was anyone ever going to tell her everything? How many things did Gustaf know that he hadn't shared? How much had Helena continued to omit from the nature and reason for their relationship?

"Jo, there is so much you do not know." The look of pity on his face finally pierced her façade.

"No shit. I didn't ask for this. I didn't ask for Helena or you and whatever carrying your goddamned god genes has done to Faron. I didn't ask to know about all this shit, and I sure as hell didn't ask to be kept in the dark by all of you who knew exactly what you were doing fucking around in my life like it's entertainment." She leaned back and pushed her cup and saucer away, barely stifling the impulse to shove the lot of it straight into Dušan's lap.

"It is not entertainment." He was still calm, and his words were even.

She leaned across the table at him. "What the fuck is it then?"

"It is war. One that has been going on for a very long time." He leaned back in his chair, looking resigned.

"I think it would be best for me and our son if you tell me everything. Uncovering these tidbits as you and Gustaf and Helena see fit doesn't give me much to work with."

A group of women clicked through the bar to a table near them.

"I think we should go somewhere else then. This is not a story that needs to be overheard."

He walked up to the bar to pay, and the two of them went back out into the snowy city. If she hadn't been following in Dušan's wake cursing his every footfall, she would've stopped and enjoyed the transformed old town. The castle hill was dressed in white, and all the terra cotta rooftops of the buildings surrounding the town square had been muted by the same blanket of snow. The central city looked like a holiday card or a Currier & Ives painting from a tin of rock-hard Christmas cookies.

Dušan led her back to her own building and across the courtyard to the always-closed accountant's office that was catty-corner from her shop. He produced a single key from the pocket of his peacoat and opened the door.

"When did you take over the lease for this place?" The interior was spotless and barren. Had there ever been furniture in there? Of course there had been.

"Years ago. About the time you and Faron moved into the building." He flipped a light switch at the back, and two rows of recessed cans flooded the room with cool light.

"Were you spying on us?" That she had been so oblivious to Gustaf's and Dušan's observation of her was infuriating. She was tired of being angry, but it was the only emotion that filled the hole inside her.

"Not you so much as Faron. I was unsure if or when, or even how, his talents might emerge, and I wanted to be able to slip in quietly to observe." He brushed his hand along a shoulder-height ledge running from the front to the back of the space on the wall it shared with Goran's antique shop. "It'll make a fine, if small, gallery."

"Wait. You were here as this accountant person before?"

She'd never seen anyone in the office and had only seen the "open" sign displayed once.

"You have seen my true face. Do you think I am only capable of wearing one mask?" He watched her, waiting for a response or a reaction.

She was tired of playing this game but refused to lose. "Of course not. You're probably the guy I buy milk from at the market and, fuck, you're probably Gustaf, too. I've never seen the two of you together."

He laughed. The warm peals rang against the bare walls and floor. It pushed her thoughts back to the exhibit at the university where they'd first met. He'd been talking to some elderly patron who had a stick jammed up his butt and was complaining about the gratuitous nudity on display. Dušan had laughed like that, genuinely amused and still somehow not condescending. When she caught his eye she had assumed it was because an American was an unusual sight at such a gathering and she exuded some kind of poise and artiness, not because she had a flashing sign over her head that screamed, "supernatural baby vessel."

"It wasn't that."

"You fucker, you can read minds." She stepped back toward the door. He had no business rooting around in her head. He'd messed it up enough in there already. And she was doubly pissed at herself for not catching it before.

"Not all the time. Only when your thoughts are especially focused and loud."

"Then what was it? And do not lay some crap on me about being young and enchanting. I will slap you again."

She turned and leaned against the wall, the toes of her boots lined up perpendicular to the planks in the floor.

"Yes. I could see you were different and perhaps troubled by it. I've always been a sucker for troubled."

"You realize that's gross, right? I have now gone from supernatural baby vessel to wounded wildebeest." Maybe she should stop him before he made it worse.

"I know you will find it hard to believe, but it is not in my nature to jump into the beds of mortal women." He stood in front of her, toe to toe.

The woodsmoke and petrichor of his cologne drifted over her, or maybe that was just him. "I do find that hard to believe."

"It is true. You are not the only lover in my long existence, but you are unique. Faron has no siblings."

"Is that a good thing or a bad thing?"

"Neither. It simply is."

"Nothing is ever simple where all of this is concerned." She waved her hand above her head, indicating all the woo-woo stuff she now swam in.

"That is true. I believe Faron exists to take the discarded mantle of the white god. My counterpart or shadow, so to speak."

She took a deep breath. "Faron is a god, too?"

"Not yet, but if he chooses it, the way is open." There was an unexpected sadness in his words.

"You don't make it sound like a party."

"It is not a party. I chose to live in this world because there are few who follow the old ways. If I did not pretend to be human, I would have very little to do."

"That seems to be the way of things." Where was all of this going? And what about his wife? Where did she fit into all of this?

"Do not let the fairy stories fool you. It is much rarer than you think. Marija has not joined me here, and she will not. She has aged, as mortal women do, and cannot stand to go out in public with me. If Faron chooses to become what I believe he is supposed to be, he will not only outlive you but also everyone he ever knows."

"Is that why you stayed away?" His words twisted in her gut. This was the conversation Rok refused to have with her before he disappeared. How many times had he buried the people he cared for? Rok wasn't a god, but his lifespan made it very difficult to be human.

"You see then." Dušan put his hand on her cheek. "There are moments when I did feel something like love for you, Jo, and for Faron, in my way."

"But you didn't want to watch us die?"

"Even gods have their weaknesses." He stepped closer to her, close enough she had to stand, her back pressed against the wall.

"When I saw you in the mountains..." He leaned in and kissed her on the mouth. It was warm and familiar and wrong. So wrong.

She pushed him away gently. "I was bewitched or hexed or whatever. Surely you could see that?" She wasn't hexed now, and she wasn't going to let herself be enchanted by what had been between them before.

"Yes. There was something, but I do not believe your feelings regarding me were clouded by that amateurish hex, as you call it."

"You could see it, and you didn't tell me?"

"I am not your keeper, Jo." He stepped back. The moment of intimacy had passed.

She wasn't sure if she was grateful or disappointed, and that she wasn't sure was disappointing. She pulled her coat around her and looked down. Their toes were no longer aligned. "What happened to the other white god?"

"He fell in love with a witch who had summoned him, thinking he would do her bidding like a common spirit."

"That seems presumptuous." And stupid. What the hell is wrong with people?

"It was, but he was drawn to the witch nonetheless. Human women do have their charms." He smiled at her. "She drew a Portal to them, whom he possessed, and he came into the world as a mortal man." He shoved his hands deep into the pockets of his coat.

"And the Portal, she died."

"Yes. That is the nature of Portals. You are a threshold that can be crossed only once. Your life for the entity you bring into the world or the dead you return to the living."

"I've had firsthand knowledge of being possessed by a god."

"I am surprised you survived. Achelous must enjoy his watery existence." Dušan laughed again.

"I figured out the dead people thing with Henry. Gustaf explained demons."

"Demons and angels are from the beliefs of Christians and Jews, but the words work. To me they are malevolent spirits or benign ones."

"Not benevolent?"

"It is rare that intervention in human lives by such entities is completely benevolent."

She nodded. She'd been mucked about by enough "entities" to be wary and, yet, she was still standing there. No matter how much she wanted to disengage with him, she couldn't change the fact he was Faron's father.

"Do I know the person the white god became?"

"He died before you could meet him. But you know his daughter and her brother, and I believe you had the pleasure of meeting their mother."

Jo dropped her chin to her chest. "Helena and Matjaž and Snippy."

"Snippy?"

"Their mother. She was awful to me, and everyone else, at Helena's funeral."

"She is very bitter. She and Mateo were in an accident some years ago. He was killed, and she was left as you saw her. I think she believed Mateo was protected from such mundane forms of harm."

"Does Helena know all of this? Does Matjaž?" That would explain a great deal. It would also raise more questions than she wanted to think about.

"Helena does, I am certain. I think Matjaž knows his mother is a witch, but I do not think he knows the whole truth."

She really wanted to sit down. Or fall down. "So that was why Helena came on to me? That was why she slept with Faron, too?"

"I suspect so. I believe Avgusta wanted one of her children to assume their father's previous role. Helena and Matjaž are not like Faron; Mateo was mortal when they were conceived. Helena is, or rather was, a powerful witch like her mother. I believe Matjaž has tried to distance himself."

"So what was the original endgame with Faron?"

"I can only speculate Helena wanted to know how much you knew — which was nothing — so she had to suss out Faron for herself. She may have sparked his gift or he, like you, may have simply repressed it."

"I didn't repress my gift. It skipped me. Maybe Helena sparked mine, too?"

"Jo." He shook his head. "You have always been what you are, as has Faron. You are both strong-willed and want to live your own versions of quiet lives. It was always there. I saw it the day I met you."

She would think on that later. "But now what? Helena is dead, and there is only Matjaž — who doesn't seem to want anything to do with their woo-woo stuff."

"I have a few theories. I think Avgusta thought she might be able to somehow use you to force Helena into the Next without dying. The lore is there, but it is murky at best. If that did not work, a grandchild from Faron and Helena would probably have some type of gift."

Jo shuddered. She was not ready to be a grandmother and definitely not ready to be that kind of grandmother. "That doesn't explain Helena trying to throw me off on Matjaž."

"Distraction. Probably for both of you."

That was far too glib an explanation. Helena could be direct, but her scheming rarely was. "Maybe. So what do I do now?"

"Release Helena. Her door will open, and she will move on to the next world. Another guide will come to you."

"And how do I do that?"

"Not my department. Talk to your aunt or your mother."

"Let's leave my mother out of this." She hadn't intended to snap.

"For now. You are going to have to deal with her eventually."

"Not today." She stood up straight and looked him in the eye. "Why didn't you tell me the whole story in Tolmin?"

"I was unsure if you could be trusted. You were holed up in the mountains with a ghost, and from all accounts you were 'not yourself.' I worried you could, like your mother, be losing your grasp."

"Not myself? Well, fuck. I'm sorry I didn't go right back to baking brownies after I buried my friends, got Milo killed, and watched my father's soul get eaten by a demon. I really fucking tried."

"If it is any consolation, I think you are very much yourself, but angry and traumatized. I did not know about your father."

"I haven't told anyone else. Not really. I can't think about him being torn into nothingness. And Milo. I haven't seen his shade since that night. I don't know if that thing got his soul, too, or if he found his door, or if he's just out there wandering around."

"Jo, your father's soul, or spirit, could not be destroyed by a demon. This is superstitious nonsense. He is probably with the lost. Milo I do not know about, but I can find out."

She really needed a chair.

CHAPTER 17

Veronika struggled with the Latin; it was archaic even by Latin standards. The spell promised searing pain to the recipient. Pain would have to do, for now. The spells to kill were beyond her abilities and required things she couldn't, or didn't want, to get. And, besides, the drawings of the fatal spells made her insides crawl. Magic was a lot harder than wand-waving and saying made-up words out loud.

She spoke the words, the best she could, over the bowl. The viscous liquid, filled with graveyard dirt and the rust scraped off iron nails, stiffened against the spoon and crystalized before shattering into a fine ochre dust. The instructions warned to be careful with this powder, as it carried the power of the emotions she had focused into the spell. Breathing it in would cause her the same pain as the intended target.

She tipped the contents of the bowl onto a piece of waxed paper and slowly folded the edges together until the dust was sealed inside. She slipped the makeshift envelope into a black silk bag she'd gotten from Avgusta and tucked the bag into her backpack. Now she'd have to wait until Tuesday and their regular night at Renegade Tea.

A knock at the door startled her. She covered her makeshift altar with a black cloth and slid it back under the bed. The room smelled like her magic and incense, but there wasn't much she could do about that. Her aunt thought she burned it to cover up the smell of pot smoke or cigarettes. She plopped back on the bed and opened a book she was supposed to be reading for class. She grabbed her headphones off the side table and draped them over her shoulders.

"Come in." Her words and the second knock met each other in the air.

The door opened a crack, and her sister Ana poked her face in. "Aunt Olga asked if you wanted any dinner."

"Sure." She unwound the headphones and set them with the book back onto the side table. "Are we having anything good?"

"Pasta. With cream sauce. Oh, and salad."

"That's fancy."

Ana opened the door wider. She looked down at the floor near the bed and then back up at Veronika. "I asked for it special."

Shit. Was it Ana's birthday? How could she forget that?

"I thought it might cheer you up." Ana looked down at her feet again.

"That was nice of you." She stood up and straightened the edge of the duvet. Working for Avgusta had made her a neat freak about her own stuff, too. "Let's go eat."

Ana smiled up at her and turned to walk back down the hall to the kitchen.

Veronika moved her backpack next to the bed in front of where her altar was hidden in the shadows. Had Ana been poking around in her room again?

———

Jo pulled a brush through her hair. It didn't make much difference; her mane had a mind of its own, and it wanted to be free. She was never one to change clothes multiple times before going out, but she had stood in front of her wardrobe far longer than usual, trying to decide what to wear on her "date" with Matjaž. She didn't want to look like she'd dressed to impress, but she also didn't want to look like she was going for impenetrable nun's habit.

After some thought, she pulled on her worn-thin Nick Cave tour shirt, a black skirt, and a heavy black cardigan. It was pretty much her uniform and a guarantee they wouldn't end up someplace fancy and romantic. She was 100 percent okay with that.

There was a light knock at the front door. Matjaž had texted to say he would swing by her place since he was going to be at the library doing research anyway. She wasn't thrilled about having him in her apartment, but if he could get into her building it was a good indication he was, as Dušan had said, benign. She smoothed the skirt flat with her palms and opened the inner and outer doors of her entryway closet to let Matjaž in. He'd made it past the wards Goran set on the courtyard entrance. That was something.

She smiled a hello and waved Matjaž into the flat. He reflexively ducked even though he wasn't as tall as Leo and was in no danger of grazing his scalp on her door. Spending a lot of time in very old buildings probably meant he'd banged his forehead on low lintels more than a time or two.

"I brought you these." He handed her a small nosegay of hothouse flowers, an arrangement of subtle ecrus and yellows bound with a heavy, cream-colored ribbon.

"Thank you." She reflexively brought them to her face, knowing they would smell of nothing, like most commercial flowers. She pulled back in surprise. They carried the scents of old leather and freshly mown grass and something she couldn't quite identify. It was a heady combo. "Wow. They smell really nice."

"I hadn't noticed, but I'm glad you like them."

She did, but it was an unexpected gesture. He watched while she rummaged through the cupboard under her sink to produce a short vase for the blooms. "Shall we?"

"What did you have in mind?" His eyes were so much like Helena's. And come to think of it, they reminded her of Dušan's pretend-people eyes as well. The thought made her a little dizzy.

"I didn't. I am hungry, though." Lunch hadn't happened. Food had been the farthest thing from her mind after her morning with Dušan and his revelations.

"Do you know about the job training restaurant? I thought maybe we could have dinner there." His gaze didn't waver as he spoke to her, and it flustered her. She needed food; her blood sugar must have been low.

"We hired our new dishwasher from there." Was her head nodding a lot or was she imagining that?

"If you've been, we could…"

"No, that's great. They have good specials." She grabbed her coat and motioned that she'd follow him out. Her hands were noticeably shaking as she locked the door. Was she nervous about being alone with Matjaž? The stupid bird hex had been destroyed by Goran. She could make her own decisions, right?

———

"I have to say I was surprised to get your phone call." Matjaž poured more wine into Jo's glass.

The restaurant was small and relatively quiet on a weeknight. Each table glowed with a candle in the dim light. Her dinner companion's face looked more angular in the shadows.

"It was the middle of the night." She feigned chagrin.

"There was that. But I've had the distinct impression you've been avoiding me." He took a sip of wine.

"I haven't been … okay. Yes, I have been avoiding you. I promised you an explanation." She placed her knife and fork at the top of her plate and pushed it a few inches away.

He didn't look hurt by her confession.

"I … you … Helena was your sister. You're her brother."

"I am aware of my relationship to Helena." He smiled. He was trying to make this easier on her, but his charm offensive only made it harder to let him down.

"It's just that it seems wrong to me." She didn't want to bring up Helena and Faron. Matjaž didn't know, and she didn't want to speak ill of the dead, at least not to the dead's brother. "And now we are in business together."

"I admire your ethics, but we aren't business partners. I'm a contractor, and technically the contract is with Olga and Gregor." Were his eyes actually twinkling in the candlelight? What the hell was wrong with her?

"Still. The brother-sister thing."

"If it's any consolation, Helena would not have given that a second thought. As I mentioned, she thought you and I were more suited."

"Yes. She has made that abundantly clear." Shit.

"What?" A shadow passed over his face, and any trace of twinkling in his eyes disappeared.

Jo put her face in her hands. This was going to be way more of a confession than she had intended. "I think we need to go somewhere more private to finish this conversation."

He nodded and went to the counter to pay the check. He ushered her into her coat and out onto the cobblestone street between the gutters full of gray and brown slush.

"I'd offer to make you coffee at my place, but I doubt you're up for the drive to Škofja Loka."

"My place is fine and much closer." She started off back toward the center.

They walked along the river in silence. When they got to the Triple Bridge, she looked down into the icy waters of the Ljubljanica. Her trip into the mountains had made her realize that no matter what she felt about Achelous' actions at the museum the night he'd scarred her chest, he had saved her and Faron from a demon. She had planned to make an offering to him on her return, but things had gotten complicated fast. It was still on her to-do list.

Matjaž followed her up the steps to her flat, his footfalls echoing up through the courtyard as a counterpoint to hers. He stood close enough to her as she opened the door that she could feel his body heat. They took their wet shoes off in the closet entryway, and she offered him a pair of felt slippers. Slovenians feared cold feet and drafts more than they feared the Devil himself.

He sat on her futon while she made coffee. She could feel his eyes follow her through the kitchen. It made her uncharacteristically nervous, and her hands shook again as she poured coffee from the *ibrik* into two cups. She crossed the small room and handed him one of the cups.

He moved his hand, and she sat next to him on the futon and turned to face him. "Sorry, my place isn't very cozy."

"It's very …"

"White?" She laughed.

"I was going to say Spartan, but it is also very white."

"I spend most of my time at the teahouse." Or she had before this hiatus.

He nodded, and his expression settled into something more serious. "So, are you going to tell me why you referred to Helena in the present tense at the restaurant?"

"Can I ask you a few questions first?"

"I didn't realize that's how confessions worked." He smiled again, but it didn't go all the way up to his eyes.

"It isn't. Or at least I don't think it is. I don't know much about actual confessions." She set her coffee cup on the deep window sill behind the futon. "How much do you know about your family?"

"I assume more than you." He was puzzled now, but there also was an inkling of realization behind his eyes.

"I assume so, too. But I think I know a couple things you don't."

He set his coffee cup on the sill next to hers. "I think I know where this is going, and I don't think I like it."

"I can't say I do, either." She looked down at her hands. They were folded neatly in her lap, and they had stopped shaking.

He was studying her face. "Did you know Helena was a witch?"

Jo didn't flinch. "Not until this morning. Did you know Helena's spirit hasn't crossed, and she is hanging around as my spirit guide?"

He flung himself back against the futon, splayed his arms across the back, and looked up at the ceiling. "Are you fucking kidding me?"

Her "no" sounded very small, even in the tiny flat.

He took a deep breath, still looking at the ceiling and decidedly not at her. "And you? You're a witch, too, aren't you?"

"Not exactly."

He looked at her then without any of the softness she usually saw in his face. "Not exactly?"

"I'm a *Vox de Mortuis*. And a Portal."

It was his turn to bury his face in his hands. "Jo Wiley, you are in a great deal of danger."

CHAPTER 18

Jo stared at Matjaž. "You know about Voices and Portals?"

"Yes. And I know what happens to them when they bring someone back from the In-Between or the Next." He looked at her and laid his hand on the side of her face.

"So you know about your father and all that?"

He nodded. "And I had hoped to put all that behind me, but it seems we cannot escape who we are."

"Truth." She took his hand and moved it from her face to her lap where she held it in both of hers. "Do you understand now why I avoided you?"

He nodded. "You thought you were protecting me." Realization dawned on his face. "And that's why you told me you knew Helena was okay at the funeral." He frowned. "I was awful to you about that."

"Please don't apologize again." She was torn between preferring a clueless Matjaž she could pretend to avoid for his own good and an in-the-know Matjaž who didn't need to be protected from anything.

"I take it from your earlier comment my sister has been

'encouraging' you to see me."

She nodded.

"I'm surprised you finally called. You don't seem to bend much to pressure."

She laughed. "Your sister is single-minded and relentless."

He didn't laugh. "I don't think it's my sister you need to worry about."

"Dušan mentioned as much."

"Wait, Dušan?" Another flash of realization. "Holy fuck, Dušan *Črnigad*. Dušan the black viper. Why had I never realized that?"

"Of course. *Belak*, the white to the black. Wait, does this mean you and Faron are related?"

He did laugh then. "No. The white and black gods are each other's shadows, but they are not brothers. Well, not really."

"You should know, Helena and Faron had a thing, too."

He didn't look surprised. "I'm sorry. I didn't realize Mother had so much sway over her."

"What does that mean?"

"Since my father was killed, my mother has been hell bent for leather to resurrect him or to have one of us, Helena or me, take his place. Neither of us wanted the gig, so Mother came up with seemingly infinite schemes to make something happen. It's part of why she and I are barely on speaking terms."

"That explains a lot. Dušan thought maybe Helena was trying to get pregnant by Faron." Saying it out loud made her shudder.

"It's possible. It's probably why she's so keen for the two of us to get together. If Helena can't produce a Belak heir by a Wiley, then maybe I could."

Jo laughed. "It never came up with Helena."

"What never came up?"

"I can't have any more children. I mean I wouldn't want to, but I can't. There were complications after Faron's birth, and without going into gory detail …"

"So much for that plan."

"Yeah." She leaned back against the futon and closed her eyes, Matjaž's hand still clasped in hers in her lap.

"Does this mean you would reconsider?"

She opened her eyes. "Reconsider what?" He was much closer on the futon, his face inches from hers.

Jo sat up and put her hand on his chest. "Matjaž, it isn't only Helena and Faron and all that white god, black god stuff." She took a deep breath. The physical attraction was still there, but now there was Leo and the business with Henry to be finished. At some point in her old age, she was probably going to regret turning him down, but things in her life were already too complicated.

Matjaž leaned back against the futon again. "Our moment's passed, hasn't it?"

She nodded. "I think so. If it's any consolation, I'm disappointed, too."

"Does this at least mean we can be friends now, and you'll stop avoiding me?" He took her hand again, but the temperature of his skin was noticeably different. "Your hands are like ice."

She shrugged. "I think we are more than friends. 'Allies' might be a more appropriate term."

"I'll take that." He sat up on the edge of the futon. "I should go."

She got up and took their cups to the kitchen. A wall of scent from the flowers on the table knocked her back. She was dizzy again, and her hands trembled as she placed the mugs in the sink.

"Matjaž, where did you get the flowers?" The scent she couldn't put her finger on had become the strongest of the smells. It was rapping its knuckles against the inside of her skull.

"An old woman was selling them along the river between here and the library."

She plucked them from the vase, dripping water across the table and floor. "I think you should take them with you. I think you got more than you bargained for." Her knees went wobbly.

Matjaž was up and grabbed her by the waist to keep her from hitting the floor like a sack of potatoes. "You okay?"

"No. The flowers. There's something in them."

He took them away from her and smelled them himself. "They smell like flowers … and, shit, like my mother's studio."

"I'm guessing your mother doesn't throw pots in her 'studio.'"

"No." He stood next to her, the flowers still in hand, away

from both their faces.

"It doesn't make you woozy? The smell?" Her insides turned to custard, and she had butterflies in her stomach. The good kind, and all the warmth that spread through her chest and nethers with those particular flutters. As nice as the feeling was, it was distinctly separate from what she wanted. Apparently, the wards kept out bad people and shades but not bad things.

"No. I think that was for you. Maybe to make you more receptive–"

"If you tried to seduce me?" She laughed.

"Something like that." He didn't laugh. "I don't want to leave you like this, but I need to get these out of here. You should probably go to bed, alone, and sleep it off."

"You should throw them in the river. Vesna said that's how Goran ended the bird hex." She needed to sit down.

"Bird hex?"

She filled him in on the bound sparrow and what Goran thought it had meant and then babbled on about the bloody heart in Faron's apartment.

"Jo, I need to go. Are you going to be okay? Should I call Gregor or Vesna?"

"I'll be fine." She followed him to the door and walked out barefoot onto the cold flags of the landing with him. She hugged him to say goodbye and inhaled the scent of him. More leather and mown grass. And he was so warm compared to her freezing feet.

He disentangled himself from her. "Jo, this isn't what you

want."

She nodded and turned her head at the noise on the wooden steps. Leo stood at the top of the stairs, his face a blank mask.

"It's not what you think."

———

Faron jumped at the knock on the door. It had to be a neighbor; anyone else would've had to get buzzed in downstairs.

Ivanka was sleeping, and he didn't want to wake her. He was pretty sure it was the first sleep she'd had since what they were euphemistically referring to as "the message."

He peered through the peephole at the back of his father's head and opened the door.

"Was the door open downstairs?"

"No."

"If I refuse to invite you, can you still walk into my flat?" He was going to ask him in, but he was curious.

"Yes, but I try not to be more rude than necessary."

Faron stepped aside and motioned him in. He watched as his father removed his pristine ankle boots and lined them up along the wall next to Ivanka's battered Chucks. How was he not covered in slush?

"I don't have much to offer. A beer, maybe, and I think there's half a bottle of wine." Faron walked into the kitchen and opened the fridge, staring at the sparse inventory.

"A beer, I think. Thank you."

Faron split the beer between two short glasses and set them on the table at the banquette by the window. He slid in facing the door, and Dušan sat opposite.

"I see Gustaf cleansed your flat."

"Goran actually." Faron no longer believed Gustaf had his or his mother's best interest at heart. It was difficult to trust someone with so many secrets.

"He's not evil. Gustaf, I mean. He is perhaps misguided. He thinks he is being protective when he keeps things to himself."

Faron shrugged. His father had secrets, too. More than he thought he wanted to know, and yet he'd let him in and trusted him in some small way because his mother seemed to. "Why are you here?"

"Unlike Gustaf, I think it is better if you know the truth."

"The truth?"

"You have a decision to make."

"I know you enjoy drawing this stuff out, but I'd like it better if you just told me what you came here to say. I'm not a child; I don't need a story."

"You aren't a child, but you are achingly young." His father's eyes changed again, but not to the black mirrors they had become at the coffee shop. They instead looked as if he was gazing at something incredibly far away, maybe even long ago. He snapped back to the present.

Faron waited for his father to continue.

Dušan sighed. He hadn't come to deliver happy news, that was certain. "It is best to simply say the thing. Faron, you can raise the dead."

"I know."

"No, you know you can reanimate a mouse or a housefly. You have the power to raise a human who has died and whose spirit has not crossed into the next world."

"I told you. I tried with Ivanka's mother, and nothing happened." Maybe his father was old enough to be forgetful.

"Her spirit had moved beyond this place."

"She went to heaven?" That felt unlikely, even wrong.

"No, she did not. Heaven is not as you imagine. Her soul, or whatever you choose to call it, is no longer on this plane."

Faron finished his beer. "I guess that seems fair."

"Fair." Dušan laughed on a single exhale. "That is neither here nor there. The important information for you is once you raise a person from the dead, you have made a choice."

Faron lowered his gaze at his father. Did he dignify his obvious statement with a comment?

Dušan continued, unperturbed by Faron's facial expression. "You will have made the choice to become the white god."

"Excuse me? That sounds pretty essentialist." Faron leaned back against the wall. His father had early-onset dementia and a mean streak of bigotry running through him. Great.

"Sometimes white is the color of a thing. It is a name, an adopted one. The old name has been lost in time. He was, and you may be, the god of abundance and life. But also of victory in war, preserving lives while I escort those shed."

"While you what? Who are you?"

"Črnobog. The black god."

"You're the devil?"

Dušan sighed heavily. "That is what the medieval Christians would like you to think. To borrow a bit from Eastern philosophy and the yin and yang, you cannot have light without darkness." He picked up his empty glass and set it back down. "The role of the white god has been empty for some time. I believe it is your job, if you want it." Dušan looked at Faron. His eyes had gone dark again, but this time they were hollows filled with stars, like looking up into the night sky in the wilderness. It was terrifying and beautiful, and Faron could not look away.

"What if I choose not to take the gig?"

Dušan blinked, and his eyes were again green and amber-flecked. "Then nothing. You have a fancy parlor trick that will probably get you into trouble at some point."

"It can't be that simple."

"Jo raised a smart man." His father looked at him with something like admiration. It was unnerving. "I believe you will have to choose under duress. You will have to choose whether someone lives or dies."

It was Faron's turn to take a deep, weary breath. "I assume this will be someone I care about."

"Fate is often a cruel mistress."

Faron thought of Ivanka and finding her balled up on the kitchen floor. Was it better to keep her close or send her far away from whatever taint his family carried?

"This is not a curse. We are what we are. We are a part of

the natural order of things–"

"Would it have been the natural order of things if you hadn't knocked up my mother?" The words tasted bitter in his mouth.

"Your mother is not unique among the long bloodlines of Voices, but she is a rare thing. Who knows what would have become of you? And does it matter? There is no way to undo the past; even I do not have that ability."

"Chronos outranks you?" There was less bitterness and more resignation.

"You could say that, though Chronos is probably more of an archetype than a god." Dušan cocked his head as if he were thinking about it.

"You don't know?"

"Omniscience does not come with the black god role. Or the white one, as far as I know."

"That's something, I guess. Knowing everything would be terrible."

"Yes. Yes, it would be."

CHAPTER 19

Leo looked from Jo's guilty face to the man's confused one.

"I should go." The man ran his hand down Jo's arm and squeezed her fingers before brushing by Leo and disappearing behind him down into the dark stairwell.

"I didn't expect you." She smoothed her rumpled shirt and skirt with her hands. "Would you like to come in?"

Did he want to go into her flat? Did he want to be alone with her after she'd been with another man? His jealousy disgusted him. She had done nothing out of character and had promised him nothing more than her presence.

He took a deep breath and looked her in the eyes. "Yes. I would like to come in." Was she drunk? Why else would she be outside with nothing on her feet?

"I can make you some coffee or tea?" She kept pushing her hair back behind her ears, her hands shaking noticeably.

"No, thank you." Had something happened? Was this man one of her conquests from the gallery in *Metelkova* that Vesna had mentioned? Had he hurt her? But there were flowers, flowers he took with him. Had Jo given the man flowers?

The air in the apartment was cloying and smelled strongly of lilies. He loathed the scent and had always hated that every church was filled with them on Easter; it made him dread his own High Holy Day.

"Your aura, it's angry." She looked like she would fall but instead plopped unceremoniously on the white-draped futon and looked up at him, her blue eyes swimming.

"You can see auras?" That was new. And troubling, for a number of reasons.

"Sometimes." She shook her head like a puppy trying to shake off water.

"Jo, are you well?"

"The flowers. Snippy..." Her head fell back and she lost consciousness.

She had been drugged. He scooped her up in his arms with the intent of putting her to bed and calling Vesna to take care of her friend. He and Jo could sort out whatever needed to be sorted between them later.

She woke enough to put her arms around his neck. "Matjaž wanted–"

"Shh. You don't need to explain anything to me." He did want her to explain everything, but not now. Not like this.

He was standing next to the bed with her still in his arms. Her eyes opened and bored into his face. "No. I didn't tell him about you. I didn't. But it was why, because of you."

Now he was confused. "That was Matjaž? Helena's brother? And you didn't tell him about me because what?"

She slid out of his arms like water and stood in front of

him in the cramped bit of space between her bed and the window sill. She was still bleary-eyed and unsteady, but she had become animated with purpose. "Because …" She put her hands on either side of his face and pulled him down to her.

Her hands and lips were cold but the kiss was warm and hungry. It took everything he had to pull away. She looked surprised at his withdrawal, and hurt.

"Not like this. You're drunk."

"Or hexed. Again. Snippy must really hate me." She laughed and wavered on her feet.

"Please sit down before you fall."

She sat, hard, on the edge of the bed. "Why does everything have to be so complicated?" When she looked up at him, the surprise and hurt had been replaced with a deep sadness. It was raw and naked and not an emotion she would have revealed if she were in control of her faculties.

He settled next to her on the bed. She leaned against his arm; he was too tall for her to lean her head on his shoulder. "I don't know that everything *is* complicated, Jo. Sometimes I think it's just me, or just you, who is complicated." He wanted to comfort her, but he didn't know how without stoking the fire that was too close to the surface in both of them.

She shook her head against his arm. "Nope. It's everything and everyone. Well maybe not Vesna. She has Igor, and they are happy — though he doesn't know about the family-business business or what a freak show her friends are." She laughed. "Okay. It really is everyone."

"I think you need to get some sleep."

"Hmm. That's what Matjaž said."

The name stung. Leo was going to have to get over himself. "Can I call Vesna? Someone else?"

"Why, silly? You're here."

He was, and maybe that was all that mattered. Rok, Dušan, Matjaž, Milo, even Helena would always have a piece of Jo's heart, but that didn't mean he didn't have a piece of it, too.

"It's not pie, you know. I am capable of caring for more than one person. That I care for Rok, shirker that he is, doesn't mean I have less … caring for you. There's enough Jo pie for everyone." She snorted. "I didn't mean it like that."

"Can you read my mind?"

"Of course not, you were just thinking really loudly."

With Jo asleep and tucked into bed, without any further revelations, he closed the door behind him and locked it with her key. He would have to leave it with Vesna, which meant talking to his niece — the one person he couldn't hide anything from. Though if Jo could see auras and read minds, even that wasn't true.

———

Matjaž pulled the flowers apart and threw them into the water. Jamming the heavy, cream-colored ribbon into his pocket, he watched the crushed petals and stems float down the river away from him, away from Jo.

He'd spent the better part of his existence doing everything he could to distance himself from his family's origins and from his mother's interference in his life. Part of him was nostalgic for the woman she had been before his father was killed, but he knew her happiness had been established on the corpse of a Portal, of someone like Jo.

Had Helena known from the beginning what Jo was? Had his mother? He hated to think his sister, whom he'd loved and tried to pry away from their mother's influence, had been as manipulative as Avgusta. Jo's sober retelling, without incredulity, of what she had learned in the past few days, even hours, saddened him. She had been betrayed by so many people she cared for. He had almost become one of those. He *had* become one of those if his suspicions about his "lost" evening were correct. His sister had used him to deliver his mother's sinister message to Jo's son.

Without thinking, he found himself halfway to Avgusta's apartment. Most of the snow had disappeared, which had left the streets dirty and icy in patches. He avoided the larger puddles and looked more carefully where he walked so he didn't wind up on his ass.

He stood on the pavement looking up at the block of flats where his mother lived. They were modern and expensive. He'd done everything he could to make her physically comfortable, but nothing he'd ever said had penetrated her sense of entitlement and the world's perceived betrayal of her. Speaking to her now wouldn't make any difference either, but he no longer cared for her comfort. This had to stop. She could not meddle in his life, or Jo's, any longer.

He rapped hard against the door and heard no answer nor any sound from within. He dug his keys out of his pocket and opened the door with the copy he'd had since the remodel. If she was out, he would wait for her, however long it took.

The lights were on in the gleaming kitchen. His mother's sense of order in her surroundings was at odds with the chaos he believed lived in her head. The march of perfectly stacked plates and sparkling countertops was marred by the stench of lilies that hung like smog in the flat. The door to Avgusta's workroom was closed, but flickering light bled from underneath it. He crossed the flat in a few determined strides.

His mother had always harped on them not to open the door to her room without knocking and even then to wait to be admitted. He turned the knob and threw the door open, banging it against the wall. His mother spun in her chair to face him, her expression dark with anger but quickly fading to something that looked surprisingly like guilt.

His sister, or a projection of her, shimmered in the air above a bowl of black water. Her sunken face registered only surprise.

"Matjaž." It was his sister's voice, but hollowed out and distant. "It's good to see you." "I wish I could say the same." He looked from her to Avgusta. Family: what a bitter word that could be.

"It's … it's not what you think." His mother's stammer was unexpected.

"That's the second time I've heard someone use that phrase tonight. I'm sure it's untrue this time." He pulled the ribbon from his pocket and threw it at his mother. "This stops. Now."

Helena's image crackled and faded in and out like a picture on a badly tuned television set. "Mother. What did you do?"

Avgusta's eyes narrowed. "I attempted to do what you could not."

"You failed before you even set out to bend Jo's will. She

can't have any more children." He spat the words out.

His mother spun again to face Helena. "Did you know this?"

"Women usually don't worry too much about knocking each other up, Mother." Helena rolled her eyes.

"Shut up! I do not need to hear about your perversions." Disgust came off his mother in waves. It wasn't his sister's bisexuality that disturbed her, it was that neither he nor his sister gave a shit about her grand schemes.

"You aren't innocent in all this." Matjaž turned his anger on his sister's image. "You dragged Jo and Faron into this mess."

"I'm less complicit than you'd like to think." Helena crossed her arms and practically pouted at him.

"Oh? You were getting it on with Jo and her kid. You've been trying to throw her at me for months. How is that not complicit in her bullshit?" He pointed at Avgusta.

"One: I liked Jo and Faron. They were fun. And two: I didn't know about all the Voice and Portal stuff until *after* I was dead and our dear mother wouldn't let me leave." She leveled her dark gaze at Avgusta.

"And me?" He didn't believe her exactly, but if the spirit Helena was anything like the living Helena had been, she didn't tell obvious lies; she preferred to leave things out.

"You two have the hots for each other, and Jo is determined to spend the rest of her life alone or seducing a string of nobodies rather than entangle some innocent in her 'messed-up little life.'" She looked at him with genuine sisterly affection; it reminded him of how much he had lost. "I figured you were already pretty close to being as 'messed up' as she is, and it would be good for both of you."

"And possessing me? That was you, wasn't it?"

Helena at least had the grace to look sheepish. "I should've asked, but it was an emergency."

"Leaving a bloody cow heart in Faron's apartment was an emergency?"

Avgusta looked from Matjaž to Helena, very confused. "Cow heart? What nonsense are you talking about?"

Helena sighed, or at least approximated one as best she could as vapor or whatever she was. "Your little witch-lette is in way over her head. She thought she was leaving a spell to drive her sister away from Faron. She does pretty shoddy work. It knocked Ivanka on her ass and would've blown them all out of the flat if I hadn't taken matters into my own hands, or rather yours." She looked at him through her dark lashes.

"You drew a circle in the blood as a containment spell." Matjaž shook his head. His sister was indeed the same in death as she had been in life.

Helena laughed. "You should get a massage, by the way. You are tense, big brother."

He wanted to laugh, too. He missed her, but this couldn't continue. "I'll take that under consideration." What he was about to ask, demand, would send her away for good, but it was as things should be. "Apologize to Jo, explain however much you feel you need to explain, and then go. Jo deserves a guide who is not tangled up in Mother's scheming, willingly or not."

His mother's mouth gaped and then set into a grim line.

"You can't do that. I need her!"

"I can ask it of her, and I will." Helena watched him silently as he turned his pronouncements on their mother. "And you will stop. Helena is dead. I do not want to take father's place. As you'll recall, he was eager to give it up. You have done enough damage to my life and to Helena's; Jo and her son are off limits."

Helena piped up. "Can I make a request before I go?" He was surprised she felt the need to ask. "Of course."

"In addition to letting me go and not calling me back into this ridiculous soup bowl, you will rein in your fledgling sorceress before she hurts herself or someone else. If you're going to train her, you need to do it properly, or send her to someone like Goran who will."

His mother looked smaller and more fragile in the folds of her blanket and the confines of her chair, but there was steel in her eyes. "Send her to someone like Goran, so she can pull rabbits out of hats? Ha."

Matjaž stared at her. "You introduced a traumatized girl to magic without filling in all the details?"

"I needed a lackey, not an apprentice." She looked up at Helena. "That was supposed to be your job."

"Well, hopefully, she doesn't have any other tricks up her sleeve." Helena cocked her head at her mother. "Can I go now, please?"

"Yes." His mother took a besom from the altar next to the bowl that held Helena's spirit. She turned in her chair and swept a section of salt away, breaking the circle and her contact with the In-Between. Helena vanished.

Avgusta looked up at him. "I'm not going to apologize. I did what I thought was right–"

"No, Mother. You did what you wanted, regardless of who it hurt. And it's done. I don't need your apology. I need your promise."

He took her ceremonial knife from the altar and nicked the fleshy part of his palm with the tip of blade. A bead of dark blood rose instantly. He motioned for her to hold out her hand. She hesitated but complied. He inflicted the same small wound on her and grabbed her forearm, smearing the blood between their hands and wrists.

"Promise me, Mother, that tonight, your campaign to resurrect my father, to confer his former mantle onto Helena or me, or to interfere in the lives of any others to achieve either of those goals, ends. Promise me, you will take no revenge on me, on my sister's spirit, or any other who has thwarted you in your mission." He locked his gaze with hers and waited.

She nodded.

"You have to say it. We both know how this works."

She was defiant still, but he could see defeat wash over her like a blanket of gray descending and muting her colors. "I promise, on our blood. If I make any attempt to break this promise, I forfeit my powers and my life."

CHAPTER 20

Rain pattered on the tin roof over her grandmother's porch. Instead of cooling the hot August evening, it brought steam up in the scorched yard and completely saturated the air. The sound of shelled peas hitting the plastic bowl in front of Jo added counterpoint to the rhythm of the downpour.

Her grandmother sang hymns to herself as she ran a thumbnail along each pea pod. Jo turned to look at the older woman. She wasn't really so old, maybe mid-forties. And so was Jo. Her dreams just kept getting weirder.

"Jolene, you should know how this works by now." She set the bag of peas aside. "You're in a mess of trouble, but I think you've figured that out already."

Jo nodded. "So what do I do?"

"Do? You still think you're in charge of this dog-and-pony show?"

"I did. I guess that's not the case."

"You are only in charge of you, but you aren't pulling the strings."

"That I did know." Was her grandmother about to impart

some Dumbledorian advice about our choices making us who we are?

"Well. That's something. She should be here soon."

"She who?"

"Who do you think?" Her grandmother pointed out into the garden covering the lawn in front of the house.

Her mother was picking her way through the tomato vines and pole beans. She was old, older than both Jo and her grandmother. Her long, gray hair hung to her waist, and she had on a sundress that left her darkly freckled shoulders bare. Her clavicles stuck out, and her creped skin barely covered the bones.

"Jolene." Her mother's voice was softer than the rain but carried to Jo from the bottom of the two sun-baked wooden steps up to the porch.

"Mother." Jo did not want to do this. Her grandmother took her hand and squeezed her fingers.

"I'm not dead yet, if that's what you're wondering. I don't think it'll be long now, though."

Jo doubted it would be, either. Her mother looked all of her sixty-odd years, plus another thirty for good measure. It was a stark contrast to her grandmother's apparent youth.

"I think you may be joining me in the hereafter soon."

Jo's heart skipped but quickly settled back into a steady rhythm. Winifred and Rebecca had hinted at the same fate, but she had *been* them in the previous dreams. She was very much herself this time.

"I don't know if she's right, but I thought you should hear

her out anyway." Her grandmother turned from her to the woman still standing in the rain. "Mary, you can come up on the porch." Another rocking chair appeared between the ones Jo and her grandmother filled.

Her mother settled into the chair, clutching the armrests like the cane-seat rocker was going to shoot off the porch, dumping her back out into the muddy yard.

"Jolene, your time–"

"It's 'Jo,' Mom."

"I'll call you by the name I gave you. Thanks for ruining my big moment."

Jo rolled her eyes. Some things never changed; her mother was still a drama queen, even in Jo's own damn dream.

"Don't roll your eyes at me, young lady."

"Stop it, you two. Mary, say your piece. You don't belong here, and I've got no intention of letting you stay any longer than I have to."

Mary shrugged. "Jo," she said it like it was a swear word. "It's time for you to move on. You've done what you were supposed to, and he'll come for you soon."

"Who is 'he'?"

"I don't know. He's the one that meets us at our end." She shivered.

"Are you sure you aren't mixing up the two of us? I barely got started with the soldiers on the mountain. There's a lot more work to do." Jo reminded herself that her mother was a Voice, not a prophet.

"He visits me. He tells me things."

Her mother's hissed words made Jo's skin crawl.

"Mary, you need to go. You aren't helping her."

Her mother stood up and started to walk back out into the garden and the rain. She looked back over her shoulder and whispered, "He's coming for us both, Jolene." She disappeared into the afternoon as silently as she'd come. A corn snake wended its way across the path where her mother had stood.

"Don't pay her any mind. If I'd known what nonsense she would bring, I wouldn't have let her in."

"You know I don't understand how any of this works, right? You're dead, but she's not and somehow you're in charge?"

"Don't think everything has to be logical." Her grandmother gave her The Eye that had sent her and her cousin Michael scampering when they were kids. Hell, it had sent her scampering when she was a teenager.

"Am I going to die?"

"Eventually. I mean that's how living works. But I don't think it's anytime soon."

"That's not what 'he' said." Her mother could deliver a creepy-ass line with some conviction.

"He doesn't warn us. He just shows up. I don't know who your mama's been talking to, but it isn't him."

"I am not really comforted by that thought, Grandma."

"Eh. You can comfort yourself or not, however you please." She picked up the bag of peas again and went back to shelling.

"Grandma, where are you exactly?"

"There's no exactly to it. I am where I am."

Shades definitely had the market cornered on being vague as fuck. "Thanks for clearing that up."

Her grandmother laughed. "I know what you want to ask. You should ask it."

"Is Dad with you?"

"No." She shook her head and pursed her lips. "He's nowhere we can go, and you probably need to accept that."

"Is Milo there?" She knew where her father was, but she was surprised her grandmother didn't know she'd been to that place.

"No, child."

Jo's heart sank into her stomach. "Did the demon get his soul, too?"

Her grandmother shook her head. "It didn't, but that doesn't mean he isn't lost in his own way."

"He's still here?"

"No, honey, he's dead. You know that."

"I mean in the In-Between."

She looked up from her peas and met Jo's gaze. "You can't save them all. That's not how it works."

Lightning struck a beanpole in the garden. The thunderclap and the flash came together and pressed the air out of Jo's lungs.

She woke up gasping in her own bed, soaked to the skin with clammy sweat and drowning in the smell of rotting lilies.

The water had been cold for a few minutes, but she still stood under the showerhead, letting it wash away the lingering floral funk. Lilacs and lilies. Why did demons and assholes think their misdeeds could be hidden behind the scent of nauseating, cloying flowers? There had to be something in that. But what did good magic smell like? Woodsmoke and the earth after a hard rain. It smelled like Dušan. That wasn't a thought she wanted to linger over too long, either. She'd spent a lot of time building a particularly high and ornate fence around those feelings.

She turned off the water and toweled herself off while walking back to her bedroom. A quick peek out the window over the futon in the living room revealed another day of slate-gray skies and more snow drifting into the courtyard. It was time to get back to work. She needed a distraction, even if the distraction was Fred telling her what to do like she was a trainee.

One other item on her mental to-do list had a bright, red ring drawn around it. She needed to choose a gift for Achelous and take it to the river; they needed to make their peace. He needed to know she was not interested in shacking up with him in his watery bower, but she did respect his power. She was grateful to him for saving her and Faron, even if he'd left the last bit of saving to her after she turned him down. Gods had their pride; that was definitely a thing.

She tapped her phone awake and started a playlist to keep her company while she got dressed. The first few bars of Gogol Bordello's "Wanderlust King" seeped out of the speakers before she could skip it; for her the song was forever linked to Rok and the last night she'd seen him. The next song was "The Ship Song," and though there wasn't a reason, it, too, had become linked with her friend in the wind. It was probably her, and she probably needed to deal with her feelings about his leaving. But it would have to wait. In her new life, there were always too many supernaturally weird things going on to deal with the emotionally troubling mundane flotsam of human existence. Though in truth, her relationship with Rok straddled the everyday and the woo-woo.

The playlist settled into the Johnny Cash cover of "Hurt," and that would have to be okay. She pulled clothes out of the wardrobe and stood staring out the window of her room. The gauzy curtains were open, and the snow outside was drifting down in fat flakes like ash from a fire. She couldn't remember the last time it had snowed so much in town. She pulled another layer out to chase away the cold.

———

Jo met Frédéric in front of the shop. He had a bucket and brush in hand.

"Wouldn't a broom be more effective?" She glanced down at the bucket of soapy water and the snow piling in soft drifts against the planters.

"It's not for the snow." He walked on toward the entrance to the courtyard.

Jo saw it then. Words and symbols scrawled in red spray paint on the heavy wooden doors standing open against the interior wall. The letters stood out like angry wounds. Goran's wards had kept the assholes away from the shop front, and they'd splashed their hate on the main door instead.

"Is there another brush?"

Fred nodded and kept walking. She went into the shop to get the brush. The bells clanged against the wooden door, announcing her entrance. Ivanka poked her head out of the kitchen and then stepped out behind the bakery case.

"Did you see Fred?"

"Yeah. I came in to get another brush."

Ivanka ducked back into the kitchen. Jo could hear her rummaging under the sink before she reappeared.

"I offered to help, but Fred said I should get started on prep." Ivanka looked down at the brush and then back up into Jo's face. "Do you think Fred's in danger?"

"No." The majority of the "*Bela Europa*" crowd were kids clinging to garbage being fed to them by scapegoaters. "I don't think it's a physical threat. They just like to rattle people."

Ivanka nodded. "It's so gross. Why would anyone do that?"

"Because they don't know anything about Fred, or Reka. They think people who are different from them are somehow taking away from them."

Ivanka exploded with emotion. "But they are angry at the wrong people. They should be pissed off at the people looting the country and leaving everyone else holding the empty bag."

Jo walked into the kitchen, hoping Ivanka would follow. "You know that, and I know that. Hopefully, when they pull their heads out of their asses, they'll figure it out, too."

"What are we going to do about it?"

"There's nothing to do about it. Clean off the paint and keep doing what we do."

Ivanka picked up her knife again. "That's what Fred said."

"Well, Fred is right. I guarantee he's had to deal with this longer than the two of us."

"I guess so." Little o's of chive fell off Ivanka's knife into a growing pile.

"I'll come help with prep when we're done."

———

Fred and Jo scrubbed paint off the door, taking brittle flakes of the dark finish with it. They'd have to repaint when it warmed up. Fred said very little, only an occasional "sorry" when they both tried to dip their brushes into the bucket at the same time.

It was a shitty thing to happen. She was quiet, too.

"I'm sorry." She scrubbed the last bit of red paint off her side of the door.

Fred stopped and dropped his brush into the bucket. "You could have told me."

Jo stepped back, still holding her wet brush in her hands. The snow had started to fall faster and was layering over the last of the dirty snow from the previous storm. "I didn't know until I got down here."

"Not about this." He gestured toward the hard-scrubbed door.

"Oh." It would've been nice to know Vesna had told him about her peculiar gift. To be fair, though, there had been a lot going on.

"It came up when the vandals broke the pots and door."

"I didn't think you'd believe me. I mean really, who would want to? And, it gets me and everyone who knows about it into trouble."

"No judgment, Jo. I understand, but it was clear something was going on."

Jo nodded. Fred was smart. She'd known she couldn't keep it from him forever, and she hadn't planned to. It just wasn't something that came up easily in conversation.

"You should probably also know something is up with Faron and his father."

"I do know. I'm just not really sure yet how that's going to play out."

"I can see that." He took her brush from her and dropped it into the bucket. "Are you going to tell Reka?"

Jo stared at him for a minute. "Probably not. She just started, and I'd like to give her a chance before we run her off. You're ahead of me in this year's dishwasher betting pool. The last one didn't last two days."

"She deserves a chance, but a Romani woman is probably not going to want to be associated with witches, Jo. I'm sure she's been pegged with her fair share of stereotypes."

"I hadn't even thought of that. Shit." Another thing on the mundane list she'd failed to take care of in some way. "Maybe we should tell her something?"

Fred shrugged. "Maybe it will be fine."

Her hands were red and chapped, and the cold enveloped her all at once. She shivered.

Fred gestured for her to walk ahead of him across the

courtyard. "I'll make some tea to warm us up, and we can get the day started." He hadn't mentioned his surprise at her return to the shop or anything else that needed to be taken care of. She'd never anticipated her business being one of the most stable things in her life.

———

Leo knocked on his friend Luka's door. He'd seen Teja, Luka's wife chopping wood earlier from the grand window of his room. The couple were among the few people in the compound he'd gotten close to. He'd learned in his line of work that it was easier to keep secrets from people if there were fewer people to keep secrets from.

Luka answered the door. He ran his gnarled fingers through his short gray hair. "Come in. The coffee is fresh off the stove."

"Thank you. I thought I saw Teja earlier, in the back."

"Yes. She got up to chop wood before I had even rolled over. Now she is off to Ljubljana to meet her sister. I never know what those two women conjure between them." Luka laughed with affection. Leo had no doubt the man loved his wife deeply.

Luka had become Leo's sounding board after both his father and his brother had died. He and Teja had invited him into the community of aging hippies and idealists. The man was a good listener and only offered his advice if asked. Leo preferred his talks with Luka to confession and was usually more relieved of his burdens by the man's thoughtful silence.

Leo sat at the heavy oak table. Luka returned with two mugs filled to the brim with milky Turkish coffee. "Have you eaten? I was about to toast some bread from yesterday."

"I will never say no to Teja's bread." Leo sipped his coffee and watched Luka slice the hard bread and lay it on the warm griddle. While the bread toasted and filled the small house with the scent of breakfast, Luka gathered butter and homemade jam and other bits from the cupboards.

The table finally groaning with his generosity, Luka sat and sipped his coffee. "I do not think you came only for my mediocre coffee."

"Your coffee is always better than mine. And you are right, as usual."

"Leo, this conversation is not new, and I don't need Teja's tea leaves to see your future." Luka spread a piece of toast with butter and his wife's apricot jam.

"I have already sent a letter to the Father to tell him I am leaving the Order. I think he will be happy to see the back of me; he has regularly reminded me I am a source of consternation and unwanted curiosity."

"I don't wonder. A brother who chooses to live in a commune instead of cloistered with the others of his faith? Teja has never believed you were truly a priest of the Jesuits."

"I did believe I was, and I have no issue with God. My work complicates matters."

"As does your heart." Luka laughed, but it was gentle.

Leo looked out through the open curtain to the snowy common area of the compound. Children from one of the flats in the main house were throwing snowballs at each other, their pink faces barely visible between their hats and scarves.

"Before Berta was killed, we spoke of having children. I

had never wanted to be a father until I met her. The thought of a family was impossible to me after I took my vows." Leo wrapped his fingers around his warm cup.

"It is still possible. To wait for a family, this is easier for men." Luka sipped his coffee and waited for Leo to speak.

"No. The time for children has passed." Leo's gaze returned to his cup.

"Jo Wiley has already had her child." Luka smiled.

"She has. And settling into a life like yours and Teja's is not something I believe she longs for."

"And you, are you willing to follow the life she will lead?"

"That is the question, my friend, the very one." Leo finished his coffee except for the small swirl of fine grounds in the bottom of the cup.

CHAPTER 21

Faron took the last few steps up onto the flat surface of the deck. Ivanka had beaten him to the top, but barely. The sun was still a rosy glow on the horizon as he reached up to turn off his headlamp before sliding it into a pocket. The cold hadn't been able to penetrate much while they were hiking up to the peak, but as his heart rate slowed a chill started to find its way through his clothes.

He and Ivanka had hiked to the top of Šmarna Gora more times than he could count. Its peaks held plague monuments, a wishing bell, and a church dedicated to St. Mary. It had been the site of warning bonfires when the Turks invaded. It was a place of refuge and safety with a view into the Ljubljana valley and to both the Julian and Kamnik Alps.

The last time he'd been there was to watch the sunset with Rok. It was probably the last time he would go hiking with his erstwhile uncle. Living that long didn't seem to have many perks, or at least not ones that could outweigh watching everyone you care about die.

Ivanka dropped her pack on the deck near the rail and looked out toward the lights of Ljubljana, where people were starting the day. She was off work until the afternoon, and he'd suggested the hike to clear her head after the new graffiti at the teahouse the day before. He guessed she felt a little helpless to do anything about it. He did.

They stood next to each other at the rail and waited for the sun to pop up over the line of fog nestled against the midnight-blue mountains. It was reassuring. The sun would come up. It didn't care if his mother could talk to dead people or that his father was an old, scary god. Daylight still came after darkness, even if he was whatever he was, or was going to be.

No one had offered to die in front of him yet, but the choice he was going to have to make hung over him like his own sword of Damocles. He wanted to keep Ivanka close, to protect her, sure she was the one he would have to save or watch die. He also wanted to tell her to run as far and as fast as she could away from him. She'd had enough death in her life already.

The sunrise shone pale gold on her face. She didn't smile or relax, but it became difficult to discern if the light was shining on her face or if she were the light. He couldn't remember the exact moment he'd fallen in love with her, but there must have been one. In his mind it looked like that moment.

She found his gloved hand with hers and squeezed. "Thank you. I needed this."

Fat snowflakes drifted down, sticking to her hat and eyebrows.

"Me, too." He moved behind her and wrapped her in his arms as they watched the sunlight move across the valley. If it was Ivanka's life or his mortality, he would choose to save her, every single time. His father probably knew that already.

———

The city still glowed orange under artificial light as Jo set out to meet Gregor at the Napoleon statue on French Revolution Square. He'd agreed to drive her to Vrhnika in the predawn hours without too many questions. It was a strange birthday request, but he had been the one who offered her anything she wanted.

She'd forgotten it was her birthday until Gregor had asked a couple days before. He'd popped into the teahouse after Vesna summoned him, pissed off Jo and Fred had cleaned away the graffiti without calling the police. Vesna had forgotten Jo's birthday, too, and the look on her face had reflected the gears spinning in her head. There would be some kind of surprise when Jo returned to the teahouse later in the day.

Surprises weren't high on her list of birthday wishes, but Helena's words about not pushing everyone away kept churning through her thoughts. And while it wouldn't hurt to let Vesna have her fun, she was absolutely not going to wear a paper hat. Vesna had a persistent idea about all Americans celebrating birthdays with "pin the tail on the donkey" and paper hats. Jo had pointed out repeatedly that more than 330 million people couldn't agree to any one thing on all occasions, and paper hats and parlor games were mostly for the under-ten set. There had to be a line.

Gregor arrived and pulled his car into the spot closest to where Jo stood, trying to shield herself against the worst of the wind and the blowing snow.

Once they were strapped in, Gregor started in on the questions he'd hedged on the day before. "Is there a particular reason you are going to hike an hour into the *barje* in the snow?"

"It's my birthday, do I need a reason?"

"Yes. It's below freezing and still snowing."

She shrugged against the leather seat. "Some things need doing when they need doing." Her grandmother's oft-quoted words took her back to the dream momentarily. She didn't plan on freezing to death in the marsh. "If you have to know, I need to make amends with Achelous."

"It can't wait until spring?"

He couldn't see the side eye she gave him, but Jo suspected he could feel it. "You are the very person who told me to figure out what I needed to do to deal with all this … stuff. I need this."

His silence indicated concession, and he changed the topic. "Are you and Matjaž a thing?"

"No. Decidedly not. He's a good guy but–"

"But your heart lies elsewhere?"

Where did her heart lie? Did her heart even know what to do with itself? She had turned down Matjaž, even with Snippy the Evil Queen's stinky lily magic trying to do its thing. Because there was still the troubling connection to Helena, and there was Leo. Leo, who would break his vows for her. Leo, who fancied himself her knight protector, even when she'd made it clear she didn't need or want that from him. Leo, who was her friend. Leo, whose presence made her as self-conscious as a teenager. And when she was being honest with herself, Leo, whom she loved.

"Jo?"

"Sorry. I was thinking."

"About?"

"Leo."

Gregor pulled off at the first available opportunity and put the hazard lights on. "Of all the people on earth you could finally fall in love with, you choose a priest?"

"Apparently."

He took a deep breath. "Jo." The anger that had underlain his question dissipated. He sounded disappointed in her instead.

"I know. I drew that line in the sand, and he walked right over it and said he'd leave the church and he drove all the way up to Tolmin to tell me and there was this roadside Madonna and we kissed and … shit. What is wrong with me? I can't do this. I cannot be the reason he leaves the church. Me? I cannot."

"Jesus. Take a breath. Maybe two."

She did, but the exhale was half-sigh, half-snort.

"If he loves you and you love him, I will dance at your wedding. Did it occur to you that if he so handily fell for you, he maybe already had issues with the church?"

"Wedding? And he's never discussed that with me. Well, not in depth."

Gregor threw his head back against the seat rest. "Did you ask?"

"No."

"It's a good thing I love you, or I'd push you out of the car."

"Thanks."

"Really, Jo. That a man, even a priest, told you he loves you in a not Jesus-like way and you haven't gone screaming back up into the mountains is progress. I'll take whatever I can get."

"Thank you, Dr. Freud. Can we get going? I'd like to get back in time to be of some use at the shop today."

Gregor pulled back onto the road and turned the volume up on the car stereo bluetoothed to his phone. Blur's "Song 2" whoo-hooed at them. At least somebody was happy.

———

Gustaf waited nervously in the courtyard. His phone had rung at what he believed to be an impolite hour of the morning. When Dušan Črnigad made a request, the Board, and therefore the Observers, answered with compliance. Ruffled feathers aside, he was eager to further discuss the advent of Faron Wiley's abilities. Resurrection was not an unheard-of gift, but the Board tended to keep an especially watchful eye on those who possessed it.

Bettine, his contact with the Board, was distrustful of anyone who could interfere in the natural order of things in such a singular way. Why, he did not understand. Bringing the dead back to life was only slightly more disruptive than speaking with them or outliving everyone currently alive. In his book, any supernatural being or ability was part of the larger whole of those things that must be kept behind the cloak of the Veil, and he differentiated little among them.

Perhaps with the exception of demons. Those he would gladly do without.

The cold made his nose run as the snowflakes fell more thickly, obscuring what little of the cobblestones remained visible from the previous afternoon's melt. He took off his glove and dug into a pocket for his handkerchief.

Črnigad caught him wiping his nose as he entered the courtyard. "Gustaf, good of you to meet me."

"I did not have to journey far." His apartment wasn't more than a few meters above their heads.

The teahouse was still dark; it was too early for Jo Wiley or any of her staff to be in. The antique dealer would not be open until closer to midday. The accountant's office had been emptied, and the New Age shop next to the teahouse had long closed. Its windows were still papered over. The residents of the building were dwindling to only those who lived their lives hidden from the mundane.

"But it is early, and the weather is miserable." Črnigad produced a single key to open the door to the former accountant's office. "I wanted to show you what will be the new gallery."

"Gallery? Here?" Had he informed Ms. Wiley he would be in a prime position to watch her every move?

"Jo and I already discussed it. The space is ideal, and if I am going to be back in Ljubljana full-time, I'll need something to keep me busy."

Gustaf nodded. "I hadn't realize you had planned to stay in Ljubljana."

"It seems appropriate, I think." Črnigad walked to the back

of the truncated space and turned on a row of can lights. The cool light made the white walls glow. It would be a perfect backdrop for the black-and-white photographs the man was famous for.

"I suppose. Will you live in town, as well?"

"Yes. Marija has decided to stay in New York. Perhaps Gregor has another flat here? It would be convenient to be close by."

Gustaf sputtered. "Are you certain that is a good idea? I mean, there is an empty flat — three in fact — but why would you choose to live so close to Ms. Wiley?"

"I hope you do not call her that to her face. She would hate it."

Gustaf caught himself staring. The man was more brazen than he had remembered. Necromancers and alchemists were notoriously self-possessed, but to move in next to the woman he had abandoned?

"I do not think I have ever known you to be at a loss for words, Gustaf. It is quite the sight." Črnigad chuckled and produced a chair out of the cold, stale air of the empty gallery. He sat on it and crossed his legs. "Sit. We have some details to hammer out."

Another chair sat facing him. It hadn't appeared so much as it had coalesced.

"That is not the trick of an alchemist or a necromancer." Gustaf stepped back toward the door and the perceived safety of the open courtyard.

"Gustaf, it is time you learned a few things even your precious Bettine does not want you to know."

———

Jo took off her seatbelt as Gregor maneuvered off the road at the closest point to Močilnik, one of the springs of the Ljubljanica, where it burst onto the marsh before winding its way into the city.

"Are you sure about this?" Gregor looked out the windshield at the leaden sky and accumulating snow.

She nodded. "Sure" was probably not the best description of her feelings. A soup of worry, fear, and determination sloshed in her gut. If it didn't happen now, it probably wasn't going to happen.

"If I come back here in two hours and you aren't standing on the side of the road stamping your feet in the cold, I'm going to call Mountain Rescue. They will be pissed."

"I hardly think Mountain Rescue will need to fish me out of the *barje*."

"You say that …"

"I am almost certain I do not meet my sticky end by freezing to death. Promise." She pulled her scarf tighter and plopped her "hideous" tam on her head. No need to rile up the local shades while she was on a mission from god. Or to a god. She laughed.

"This isn't funny, Jo."

"It's not funny, but the Blues Brothers are."

"Is that where your head is this morning?"

"Hey, I take my humor where I can find it." She kissed him on the cheek and opened the door into the cold. It felt like a much worse idea than it had yesterday, but she had to go. She sensed Achelous was waiting for her now, and he would be less than pleased if she bailed on him.

"Call me. I will call out the dogs or whatever is necessary."

She nodded again and closed the door.

Walking along the river through the frozen marsh was not her idea of a good time. The earth crunched with every step, and the wind continued to whip up the snow from the ground to meet the flakes falling from the sky. The canopy kept most of it from settling, but it still made the frozen, muddy spots slicker than owl shit, as her grandma would have said. She needed to find a stick, or she was going to wind up on her ass or in the water.

The stone Leo had given her after Helena's death was tucked into her coat pocket. She wanted to hold it but was afraid it would slip too easily from her gloved hands and be lost forever. There was a small possibility Achelous could still want to drag her into the river to be his drowned bride, and her judgment and senses had been manipulated too much lately for her to trust her instincts. The rock was the best substitute, unless its power to point out dangers didn't apply to the machinations of gods.

When she'd finally picked her way through the snowy forest to the source, the pool was calm and edged with a frozen crust as thin as waxed paper. It had been years since she'd come with Faron and Rok to see Jason's Fist, the impression above the spring that looked like a giant had punched the rock wall. Legend named this place the end point of the Argonauts' trek up the Ljubljanica River. They'd had to overwinter, then portage to the Adriatic to get home. Apparently Jason wasn't too pleased about that.

Her visit had been in the springtime, after the rains and melt. The trail she'd come in on had been underwater then, and the springs were bursting from the rocks. It was a dramatic setting in which to meet with a god, but Achelous was a bit of a drama queen.

She couldn't remember the last time she'd prayed, at least not when either she or Faron hadn't been in mortal danger. The words didn't come easily. Choosing a gift for Achelous had been difficult, too. It needed to be something precious and irreplaceable, at least to her. She wanted whatever she sacrificed to the river to be connected to her father. Whether Achelous could help her recover him was up for debate, but he had a connection to this place, and she had to believe as a god he had more power than she did.

The spoon was heavy in her hand. "U.S. Navy" was stamped on the handle, though the years had softened the imprint and it looked like someone had hand-lettered the words. It was the one thing she had of her father's. She'd carried it from Chattanooga, to India, to Ljubljana. Her father hadn't even been in the Navy. The spoon came from a junk shop in a bundle of flatware her mother had purchased for their first kitchen, and he'd simply liked the heft of it. He'd eaten his Cheerios with it every morning.

Jo stepped to the edge of the pool and crouched down, knees popping.

"Achelous, um, thank you for mostly saving me so I could save Faron. I'd like to ask you to help me save my father, if that's something you could do. I'm still not interested in shacking up with you, but I believe, no, I know you exist and protect this river and place. Amen?" The spoon slid from her fingers into the pool, hardly disturbing the surface at all. She hoped stainless steel wasn't bad for the local ecosystem.

"It is one of the more interesting gifts I have received."

Jo stood and wheeled around toward the voice, almost toppling into the freezing water before regaining her balance. Achelous no longer sounded like Tom Waits' morning voice after a cigarette bender. He looked different from what she'd imagined, as well, a pastiche of his description in "The Waterman" poem and every portrayal of a god on a Grecian urn she'd seen. He was tall and athletic-looking, and his hair was dark, but that's about all she'd had right. His eyes were an unnerving color, the same milky green as the water in the pool.

"You seem surprised."

"A little."

"Surprised by my appearance, or that I appeared at all?"

"Both."

He crunched across the crusty snow and hoarfrost toward her.

It took more willpower than she thought she had to not back away from him.

"You needn't fear me. You have made your wishes clear."

"Thanks?"

"I wish I could say I missed the formal prayers and reverence, but it does get old. I think I prefer your reluctant admiration." His laugh bounced around the iced-over glade like handfuls of glass beads dropped into a crystal bowl.

"Reluctant admiration is about all I've got. I'm still not

quite okay with you almost letting me drown in the museum."

"I saved you from the demon. It is not my domain to save you from yourself."

"And my father?"

"You already know where he is. That, too, is beyond my domain. And you knew that, as well."

"It never hurts to ask."

"It does not, as long as you can live with the answer."

She nodded. She guessed gods did have a few things going for them on the wisdom front. "I can live with that, but I'm not sure how to continue this."

"Continue what?"

"I don't know, veneration? I'm really not comfortable with the concept of 'worship.'"

"It's been many generations since my priestesses lingered in the marshes of the Dodona."

"I don't want to be one of your priestesses, or anyone else's, but I will honor you in some way."

"Jo Wiley, your prayers are enough. My days of taking what I want are behind me."

"Really? What was that business at the museum then?"

"I did not take you, though I could have. I could take you now. It is not often a mortal offers herself up in such a secluded place. But I gave you a choice, and I respect the one you made."

"Thank you, for that. I guess I should be going." The snow had kept falling, so the walk back to the road was going to be more of an adventure than the trek in.

"There is something more you would ask."

"There is."

Petitioning a god, even on another's behalf, was an awful lot like asking for help. She still struggled with it, struggled with putting her faith in another person, another being, to do what they promised. "If my prayers are enough, will you offer your protection to Faron?"

"I offer my protection, such that it is, to you and, by extension, to your son. I doubt he will require it much longer."

"What–"

"Do not ask if you cannot live with the answer."

———

Henry watched storm after storm wade through the mountains, wrapping the world in a blanket of dazzling whites and pale blues and grays. The cold could not reach him, but he remembered it and remembered the warmth of Jo's skin against his flesh. Flesh she had the power to bring back into existence. He drank her wine and ate her food and loved her body, but she was as much a ghost to him as he was to himself.

She would return. He could believe that much. Her return would put an end to his miserable existence here in the purgatory he had made for himself. He hadn't earned her pardon, but it was her lot in life to offer it to him regardless. For the others on the mountain, his hell would be the genesis of their release. His final coin paid at the table and in the bed of a woman born after he had died. Were he a physical person, and if his prison had walls he could touch, he could scratch the days until she came back onto the stone. Instead there was waiting and the counting of suns as they passed overhead and sank back to the valleys beyond the peaks.

CHAPTER 22

Vanilla and cinnamon and the vegetal haze of black tea greeted Jo like an old friend at the entrance to the shop. A muscle in her chest relaxed when she tied on the long, black French apron, crisscrossing the ties under her breasts and finishing the bow in the back. Her tongue softened in her mouth, and her jaw unclenched as she read down Fred's prep list for the day. It was a temporary reprieve. That's probably all she would ever get. But she'd take it today, or however many days it lasted. Grandma and Achelous had made it clear in their individual ways that she wasn't piloting this ship. All she could do was steel herself against whatever, or whomever, was coming for her family, this time.

"No music this morning?" Fred stirred the day's soup before tasting it.

"What are you in the mood for?" She would be in the mood for that red lentil soup long before lunchtime.

"Your choice. Igor came by to see Vesna this morning and dropped off a stack of CDs he thought you might want."

"We don't have anything to play them on here." She didn't even have anything in her flat she could play CDs on.

"He was a step ahead of you." Fred walked out to the service area where the tea bar was arranged and pulled a beat-up MacBook off the shelf where she usually stashed her iPod to play music for the shop. "He said he'd come and get it after you ripped whatever you wanted."

"Cool." She took the laptop from him and set it on the bar to pick up a stack of CDs in plastic jewel cases.

"Pick something, and I'll pull the *mise* for the scones and shortbread for you."

"Sure. Thanks." She was distracted, already swimming in the nostalgia of music from her formative years. She had a lot of what Vesna's boyfriend had brought, but not everything. Halfway through the pile there was a copy of XTC's *English Settlement* with the white outlines of the Uffington Horse against a forest-green background.

She pulled the disc from its grippy little circle and slid it into the slot on the side of the computer. She figured out how to open the disc file and get it to play. The speakers in the shop popped when she plugged the line in. Andy Partridge's voice was almost lost in percussion, layered 12-string chords, and soft synth mesmerism as he implored an abused runaway to come home on the opening track. She was dragged back to her college boyfriend Turner's dorm room, draped over his bed, stoned out of her gourd. At 17, every lyric had some import directed solely at her. Her father had never hit her, but he'd left her with a mother who had. She tucked the laptop back onto the shelf and stacked the jewel cases next to it.

The bells on the front door banged against the wood. Faron came in with Ivanka. She hung her snowflake-sprinkled coat on a peg by the door. "Did Fred pick the music this morning?"

"Nope. Reliving some college nostalgia." Jo smoothed her apron.

"This doesn't sound like something you'd be into." Ivanka headed for the kitchen and threw a look back at Faron.

"What can I say? My interests are multitude." Jo watched her son fidget nervously next to the coat pegs. "You look like you need to talk."

"Yeah. I'm just not sure I want Fred to hear. Or Ivanka."

Jo walked back to the MacBook and cranked up the sound a bit. Andy and the band had moved on to "Jason and the Argonauts." She'd forgotten about that song.

Faron sat at the table nearest the door, his coat still on like he would flee at any moment. She pulled a chair out and sat next to him.

"I'm sorry I didn't tell you about Helena and the mouse and—"

"You don't need to apologize. I get it." They were cut from the same weird cloth.

"I'm still sorry you had to hear it from Dušan."

It was petty, but she was glad Faron didn't call him Dad. "That was unexpected, but not any more than–"

"Than everything else. Yeah."

"How much did he tell you?"

"All of it, I think. If I bring someone back from the dead, I'm the white god." Faron played with a leather bracelet tied around his wrist.

"That was the overview I got, too." This was more awkward than the sex talk and the drug talk combined. She couldn't help but swim around in her guilt: If she hadn't been attracted to Dušan. If she hadn't let herself be drawn in by him. He'd used her, however he rationalized it, and Faron was paying for it.

"I've tried to send Ivanka away or break up with her. I can't do it." He looked anguished by his failure.

"Why do you think it will be her?"

"Just feels like it would be." He was waiting for her to give him the answers, and she didn't have them.

"This stuff … I don't know. I don't think you can out-think it. Don't make yourself miserable in an effort to try." She put her hand over his. "I can tell you one thing though: if it's me, let me go."

"I couldn't do that, either. How can you say that?" He pulled his hand away.

She hoped he could see the empathy in her face and didn't mistake it for pity. "I think Ivanka would tell you the same thing, if you asked her." He had already made up his mind, she could see the determination in the set of his shoulders. His body language was so like Dušan's, though they'd never even spent a whole day together.

He leaned back in his chair. "She would."

Jo stood up. "Are you going to be late for class?" She wanted to keep him there, keep him safe, whatever the cost to her. She couldn't try to out-think it either, though. There were too many variables, and in her effort to prevent one thing, she would invariably cause another, possibly worse, outcome.

"Maybe." He stood up and pulled her into a hug.

"Faron, you know whatever happens, whatever choices you make, I'll still love you. I'll still be here for you." Somehow. If her great grandmothers could get to her, she'd figure out how to get to him. "Even if I'm not here, here."

"I know." He kissed her on the forehead and headed out into the morning.

Jo remembered the thing her Aunt Jackie had said to her when Faron was born, something like having a child was like watching your heart walk around outside your body. She had thought she'd fear for him less as he got older, but no pithy quote could have prepared either of them for this.

———

Vesna and Reka appeared in time to join them for family meal. Jo was deep into a bowl of Fred's spicy lentil soup pondering her conversation with Faron when Vesna dropped her birthday surprise bombshell.

"We're closing the shop a little early. Say 9?" Vesna took a bite of a smoked salmon sandwich and beamed at Jo.

"And why would we do that?" Jo leveled her gaze at her friend and birthday nemesis.

"So we can all go to your birthday party."

Jo had promised herself she would go along with Vesna's weird idea of birthday celebrations and thus kept her eye-rolling to a minimum. "And will there be paper hats and parlor games?"

"No. I'm pretty sure Niko would have a shit fit about blindfolded, drunk people poking holes in the gallery walls."

Reka snorted. "He'd probably paint a frame around it and call it art."

Vesna sat up straight in her chair. "But seriously, birthday party. 9:30-ish at Niko's gallery."

"If you insist." Jo went back to her soup.

"Could you not be that way?" Vesna was snippy in lieu of being hurt.

"I'm sorry. It's just that celebrating my birthday is the last thing I'm interested in doing."

"Maybe your friends would like to celebrate you." Fred looked at her over the rim of his teacup.

Jo sighed. "Point taken."

"Good. Then you should leave about 8 or 8:30 and shower and change or whatever you'd like to do. We can wrap up here and walk over together." Vesna stacked the dirty dishes and got up to take them to the sink.

———

Tuesday. Again. There was no backing out this time.

Veronika was determined to complete her spell that evening. Avgusta had grilled her about how she would release the spell, but she'd also been distant and withdrawn. Veronika hadn't remembered messing up more than usual, but she never knew with Avgusta. She'd finished the few chores Avgusta had for her and taken off. If this spell worked, Avgusta might trust her to help with more-powerful workings. Maybe she would trust her enough to show her how to pull her mother or her father up into that bowl.

Ivanka was at work, and the Tuesday night crew was

supposed to meet around nine, despite the weather. The snow had stopped, at least for the time being, but the roads were kind of a mess and the buses weren't running. She'd rather walk, anyway. Being crammed into an overheated bus wasn't her idea of fun.

She hitched her backpack up on her shoulder and looked behind her. She had a sense that someone was watching her or following her, but nobody had a reason to, as far as she knew. Avgusta didn't have any other assistants, and she hadn't told anyone else she could do magic. She headed on to the tea shop, her stomach fluttering. There was excitement, but she was nervous, too. What if the spell didn't work? It would be hard to deny what she'd tried to do. She was also anxious about finding Jo alone. Her best bet was to catch her if and when she took the trash out to the receptacles down the street. The shop was too small to catch her alone unless Veronika managed to meet her on the stairs down to the basement toilets.

Veronika had to admit to herself that the nerves came partly from worrying about what the curse would look like. She'd never been the cause of someone else experiencing physical pain. What if she was too weak a witch to bear what she'd done? She needed to let that go. Jo Wiley deserved whatever she got.

Faron, Aleš, and Marko were walking out to the courtyard when Veronika got to the arched doorway. She tried to walk toward them but couldn't move past the entrance. The air was dense, and she bounced off it.

Jo must have warded the entrance after the vandalism. Shit.

"You okay there? We didn't mean to startle you." Marko joined her on the street. "Hey, Vesna's closing the shop early. We're all going to Niko's in *Metelkova* for a birthday party for Faron's mom." The others followed out through the arch and clustered around her.

"Okay." So much for ending this tonight.

"Don't look so disappointed. You're invited. We're walking out there now. The buses still aren't running." Faron joined them and chucked her lightly on the arm.

Veronika moved away from him. "I know. I walked." She adjusted the backpack. It wasn't heavy except for the weight of what she planned to do. Still, the straps dug into her shoulders. "Where's Ivanka?"

"Closing the kitchen. She's going to walk over with Mom and everyone else."

She followed the men out to *Breg*. This was not the plan, but it would probably be easier to get Jo alone in *Metelkova* than at the teahouse. Maybe some god of witches was smiling on her.

———

Jo pulled her heavy coat on over a layer of silk long underwear and a black ballet dress. It was her birthday, whether she was overjoyed about it or not, and it was cold. If the phones were going to come out for pictures, she might as well look nice. Vesna hadn't shared the guest list with her, but she assumed it would include Leo. Jo wanted to see him, and yet she didn't. There was no denying her feelings about him, even to herself, and she was a gold medalist in emotional denial. She couldn't dismiss him for not knowing the darkness she attracted, the darkness she was. The thing she could do was fret about him leaving the church for her. Gods were jealous. What would breaking his vows unleash on him? On her? Maybe Leo's god had mellowed like Dušan and Achelous. Or maybe he had enough swagger still, with his millions of believers, to smite those who turned away.

The mail was scattered on the futon where she'd dropped it when she came upstairs. A fat envelope with brightly swirling foreign stamps caught her eye on the way out the door. Her name and address were written in Rok's slanted hand. He'd remembered her birthday and taken the time to send a gift from wherever he was — somewhere in the Middle East, given the Arabic on the customs form. She paused at the door holding the slim package. Her disappointment at her friend's departure had ebbed, but the hurt over how much he had hidden from her still stung, even after Dušan's revelation of the heartbreak of the Long-Lived.

The paper and tape gave away easily to reveal a small box and a letter. She couldn't face his words just yet, so she laid the letter back on the futon to open the box. A medallion on a silver chain was nestled in a wad of crumpled paper. The image was worn and faint, but the horns of a bull were still decipherable. The reverse was worn smooth, as if it had spent a lifetime against another's skin. She set the box on top of the letter and fastened the chain around her neck. A clear image of Rok at a counter sliding the package across zipped through her thoughts and was replaced just as quickly by an aching cold and the sensation of her own limbs floating out from her body. She really needed to ask Jackie or Gustaf about the side effects of being a Voice or a Portal, or if something else was causing the new intrusions.

She locked the door behind her and made her way to the courtyard where Vesna, Ivanka, and Reka waited for her with Fred. They'd been joined by Goran and Gustaf. Vesna had been generous with her invitations. Niko would laugh at Jo's poaching prospects for the evening, but she knew who she wanted in her bed and it wasn't a nameless, faceless person to keep her warm.

"*I winsch da ois guade zum Gebuatsdog.*" Gustaf extended his hand to her.

"Thank you." Gustaf: guaranteed to be awkwardly formal.

CHAPTER 23

The muffler of snow banks and still-falling flakes spotlit by the street lamps left Jo feeling as if she and her companions had stepped out of the courtyard into a different city. Familiar landmarks on the pavement had disappeared, and people weren't venturing out in the streets. The few they passed were rushing home with their heads down against the cold.

Vesna must have promised Niko a crowd to get him to open the gallery on a night like this. His loyalty to Jo was as amorphous as his affection had been. He would never have offered to host a party for her unless a significant amount of cash was going to pass over his bar.

Forty-four. There wasn't anything significant about it as a birthday, other than it was her first as a Voice. The jury was still out about whether that was a reason to celebrate.

No one offered to speak on the walk or to break the spell of the silent street. They hugged the river embankment until they reached the Dragon Bridge to turn north toward the former squat. Jo felt the water moving alongside them, its icy run echoing in her veins. She needed to think of things besides lost friends and previously forgotten gods if she was going to work herself into any kind of celebratory mood. She reached out for Ivanka and Vesna and took them both by the arm, walking on to the gallery between her dearest friend and her son's love.

———

Light cracked out into the frozen air through the gallery windows and onto the snow-covered central courtyard of *Metelkova*. Footprints had tamped down the first of the snowfall into a compressed gray lawn. The party had started without them. PJ Harvey's driving guitar and voice followed the light out to reverberate off the concrete and steel of the old Army barracks.

Vesna rushed ahead through the door. "Down by the Water" abruptly ended and was quickly replaced with The White Stripes' cover of "Jolene." At least it wasn't a stupid party hat.

Jo smiled at the faces connected to the clapping hands gathered to wish her well until she looked behind them. A new mural, Igor's work, took up the entire back wall of the gallery. Jo walked toward it, and the crowd of friends, still clapping, parted as she moved through them to stand in front of the painting.

She sensed Vesna at her side and Leo hovering behind her, his height casting part of the swirl of spray-painted images in shadow. Her image was there in the center, pot in hand, pouring darjeeling into the river of tea she stood in. Her dark blonde hair drifted out around her like an underwater crown. Behind her were the faces of friends and family. Vesna, Gregor, and Leo stood, arms linked behind them. Rok and Faron were clinging to a mountainside waving. Ivanka, Fred, and Reka were lined up in front of Renegade Tea each holding a plate of fantastical food. Swirls of color moved between each snapshot of the people she loved. Above those faces a storm cloud of dark grays and blues hovered, releasing snowflakes onto the scene below. Some of the flakes were images — logos from bands she liked or who had played at the teahouse, a tea bag, a medallion with a bull's head, lilies and carnations, stars, skulls and bones — all raining down on her and into the river of tea. The storm cloud was made of wings and eyes hidden in the billowing curves.

Jo stumbled back away from the wall. Leo caught her arm when she tripped over her own boots.

"It's amazing, isn't it? Igor finished it last night." Vesna was beaming with pride at her birthday surprise.

"Did you tell him …" The question died on her lips. Achelous' face, the face she had first seen that morning at the spring, was hidden in the current of the dark river.

"I asked him to do a birthday mural for you. I think he and Niko discussed where it could go."

Jo realized Leo was still supporting her, and she planted her feet underneath her.

Igor joined them in front of his artwork.

"*Vse najboljše.*" He kissed her on both cheeks.

"Thank you. The mural. It's …" She reached out and touched the painted medallion that matched the one around her neck. "How did you know?"

"Know what?"

Vesna raised an eyebrow at Jo, warily awaiting an answer.

Jo fished Rok's birthday gift out of her dress and showed it to Igor. "It came today in the mail."

Vesna's eyes went wide.

Igor shrugged. "Hmm. I remembered you wearing one before. Must have been someone else." He picked up Vesna's hand and kissed it. "Would you like a drink or something?" Vesna nodded, and Igor disappeared through the crowd toward the bar.

When he was gone, Vesna visibly crumpled.

"Vee, what the fuck is going on?" Jo tucked the medallion back into her clothes.

"So much for ignoring it."

"Ignoring what exactly?"

"He's a seer, too. Not auras like me. He sees the future, but he won't talk about it. It shows up in his drawings and murals. I knew it when I saw him the first time at the shop, but I didn't want to admit it, either."

"Are you fucking kidding me?" It was a rhetorical question. She'd figured out nothing in her life was untouched by, untainted with, the woo-woo crap she had fallen into. That Vesna was firmly bound in the same net hadn't occurred to her. Helena was right; she had been a shitty friend.

Leo coughed above them. "Let's discuss this later. We're here to celebrate tonight."

Faron and Gregor emerged from the crowd, and her son threw his arms around her. "Happy birthday, Mom!"

"Thanks." She hugged him back. Maybe it was better to

continue to take the day as a pause in everything. How many quiet days would they get?

Gregor leaned down and kissed her cheek. "Happy birthday, love."

A few bars from "Whatever Lola Wants" slid through the strains of Sinéad O'Connor's "Just Call me Joe," surely Niko's idea of a joke, blaring through the gallery speakers. Helena's tall form stood by the bar right next to her brother, Matjaž, getting a beer. Helena smiled her dazzling smile, but there was a sadness in it that caught Jo off guard. Even the quiet days weren't.

Matjaž turned and walked toward the three of them looking out over Jo's party. He handed Jo a beer bottle emblazoned with one of the Four Horsemen of the Apocalypse.

"Happy birthday, Jo."

"Thanks. It was sweet of you to come." She took a sip from the bottle.

He nodded and turned to talk with some of Niko's friends clustered in the corner.

"So, it's your day, what would you like to do?" Leo, leaned down to ask the question in her ear. The music had gotten louder over the din of people talking and drinking.

Her thoughts were spinning with the mural, and Helena, and Rok's cryptic gift. She wanted to be alone, for a few moments, to catch her breath and fashion a fake party face. "You know what? I'd really like a cigarette."

Leo shrugged. "I'm not a smoker."

"Reka is."

Jo found her at Faron's table with Ivanka and their friends. Jo tapped Reka on the shoulder and asked if she wanted to go outside for a smoke.

"It's freezing." Reka handed her a lighter and her pack of cigarettes.

Jo tucked them into her coat pocket and wended her way back through the throng of well-wishers and out into the courtyard.

The weather had driven everything inside for the night. The courtyard was quiet except for the bass line of 1980s punk pulsing from the gallery. Jo stepped into a protected corner and pulled a cigarette from the pack. The lighter struggled against the wind but finally caught the paper and tamped tobacco. One benefit of being cold all the time was not feeling any more chill outside than inside. Maybe a little, since she had to take her glove off to smoke.

How many of those faces inside knew what she was? How many of them had spent a night with her and only showed up for Niko's questionable DJ skills and a few drinks? How many people were missing because of her? She hadn't answered any of her questions before the surge of music indicated someone had opened the door to join her in her illicit birthday smoke.

Veronika appeared from behind the corner.

"Sorry, I was trying to get out of the wind. I didn't realize you smoked." She held out Reka's pack.

"I don't." The girl brought her hand to her face.

A flash of bright pink scarf ran between them from the under the cover of a nearby table. "Stop!"

A shower of brown dust fell over Jo and the person wrapped in the flashy scarf.

Jo dropped her cigarette into the snow as her body seized, throwing her head back and onto the ground. Every nerve ending was open and screaming. Air came into her lungs and seared all the way down and out again before stopping. The child's wailing at her side blocked out any other sound. Jo's heart muscle tensed in her chest. This is what dying felt like, to burn to death inside her own body.

———

Faron looked around for his mother. She'd been gone too long. He went to look for Reka and found her at the bar getting another drink.

"Did Mom give your cigarettes back?"

She shook her head. "No big. I'll get them later." She took her beer from the bartender and headed back to the table.

Leo towered above the crowd, his head bent down to listen to Gregor above the noise. Faron made his way to him.

"Hey, have you seen Mom?"

"Not since she went to smoke."

"She hasn't come back." She could take care of herself, but too much weird shit had gone down for Faron not to worry about her.

"Let's go get her. She shouldn't be pouting at her own party." Gregor motioned toward the entrance.

Faron opened the door to a child's screaming audible above the music from inside. The three men rushed into the courtyard trying to locate the source.

They found Veronika on her knees in the snow cradling her sister Ana's writhing body the best she could. She kept repeating, "I'm sorry." A few feet away, Jo's body lay in the snow. She wasn't screaming like Ana, but her eyes were wide and unseeing in fright. Her muscles bowed her body into an arc on the snow, only her shoulders and heels touched the ground.

"What the fuck did you do?" Faron pulled Veronika from her sister onto her feet and shook her.

The girl was hysterical. "I just wanted to make her hurt. Make her pay for what happened … I didn't know Ana …"

Leo put his hands on Faron's shoulders. "Faron, let her go. She can't help us. Go find Goran."

Faron let go of Veronika, and she collapsed to the ground and scrambled back to Ana still twisting in agony.

He stood there staring at her, anger taking away any rational thought.

"Faron. Go get Goran." Gregor turned him back toward the gallery.

Leo and Gregor knelt beside Jo's body as Faron took off at a run.

———

Jo stood across the courtyard watching Faron, Gregor, and Leo interact with Veronika. Leo stepped past the two girls in the snow and knelt beside the body she had been in seconds before. Gregor got on his knees on the other side. When he touched the body's face, it crumpled back onto the ground, and she could feel a warmth like the sun shining on her through a car window.

Helena was next to her, without any Sarah Vaughan fanfare.

"Jo. I'm so sorry. I didn't realize Veronika had figured out anything this advanced."

"Veronika?"

"She's been working as a lackey for my mother. It's a long story. I didn't realize she had any real ability."

"What was that?"

"I have no idea what she thought it was supposed to do, but I don't think it was supposed to kill you."

"Am I dead?" Being dead was much less concerning than she'd imagined.

"Well, kiddo, your body is over there, and you are decidedly not in it."

"Hmm."

An uninviting door opened a few feet from them. Jo could feel Helena's smile.

"I think that's for me." Helena sighed. "The dead, even dead Voices, don't require a guide."

"Where's mine?" Would her door be more inviting? A lit arrow flashing "this way, please"?

"Do you want me to wait with you?" Helena's voice was soothing. How did that work? Neither of them had bodies, vocal cords, eardrums, or even brains to hold a mind. How did the connection work? It didn't really matter at this point.

"What if yours closes?" Jo could no longer open another's

door with her words. What a simple spell it had been: she said someone's name and released them from this plane of existence. Well, she could before.

"I don't think it will close."

"I don't know how any of this works." Faron came back, Goran in tow.

"He can't touch my body." She would not be the choice he had to make.

"What?"

Jo reached out for whatever Helena was with whatever she had for a hand and pulled them both through Helena's open door.

"I guess you got your wish about pushing me through the first opening." Helena's laugh sounded flat as they tumbled into the nothingness beyond the threshold.

CHAPTER 24

Jo had dragged Helena into an abyss as cold and complete as the place she'd fallen through with Dušan. Maybe falling back to his realm was the penalty for jumping through a door that wasn't hers. She'd managed to ruin Helena's grand exit, as well.

The two of them floated more than fell, suspended in a space beyond stars or time. There was no way to tell how many minutes or hours passed. She tried to speak to Helena, but the words were snatched away as soon as they left her.

Ravaged soldiers' faces came to Jo in the darkness. She wouldn't be returning to the mountain to mourn Henry's remaining dead or to release him. There was guilt and sorrow for having found her purpose so close to the end. There were no other Voices, aside from her mother and Jackie, who could help him. One was too addled and, at her own insistence, too close to death. Neither had a clue Henry needed saving, anyway.

Her mother had been right. She was dead, but it wasn't the man she had seen in her dreams who had come for her. Veronika had been giving her the evil eye for weeks and had disappeared from the Tuesday night gatherings. Jo blamed herself for leaving the girls, but she had no idea Veronika harbored such hate for her.

There wasn't even wind whistling in her ears, but there was Leo's discarded black cassock floating above her. It looked close enough to catch but she couldn't grasp it. He wouldn't have to leave the church now. Vesna would no longer have to cluck after her like a mother hen, and Gregor wouldn't feel the need to clean up any more of her messes. Rok could mourn her, or not, and continue on the journey his long life forced him to undertake. But Faron, Faron would be alone. Alone, yes, but maybe safe, too. Everything started to run together in her mind, a cascade of images and thoughts carrying her on. Helena's tight grasp was the only solid point.

As before, they didn't so much stop falling as the ground rose up to meet them. The dark outlines of naked trees reaching up into a gunmetal sky, like a quickly drawn sketch, grew sharper as her eyes adjusted to the dim light suffusing the landscape. She and Helena were alone. There were no throngs of lost shades, as there had been on the previous visit. And there was utter silence, until Helena laughed.

"Jesus, Jo, what did you do to deserve this?"

Whether or not the punishment fit the crime was beyond her reasoning. She had a laundry list of trespasses in her head to work through, including taking the exit not clearly marked for her. She'd watched her however-many-greats grandmother, Rebecca, make a similar choice on a Civil War battlefield. Was she down here, too? What punishment had her whatever-great gran gotten for jumping through her own door before she was actually dead?

There was no way to tell how long they stood there. Squinting out at the dark horizon, Jo plopped on the ground. Fine, gray ash rose around her then settled quickly, without wind to disturb it. Helena sat down beside her.

"It looks like we have plenty of time for you to tell me what the hell all that was about." Jo pointed up, though there was no way to know if direction meant anything between here and there.

"I'm not sure where to start exactly."

"You could start by telling me what your plan was. Did you know I was a Voice and a Portal when we met? Were you trying to get knocked up by my son? Were you ever going to let me in on your plan with Matjaž? Or were you going to go on betraying my trust until I cottoned on and fired you as spirit guide?"

"It would be easier to tackle these one at a time."

"Take your time. I'm definitely not going anywhere."

"I did not know you were anything but a teashop owner and a photographer, or that you used to be a photographer. I did maybe know you had been tangled up with Dušan Črnigad."

"So were you actually attracted to me, or was this some starfucking-by-proxy garbage?" She regretted the question as soon as she asked it. If it was the latter, it would make all of this bullshit even worse.

"Starfucking was hardly my thing, love. I was attracted to you. And I was attracted to Faron. You were both a bit of fun."

"So there wasn't any grand scheme to produce some Wiley/

Belak heir to the white god throne or something?"

"That came later and was entirely Avgusta's doing. My mother figured out what you were at my funeral and hatched her plan from there."

"So it was her idea to get Matjaž and me–"

"Again, no. I thought the two of you would be good together. He broods for weeks at a time, and you are about as interested in commitment as I am. Perfect match." Helena laughed again. Of course she would be undaunted by the possibility of spending eternity in a barren wasteland hashing out their relationship.

"So what was your role in all this?"

Helena pulled her knees up to her chin. "Reluctant Radio Helena."

"Do tell."

"Avgusta would call me up into her studio and grill me for information."

Jo looked out to the horizon and the miles of bleak surrounding them.

"You could've told me."

"To what purpose? I had no intention of helping her. I had my own plan."

"Which Avgusta thought she could subvert to produce a supernaturally inclined grandbaby?"

"Avgusta was rather single-minded in her pursuit."

"I guess you come by it honestly, then." Jo stood up. "What do you think would happen if we just started walking?"

"I think we'd be moving, but the landscape wouldn't change much."

Jo shrugged. "And how did Veronika get involved in all this?"

"Mother needed someone to be her errand girl, and who better than a traumatized teenager who'd probably already had her lifetime's worth of bad shit happen to her? Avgusta was never one not to meddle."

"I see you come by that honestly, too."

Helena laughed again, but it was more sarcastic. "Except I should've meddled more this time. After the heart business, I should've paid more attention to what she was up to."

"That was Veronika?" The flash she'd had of Matjaž at Faron's door made even less sense.

"Yes. She fucked that one up, too. I hijacked my brother's body to defuse it. I'm sorry Ivanka caught part of it, but it would have been much worse."

"No wonder he was so angry about the flowers."

"He was angry about a lot more than that. Rightly so. If it's any consolation, Avgusta's days of scheming are done. Matjaž put paid to it."

"Matjaž and I put paid to your scheme, as well. Not that it matters."

"I know. I saw you with Leo." Helena took Jo's hand and pulled her back down to sit next to her. "I have to admit, I was a bit surprised you fell for the priest. But you don't seem to know how to take the easy way out, either."

"It doesn't matter now." It might not matter to Leo, whether

Jo loved him or not. It did matter to her. Death probably left everyone feeling unfinished.

Helena put her arm around Jo's shoulders. "It should have mattered. I failed you as a guide and a friend, too."

"You protected Faron and Ivanka, so I'll give you a pass." Jo laughed. "Besides, if you and I are stuck here together forever, there's no point in being pissed off at each other."

"I'm glad to see you are taking a practical approach."

"If we are in Dušan's version of the Land of the Lost, it means my father is here somewhere."

"That's why you wondered what would happen if we started walking?"

Jo nodded.

Helena stood up and offered her hand. "Well, I might not be your spirit guide anymore, but the least I can do is help you look."

Dušan, decked out in his black god regalia, appeared in front of them, glaring down at Jo as the two women landed on their butts back in the dust.

"You do not belong here."

"That's comforting, but I seem to find myself here anyway. And, look, I brought a friend."

Gods didn't sigh exasperatedly, or she guessed they didn't, but that was the mood drifting off Dušan nonetheless.

"You have, and now I must take you back."

"I don't want to go, not to where Faron can revive me. Besides, I'm not going anywhere without my father." She pushed herself off the ground and stood in front of Dušan as defiantly as she could. She barely came to his chest. Helena stood silently beside her.

"There is no time to find him." Dušan's voice reverberated as much in her chest as in her head.

"I'm not going. He sacrificed himself for me and–"

"You do not understand. You are in no position to bargain."

———

The party had followed Goran and Faron out into the courtyard and now stood pressing in against Leo as he tried to keep them away from the grim tableau. Goran knelt beside Jo first, but quickly turned to Ana, moving his hands over her and chanting softly under his breath.

Gregor called Investigator Marta Klančnik. She would be able to disperse the crowd and keep things as quiet as possible.

Leo tried to close Jo's eyes, but they wouldn't stay closed. He tried not to imagine the pain she had been in, given the condition of her body when they found her. He was focusing on mechanics and facts, but his thoughts were crowded by his own silent keening. She couldn't be dead. In all the possible futures he had mulled over in his indecision, Jo lived, with or without him.

Piercing sirens and flashing blue lights transfixed the crowd. Police officers, usually unwelcome in the semi-autonomous enclave of Metelkova, were greeted with silence. Uniforms herded the crowd back into the gallery, leaving a half-moon of the directly involved standing in the snow around a raggedly screaming Ana, a sobbing Veronika, and a dead Jo.

Marta stood among them, questions forming then dying on her lips. She finally asked Gregor what happened, but he redirected her to Leo. Leo could see Jo's oldest friend was using every ounce of his strength to remain calm and helpful, but the shock and sorrow on his face was as clear as the night air around them.

"We found them like this. We haven't had any luck getting Veronika to speak, but best I can tell she tried to curse Jo. Ana got in the way."

"Is that possible?" Marta looked to Gustaf, who had taken a few steps back from the others. His face was pained and grayer than usual.

Gustaf stared at Investigator Klančnik like she had fallen there from space before coming back to his senses. "Yes. Of course." He stepped closer and looked down at Veronika, still rocking back and forth unable to comfort her sister.

The younger girl's voice finally gave out, but she still thrashed in her sister's arms.

"I had no idea Veronika was a witch, or that she had taken up training with one." Gustaf continued to stand, staring at the two girls as if he were looking through them to the center of the earth.

"My mother wasn't training her so much as using her to do her bidding." Matjaž's comment raised more than one eyebrow, but the focus quickly turned back to comforting Ana.

Leo watched the discussion in a detached way. He alone was comforting Jo. Was he the only one who believed she couldn't be gone? Or maybe the disposition of her body was too much for anyone else to bear. Faron stood over them, his face determined.

"I can bring her back." Faron knelt in the snow and started to lay his hand on his mother's chest.

Gustaf rushed to Faron and pulled him away. "Stop! Your mother would not want this."

Leo looked at the two men, confused. Jo had told him about Faron's ability, but he'd assumed at most he would be able to revive a house cat. It never occurred to him Faron could raise the human dead. In his experience, Death never gave up his quarry without a price.

Faron ripped his arm away from Gustaf. "It's what I want."

The others stared at the two men.

"Your father told me what he is, what you are. You cannot undo this once it is done. Would you give yourself to him to save her?"

Leo looked from Faron to Gustaf and then around at the faces gathered. Almost any one of them would have given themselves to save Jo. These people were Faron's family, the family his mother had chosen.

"Yes." Faron turned away from the Austrian and his warning and knelt again in the snow across from Leo. "You should put her back on the ground. I don't know what will happen if she comes back."

Leo laid her back onto the packed snow as tenderly as possible. He'd seen her body seize, her hands curled into fists. He would be surprised if the tension in her muscles hadn't broken bone.

Vesna knelt with them, as if Jo were an altar they had all come to tend. "Faron, she's not here. You won't bring her back now."

Faron turned on her, tears freezing to his reddened face. "How can you know that?" He ran the back of his bare hand over his cheek. "She has to still be here."

"I can't explain how I know. I only know she isn't back yet."

———

"Goddamnit, woman. Will you not listen to me?" Dušan, god of the darkness, her son's father, looked down at Jo as if she were a child he could scold into obedience.

"I will not leave without him." She would not do as she was told. That hadn't worked out any better than doing things her way, and she sure as hell wasn't going to choose getting ordered around.

"Now is not the time."

"Then promise me you will find him so he can cross into the Next."

"Gods do not make promises to mortals, or if they do, it is never the bargain the mortal wishes. Have you not read enough mythology to know that?" The frustration in his voice was gone. It had been replaced by the arrogance she was more familiar with.

"I will take your promise in whatever form you are willing to give it. At this point, I don't have much to lose."

Helena laughed. "She has a point there."

Two shades struggled toward them from the dark horizon. As they got closer, Jo recognized them as Katarina and

Tomaž, Ivanka's parents. Both were wan with haunted eyes and reached out to her pleadingly without speaking.

She was repulsed by them. Their appearance and demeanor were nothing like they had been in life. Katarina's cascade of dark hair was matted and stringy, and her clothes were rags. Tomaž was a whimpering husk, belying his life as a swaggering womanizer. Her revulsion was quickly replaced with anger at herself and empathy for them.

Whatever they had been in life, they, like her, had been at the mercy of supernatural forces far beyond their control or understanding. They had not deserved the deaths they had received. Jo still wrestled with her own guilt, for in the end, she had been the instrument of Katarina's demise. Leo and Gustaf could argue into the following week about how it wasn't true, the demon had already consumed her life, but Jo had heard Katarina's neck snap as they fell.

The memory of it sent slivers of ice down her spine, or where her spine had been. Maybe someone in the Next could explain the physics of shades to her.

"You can take them back with you. They have suffered, as have their daughters. It would do well for them to be at peace."

It wasn't what she asked for, but it was its own solace, to be Tomaž and Katarina's "get out of jail free" card. She nodded.

Relief flooded their drawn faces. Dušan gathered the four of them into his cloak, and the bottom dropped out of Jo's stomach. Even her shade wasn't cut out for inter-dimensional travel, assuming this was another dimension. Her understanding of what constituted reality, her own especially, had taken a beating.

CHAPTER 25

This was not the person Faron was supposed to save. He sat back on his heels, his face burning with tears and anger. He couldn't say Dušan lied to him, but he hadn't told him the truth, either. There was no way his father hadn't known it would be Jo when the decision came.

Vesna took his hand. "She is coming back."

"How can you tell?" He wanted to scream but he spit the words out at her instead.

"There are things that haven't happened yet. Things Jo has to be here for."

"What does that even mean?"

"It means you have to trust me. And we have to wait."

There was so much pain in his mother's face. Could he bring her back into that? Goran was still murmuring behind him trying to undo whatever Veronika had done to her sister.

Across from him, Leo clutched Jo's hand. "Faron, there is always a cost. You can't bring her back if it means your life. She would rather be dead." The words pained him to say; Leo wanted her to be alive as much as Faron did.

"I won't die." And that was the problem wasn't it? He would be like his father, like Rok. He would eventually watch them all die. He sat back on his heels. "Vesna, can you really tell me when she's back?"

"I think so."

He nodded. More words weren't going to change the situation or make him feel any better.

Gregor and Matjaž joined them in their vigil. Faron could feel the others standing behind them, watching. Ivanka's hands rested softly on his shoulders. He shrugged them off. "Not now."

After this, he would have to end it. He couldn't ask her to stay with him. He felt her move away again, and he went back to waiting, watching his mother for a sign.

———

Jo settled back on the snow-covered ground as Dušan let go of her arm. The scene in the courtyard had changed only in the number of people standing around her corpse and the miserable child.

Helena stood next to her and grabbed her hand again. "What are they waiting for?"

Jo shook her head. Ana needed medical attention.

Jo was waiting for her door. She imagined it arched like the entrance to the courtyard, and maybe purple like her grandmother's front door had been. Dušan the God disappeared from her side and reappeared as Dušan the Man walking toward the group huddled in the snow.

The realization landed on her like an avalanche, and

there was nothing she could do. There was no door to run through this time. Dušan had orchestrated his plan perfectly, maneuvering them all into place so very carefully. She had trusted him again at her peril, and Faron's.

Dušan knelt in the snow next to Faron. She couldn't see if he spoke to him, but Faron looked to Vesna, who nodded. Faron put both of his hands on her corpse's sternum as if he were going to start CPR, and Jo snapped back into her body, and into a pain she would never be able to accurately describe. It was nothing, though, compared to looking up into her son's completely white and glowing eyes.

"River." She could barely get the word past her lips. There was a flurry of activity around her, but she couldn't focus on anything except the screaming in her nerves and the hole punched through her heart. Leo's face came close to hers. "River. Take me. Take us."

———

Leo could barely make out the words. She was still on the edge of death; he wasn't sure how hypothermia would help.

"She said to take her to the river." He looked at Gustaf, as if he could translate.

Goran stood up from his ministrations over Ana. "Of course."

"Can't we put them under a hot shower or something? The river is nearly frozen." Matjaž pushed in tighter to the group.

"No, the river is sacred. She's right." Goran nodded his head.

Getting Jo and Ana to the river and into the water in the city wasn't an easy task. Plečnik's architecture was designed to keep the river out of the city, but his canal design also made it very difficult for anyone in the city to walk into the river.

Gregor looked at them, incredulous. "Have you lost your minds? Throw them into the river? You might as well leave them out here to die in the cold. Gustaf, can't your witchdoctor friend help them?"

"Dr. Struna is not a witchdoctor, and this is beyond her capabilities. If Goran cannot reverse the curse, the river is the safest option." Lichtenberg's words were much calmer than his expression.

"Then we go." Leo picked Jo up as gently as possible.

She wasn't twisting and screaming like Ana, but every muscle tensed, including those in her face. Tears tracked down her temples into her hair, but it was her silence that unnerved him.

He started toward the river, out of *Metelkova*. Faron picked up Ana, and the others followed. What had been a celebration was now a gruesome parade through the empty, frozen streets. A mantle of white covered every surface and reflected the light of the street lamps. They encountered no one on their grim errand.

"There's nowhere close you can get into the river easily." Vesna walked beside him, taking two steps to his one.

"If you insist on doing this, the closest place is *Trnovo pristan*." Gregor joined them. "But the steps will be icy from the snow."

Leo would figure it out. If he had to jump into the river with her, he would.

Fat snowflakes landed on Jo's clothes and in her hair without melting. He wanted to brush them from her face, but he couldn't stop before the river. If he were a different man, he would have bargained with God, offered to stay in the church to spare her life. But whether Jo lived or died was in the hands of other gods, and he was past bargaining. He had broken his vows the moment he believed she could love him. They only lacked the official ceremonies to cement it. If Jo lived, and she still felt the way she had when she'd kissed him in her bedroom, he would choose to be with her every single day she let him.

The band of souls who lived on the shadier side of the Veil walked the embankment until they reached the wide concrete steps of the Ljubljana "beach" that descended to the river's edge under the bare branches of the willow trees. There was a drop-off from the last step into the icy river.

Gregor had been right about the concrete being slick with snow, but Leo made his way to the water's edge on the lowest step and knelt, still cradling Jo's rigid body. Faron joined him and laid Ana in the water.

The girl gasped from the shock of the cold before she went under. She came up again quickly and flailed against the embankment, trying to scratch her way out of the water. Her lips were blue, but the look of agony was gone. Faron pulled her back onto the steps, and someone passed him a coat to wrap the girl in.

"Get her and Veronika out of here." Faron's anger hadn't faded.

Leo didn't wait to see what happened with the girls. He lowered Jo into the river. As her face slipped under the surface, the water surrounding her turned a luminescent, milky green. Something, or someone, in the water pulled her out of his grasp.

He dove in after her, searching the river lapping at the edge of the step and shouting her name, but she was gone.

CHAPTER 26

The cold went to Jo's heart. She wavered between life and death, between freezing and the fire in her nerves. Leo's arms had supported her weight, but now she floated free. It would have been easy to drift off again, away from life and the pain, but she was tethered to her body by Faron's magic.

She sank through the depths of the river. Her coat and dress billowed out around her, obscuring her ability to see what might be in the water with her. Her limbs were too heavy to attempt to swim, and even after the envelope of pain passed, her left arm still felt wrong.

A face swam into view in the murk. Achelous smiled at her, nose to nose, and took her hands. He pulled her along until they passed through a shimmering curtain of water into a dry bower.

"You flatter me, Jo. I did not expect you to give yourself over so completely to your 'reverence' so soon." He smiled, but there was more than mirth in the gesture. He lifted the bull head medallion from the hollow of her throat. "And wearing my emblem, as well."

She stepped back from him. The necklace was warm

against her skin after his touch. "I didn't know what else to do. Running water dissipates magic. Even shitty teenage revenge magic, right?" Jo rubbed her upper arm. Something was definitely wrong. And Rok had way more secrets than she'd imagined.

"Your arm is cracked. Broken? I do not always know the words." He rubbed his palm over her coat, strangely dry after the snow and the river. Warmth spread from his palm down through her fingers. "There. It is not healed, but it should trouble you less until it can be seen by one of your doctors." Achelous' magic filled the air around them with the heavy scent of orchids.

"Thanks." She flexed her fingers and turned her wrist. "So what happens now?" In just the past few hours, she had been killed by Veronika the Teenage Witch, transported to the land of the dead, tricked by her ex-lover, and thrown into a river in the depths of February. Really, what could happen next?

Achelous took her hand and led her to a stone bench carved into the wall of his barren keep. She sat next to him and looked out at the rippling water. The magic of gods was fascinating. At some point, she'd like to have enough time to enjoy the good things that came with this gig.

"If it were up to me, you would stay." He tutted her protest. "But it is not up to me. You made your intentions clear, and you have obligated yourself elsewhere."

She'd offered no other gods any kind of loyalty. Dušan sure as shit hadn't earned her devotion.

"You knew what Dušan had planned for Faron, didn't you?"

"'Planned' is a very precise word."

"What does that mean?" She pulled her coat more tightly around her.

Achelous tapped the ground in front of them with the toe of his soft leather boot, and a blue flame sparked into existence.

"Jolene Wiley, some things simply are. No planning involved."

"What? I'm supposed to resign myself and my son to the Fates, and whatever happens, happens?" The fire warmed the air quickly. Jo stood to face Achelous.

He pulled her back down to sit next to him and turned to look at her. "You act as if you are the only person troubled by the hand she was dealt."

"I do not." A lot of shitty things had happened in the past few months, but there had been good things, too.

"It is the nature of humans to place themselves at the center of the world. You can only see out of your own eyes."

"And whose eyes can you see out of besides your own?"

"Only mine, but they have seen millennia."

"Okay, I'm selfish. Other people have it just as bad as me, and–"

"You are not that selfish, for a human, but you are as short-sighted as humans usually are."

"Thanks, Lord of the River Dance, I'll take that under consideration. None of that answers my question about what happens next."

"I will take you back, and you will have to figure the rest out on your own. I will give you this piece of advice, though. Dušan may seem like your enemy now, but he will be your biggest ally in all that is to come."

"You'll have to excuse me if I find that hard to believe." She cocked her head at him.

"You may believe whatever you choose, but do not let your anger stand in the way of your safety." He stood up and offered her his hand. "This part will, as you say, suck."

"No magically depositing me on the shore, dry and unscathed?"

"No." He walked into the water, pulling her behind him.

The shock of cold took the breath out of her lungs. The river quickly found its way into her clothes and chilled her to the core. Achelous pushed her in front of him as they neared the surface and put his arms under her as if he would carry her out of the water.

Her knees and face hit the air first. The cold was stultifying, and someone else was in the water with them.

Leo reached for her. "Jo. Oh, God, Jo. I thought you were gone."

Achelous released her and disappeared into the depths with a faint glow that faded beneath them. Fucker. He was going to leave her to save herself again.

Leo pulled her into his chest and paddled his legs with the current back toward the embankment. They hit the concrete, and other hands reached in to pull her onto the steps — scraping every bony bit over the edge of the concrete.

Gregor pulled her to a standing position. Dr. Struna appeared with a heavy blanket on her arm and a concerned look on her face.

OK. She had some help with the saving.

"It's nice to see you conscious, but I'd prefer it if you stayed out of the water. Now strip, you two."

"What? Here?" She was shivering, and her face was numb.

"You have to get out of those wet clothes now."

Vesna joined them and helped Jo out of her coat and sodden clothes. Her arm didn't want to cooperate.

—

Leo tried to shrug off the wet coat but needed Gregor's help to free himself. He turned and bent over so Gregor could pull the sweater over his head and down his arms. The air was freezing, but less so than the water had been. He stood up and pulled the blanket around himself.

Jo was facing him, pulling her own drenched clothing off with Vesna's help. He looked first at the tattoo between her breasts and down her stomach. An eclipse with the sun's corona snaking its way along her ribs and down to her navel. He met her gaze and couldn't look away. Was she the sun or the moon in that scenario?

Dr. Struna ushered them up to the street from the embankment to where Faron and Gustaf waited by a white panel van with its flashers on. Faron's eyes had returned to their regular blue, but the cast of them was ten years older.

"Where have the others gone?" Veronika and her sisters, Goran, and Matjaž were nowhere to be seen.

"They went with Robert, Dr. Struna's assistant, to her surgery." Gustaf appeared calm, but there was an unsettled quality to his posture — like a man with shell shock attempting to cover it. Leo felt similarly, immensely relieved Jo was alive but deeply disturbed by the night's events.

"It's where you two are going now." Dr. Struna motioned for Jo and Leo to get in the back. "I've only got room for one up front."

Everyone deferred to Faron for the second seat.

"We'll walk." Gregor motioned at Vesna and Gustaf.

Leo and Faron helped Jo up into the back of the disguised ambulance, and Leo clambered in after her. Gustaf shut the doors behind them while Dr. Struna and Faron settled into the front.

The doctor stuck her head in the back. "You two need to lie down on the gurneys. You'll bounce around too much back there otherwise."

Leo's fingers were numb, but he reached across the space between them to find Jo's hand. Her fingers must have been frozen, as they felt colder still than his. She squeezed back but didn't speak to him on the slow ride to the surgery.

———

Jo felt every cobblestone under the tires until they got onto the asphalt-paved street. Leo's hand was warm, but the rest of her was an ice sculpture. She could've used three more blankets and a space heater. Dr. Struna probably didn't have a hot toddy, though, for the existential glacier inside her.

Dušan had gotten what he wanted. She was more indebted

to Achelous than she had been that morning. Helena was still lingering about, and she had Tomaž and Katarina's shades to deal with after she got her arm cast. She stared up at the white metal ceiling and caught herself humming "Whatever Lola Wants" — thinking of Dušan, but summoning Helena.

"It's tight in here. Even for a shade." Helena squeezed herself into the space and sat on the gurney by Jo's head. "You don't have to speak, but I'd like to fill you in on the way to the good doctor's."

CHAPTER 27

Veronika sat in the lobby of Dr. Struna's surgery. It looked like a regular house until you got past the front room, which did an adequate job of masquerading as a den. Ana was quiet now. She didn't have any lasting magical damage, and she'd been treated for hypothermia after the river.

Swimming the witch. That's what had been done to women accused of witchcraft, at least in the books she'd bought. If they died, they were innocent. The logic was stupid. And it should've been her in the water, not Ana. Her sister had turned to face the wall when Dr. Struna let Veronika in to see her. Ivanka didn't speak to her, and Ana wouldn't look at her. She might be better off taking her chances in the dunking machine.

Veronika had killed Jo. She'd nearly killed her sister. That had not been the plan. It was stupid to not be more careful around Ana. She was probably going to witch jail. That had to be a thing, right?

Matjaž, Avgusta's son, came and sat next to her on the hard couch.

"More than you bargained for?" He didn't sound as angry

as he probably should have been.

Veronika nodded.

"It was careless of my mother to drag you into this."

"She didn't drag me into this. Jo and Faron did." Avgusta might be a bitch, but she was the first person who had tried to help her.

"I can see how you would reach that conclusion, but you're wrong." He didn't talk to her like she was a child. That was something.

"If my parents hadn't been friends with her–"

"I've been around magic and the supernatural my whole life." He put his elbows on his knees and looked down at the edge of the busy rug and the shiny wooden floor before looking back up at her to continue. "Some people handle it well, and some people try to use magic to make the world what they want it to be."

"Isn't that what magic is for? If I can make something better for me because I have magic, I should do that."

"You can, and many do. But magic has a price. Someone pays when you meddle in the story line. Sometimes that person is an enemy and sometimes it's–"

"My sister."

"Exactly."

Veronika didn't know what to say.

"I don't think you know the whole story of what happened to your parents, but I think you should."

"I was there." Veronika crossed her arms. Now he was going

to talk to her like she was an idiot.

"Not for everything. A demon killed your father. It killed my sister, Helena. It killed Maja, who worked for your father and Jo, and Milo who was Jo's friend. It took Faron to lure Jo. And it killed your mother because that's what demons do."

"How do you know all of this?" Veronika was unwilling to accept a demon, something she couldn't imagine or lash out at, was responsible for her parents' deaths.

"Because I've watched my mother my whole life. I've watched her anger and bitterness eat at her, like a demon would. She used her power to get what she wanted, and she's been paying for it for a long time."

"But my parents didn't have any magical powers. They didn't try to manipulate anyone."

"They didn't. They were victims. Just like Helena and Maja. Just like Faron and Jo."

"It isn't fair. Jo is alive, and my parents are dead."

"Veronika, you are old enough to know life isn't fair. Faron and Jo survived, but not without scars." Matjaž looked tired.

Ana had tried in her way to move on from their parents' deaths, and Veronika had single-handedly given her a bunch of new trauma to deal with. She'd created some of her own, too.

Avgusta. She was the one her gave her the spell book and told her what to do.

"I guess you're right. I shouldn't have gotten tangled up with Avgusta."

"It won't help you to blame my mother next. You have to

take responsibility for yourself." Matjaž stood up. "Trust me, Avgusta has enough sins to pay for."

"I guess that means no more magic." Maybe she could continue to study quietly on her own.

"You have a natural talent. It would be a shame to waste it. If you'd like to study magic, I can introduce you to someone."

"Can I still study magic in witch jail?"

"Witch jail?" He laughed. "You aren't going to witch jail. I won't say you aren't in trouble, but witch jail isn't a thing." He left her.

She heard the front door open and close. Matjaž must have gone outside to smoke or wait for the others.

The front room quickly filled with a new batch of people. Jo was with them, wrapped in a blanket, her lips still blue.

Jo walked over to where Veronika sat on the couch. Veronika wanted to crawl between the cushions and disappear with the loose change and lint. Jo looked around for someone. Veronika was sitting right there.

"Where's Dušan?"

"He said he would meet us here." The little gray man moved from the door to the center of the room to answer Jo.

"Call him. I need him here now."

The man got out his phone and tapped the screen a few times before stepping back to the edge of the room to talk. "It's Gustaf."

Jo looked around again and nodded at another corner. "When Dušan gets here. I need everyone to leave us alone for a bit."

Heads nodded around the room. Including Veronika's.

Jo looked directly at Veronika for the first time. "Except you. You need to stay."

———

Jo stood in the middle of what looked to be Dr. Struna's lobby. Leo disappeared through a door with the doctor. Veronika was trying to climb up the back of the couch to get away from her. Gregor, Faron, and Vesna took Jo's request as an excuse to go back outside, out of the stifling, overly floral sitting room. They joined Matjaž, who was out there smoking.

Helena stood in the corner, flanked by the shades of Tomaž and Katarina. The anguish on Katarina's face as she watched her daughter squirm was almost unbearable. Jo had reason to hate mother and daughter equally for what they had taken from her. She wanted to hate them. Not caring about their fates would have made her life a whole lot easier, but she knew too much to hate them. They had all been manipulated by beings with agendas that disregarded human lives. Or worse, if Achelous was right, Jo was destined to be standing on this godawful rug with the weight of the night's events pressing on her heart.

If she had a choice, she'd prefer to believe they had all been part of a chess match between gods and demons than believe that things were already written down somewhere. She knew gods, if not demons, could be reasoned with.

Dr. Struna interrupted her thoughts. "Ms. Wiley, I have some scrubs you can put on if you'd like."

Jo nodded. She caught Katarina looking at her. There was

still pleading, but the quality had changed. Katarina wasn't pleading for herself, but for her daughter. But Jo didn't have any say over what would happen to Veronika now. That was up to Gustaf and the Board.

———

The scrubs were dry. Though they were not as warm as the blanket had been, they definitely were more practical. It was a little awkward not to have on any underwear, especially given how tight the pants were across her butt. The sling for her arm wasn't exactly a fashion accessory, either, but Dr. Struna had assured her that she should be happy her arm had only a hairline fracture. There's no way Dr. Struna had scrubs for Leo. Hopefully she had a dryer.

Jo peeked in on Ana. Ivanka was sitting next to the bed and looked up when the door opened.

"How's she doing?"

Ivanka's eyes were red, but her voice was calm. "She's okay, as far as I can tell. Whatever Dr. Struna gave her finally put her to sleep."

"Sleep is good." It would be better if the drugs put her past dreaming. Jo started to duck out and close the door.

"It's not going to stop, is it?" Ivanka stood up and walked closer to the door. "This supernatural stuff."

What could Jo say? She hated the word-puzzle approach Dušan and Achelous offered. Best to be straight up. "If you stay with Faron, it's not going to stop for you."

"He's different now, isn't he?" She looked so young, but all of the fragility and brittleness was gone. Ivanka was much stronger than Jo had given her credit for.

"He is. I think it best if he explains it to you."

Ivanka nodded. "Thank you."

"For what?"

"You saved Ana."

"Not really. The river saved Ana. I can introduce you to Achelous, if you'd like to give thanks where it's deserved."

"I'd like that."

Jo closed the door and leaned against it. Maybe she was going to be a priestess for her river god after all. She was apparently proselytizing already.

"Okay, time to do this." She pushed herself off the door and went back out into the lobby.

Dušan had arrived, looking human except for being preternaturally clean compared with the rest of them. Veronika sat on the edge of the couch, her fingers clutching the cushions. Everyone else had stayed out as she'd requested.

"You look fetching in doctor's attire." A smile crept into the corner of Dušan's mouth as his unsaid words found their way into Jo's thoughts.

"Shut up, Dušan. You aren't getting in these pants. Again. Ever." Jo could play this game, too, though she would have preferred to say the words out loud to him, as close to his face as humanly possible.

"Ever is a long time." He laughed, to everyone else's confusion, but got serious again quickly. "What did you ask me here for?"

"I know gods don't bargain with humans, not really. And I know I can't command you to do shit, but I would like to ask you for a favor."

"A favor?" He smiled. "This favor?"

Veronika gasped and tried to climb back up the couch as the shades in the room became visible to everyone.

"Mind-reading shouldn't be allowed, but yes, that favor." Woodsmoke and petrichor. It was deeply unfair for Dušan's magic to carry her favorite scents.

Helena was her radiant, toga'd self. Her skin even looked warm. Tomaž and Katarina were still hollow-eyed and bruise-colored. Now that Veronika could see her parents, too, Jo wished they didn't look quite so dead.

Veronika stared.

Katarina ran to her daughter, but Veronika wasn't having it. She turned on Jo. "What horrible trick is this? What kind of monster are you?" Her voice filled the room, adding to the uncomfortable closeness.

Jo started to speak, but Dušan stopped her. "Jo did not bring your parents back. I did."

"And who the fuck are you?"

Dušan laughed, and his eyes turned black and star-filled. "I would have thought Avgusta would have instructed you better in the *deus loci.*"

"*Deus?* You're a god?" Veronika crumpled back onto the couch. "Fuck."

Dušan's eyes returned to bottle green and amber. "Your parents, because of the circumstances of their deaths, found themselves in my realm, as did Jo when you tried to kill her. I asked her to bring them back."

"I wasn't trying to kill her." Veronika whispered it to the hideous gladiolas on the area rug.

"You are either a very powerful natural witch or a very bad ceremonial one. But that is for later. Now you will listen to Jo."

Veronika nodded. Katarina sat next to her on the couch but didn't touch her. Veronika had the sense not to move away again.

"I asked Dušan here so you could say goodbye to your parents, properly, before they cross into the Next. If you want to be pissed off at someone, it isn't me or them you need to be pissed off at. You can be pissed off at the Fates or the gods, depending on how you choose to look at it."

"Matjaž kinda said the same thing."

Helena stepped next to Jo and took her hand. "My brother was always the smart one."

Veronika looked up at Helena. "You're the sister."

"Yes. And Matjaž and Jo are right. She isn't responsible for what happened to me or your parents. Your mother isn't even responsible for what happened to me." Shame radiated off Katarina at Helena's remark.

"Katarina, I wanted you to see there is nothing to forgive. I know it was the demon. I'm sorry you were so unhappy and that it took advantage of you." It wouldn't do for Jo to cry. This reunion she'd arranged was definitely not about her.

"You were so nice to me. Even when … I remember that."

Katarina bowed her head again — whether out of shame or to hide her tears, Jo didn't know.

"I'm sorry I couldn't save you, or Tomaž." It was good to say the words to the people, but it didn't make them not dead.

Tomaž finally joined them. "You tried."

Jo laughed a tiny, rueful laugh. Trying wasn't doing, but it was all she had.

"Jo, you need to wrap this up." Dušan opened the door and waved Matjaž in. "I will leave you to it."

Matjaž stood at the door. "Helena?"

She ran to her brother and threw her arms around him. "I'm so sorry." Matjaž patted his sister's hair and held her.

"Veronika, this is your last chance to say your goodbyes." Jo took a deep breath. This hadn't gone exactly as she'd planned, but apparently that was a thing.

The girl turned to look at Katarina. There was an awkward second before Veronika fell into her mother's arms sobbing. Tomaž joined them on the couch and hugged both women to him.

"Okay. It's time." Jo stood up straight, the strap of the sling rubbing over her shoulder. Katarina and Tomaž were not unmourned, but their doors had not opened. Jo was going on intuition.

"Katarina and Tomaž, are you ready?"

Katarina was shaking her head wildly. "I won't go back to that place."

"I don't know where you are going, but I can promise you it isn't there."

Tomaž stood up and Veronika with him, holding his hand. Katarina stood then, too, and grabbed her daughter's other hand. "Thank you, Jo."

"Don't thank me yet." She looked at Helena and Matjaž out of the corner of her eye. They were standing much like the Novaks, watching and waiting.

"Katarina and Tomaž Novak." The words spilled out of her and coiled in the air before swirling around the two people she'd named. That was not how it had worked in the mountains. She had only sensed a door opening behind her.

Tomaž and Katarina both glowed with a faint blue light.

When she looked behind her, Jo could see their door this time, as clearly as she had seen Helena's earlier. It was arched like a church door and glowed the same blue as the couple. Each half had its own ornate, wrought-iron handle and was set with a leaded pane spilling more blue light into the room. Only Tomaž and Katarina were looking behind her. That was consistent at least, but it didn't explain why she could see it.

Tomaž kissed his daughter on the head, and Katarina squeezed her around the shoulders before the couple walked toward the door holding hands.

Veronika gasped through tears. "Wait! What about Ivanka and Ana? Don't they get to say goodbye, too?"

Katarina dropped Tomaž's hand and turned to her daughter. She ran her hand over Veronika's dark crown. "Your sisters already said goodbye in their way. This was for you." She turned and took Tomaž's hand again, and they walked through the door, each opening their own side.

Their light flooded the room before the door closed and disappeared.

Jo turned to Matjaž and Helena.

"I guess it's my turn." Helena dropped her brother's hand and stepped up, shoulders back. "I'm ready."

"Ready for what?" Jo looked at them both, confused.

"The Next. I promised Matjaž I would apologize to you for my unwilling part in Mother's schemes, and I would bow out so you could get a new guide with a clean slate."

Jo looked at Matjaž, who nodded in reply to the question on her face.

"Do I get a say in all this?" Jo cocked her head at both of them.

Matjaž sputtered. "I guess," he said, his forehead furrowed. "I assumed you would want her to leave after you knew everything."

"Your sister and I have been to Hell and back, literally, and I'd like her to stick around for a bit."

Helena's eyes were shiny. "I'd like that, if you mean it."

"Of course I mean it."

Helena rushed her into a hug. Jo flinched for a moment at the pressure on her arm and at Helena's warmth. There was no breath on Jo's neck, but Helena felt alive.

"I'll let Dušan know." Matjaž turned to let the friends have their moment. The door opened as he reached for the handle.

Jo caught Dušan's gaze over Helena's shoulder. The warmth slid out of Helena and it was Matjaž's turn to gasp. His sister had disappeared again, visible only to Jo.

Helena stepped back and took Jo's hand. "You should go home and get some rest."

Jo yawned, nearly cracking her jaw in the process. "Yeah. Sleep sounds good. Walking home in scrubs and wet boots, not so much."

Dr. Struna rejoined them. "Your clothes and shoes are dry. You can change in the exam room if you like. Are you up for the walk?"

"I think so. I'd rather go home. That couch is too loud to sleep on."

CHAPTER 28

Jo walked with the others back toward her flat. Dr. Struna had offered transportation, but the snow was deep enough and her apartment centered enough in the pedestrian-only core of the city, it was silly to drag Robert out into the weather again. Between Achelous' ministrations and Dr. Struna's sling, Jo's arm felt about as good as could be expected.

Dušan had disappeared again before she finished changing clothes. He probably needed to crawl back to his lair to dream up some other way to fuck up her and Faron's lives. Ivanka and Veronika stayed with Ana. Dr. Struna had insisted Ana be there overnight due to her more severe case of hypothermia. Jo marveled she wasn't in the same boat and worried that her being relatively unscathed by the cold was less luck and more woo-woo. The true bystander in all of this had taken the brunt.

The apartment was only another block or two, but it felt farther away. Exhaustion dragged at her, and she watched her son, neighbors, and friends disappear around the bend of buildings in *Mestni trg*, the town square. Only Leo stayed back with her. They were in front of the Robba fountain, boarded up for the winter and filled with snow. The cobbles were arranged in a repeating scalloped pattern that always made her think the square and the street were a great gray dragon sleeping under the castle hill. They had disappeared under a white duvet. As achingly beautiful as her town was, it held its dark secrets. They were looking at a snow globe diorama but standing on what had been the place of execution.

Leo nudged her gently out of her daydreaming, and they started walking again. Jo took two steps before dread overtook her. She grabbed Leo's arm.

"Something's wrong."

"You're just now figuring this out?" He chuckled and put his hand over hers.

"I'm not being funny." The words were still hanging in the cold air when Jo felt a pull through her sternum like someone had a rope looped around her heart.

She kicked out at empty air as her boots left the ground. The strap of the sling came undone, and her hands were wrenched behind her as if she were bound at the wrists. She screamed as her left arm twisted.

Leo tried to grab her foot but jerked his hand back. "Your boots are like fire."

Her feet were warm, and the heat moved quickly up her legs and torso. Her hair lifted on thermals in the air around her. Fire crackled and licked at her face as the smell of burnt hair and flesh filled her nose.

There was a lot of screaming, though it was hard to discern how much of it was hers and how much was Leo's as it bounced off the surrounding buildings. She caught her breath for a moment.

"I'm burning." The words didn't seem to make it very far, but Leo answered.

"There's no fire. Jo, there's no fire."

She would suffocate before she burned. What had happened earlier in the evening was a cozy nap compared to the way the superheated air snaked into her lungs. There wasn't enough air to scream anymore.

Leo's footfalls pounded away from her.

Faron had given up his mortality and humanity for a couple extra hours. All of Dušan's maneuvering had been for nothing. She was going to burn to death like a common witch in a fire only she could see. Fucking figured.

The flames in front of her face parted like a painted tulip. Mary, the one of the crossroads who had watched her and Leo kiss, walked through the orange and yellow petals of flame to stand in front of her.

That was not the god she thought would come to claim her in the end. She would've bet on Achelous, or even Dušan, but not Leo's Mary.

Now she was Jo's Mary of the Crossroads, her very own Lady of the Various Fucking Sorrows. Mary nodded and held out her hand for Jo to take it. Perhaps Our Lady had missed the magically bound wrists bit?

Mary was insistent, and Jo didn't want to keep her waiting or hang around for the part where her eyeballs melted onto her cheeks or her molars exploded in her jaw. She wrenched her good arm free and took Mary's hand. A thousand prom corsages of curled, baby-blue carnations choked out the fireball around her, and she crashed back onto the street like a bag of doorknobs, right onto her shoulder.

"God damn fuck shit fuck." Jo squeezed her eyes shut against the pain.

When she opened them, Mary was gone. The whole square smelled like burning lilies overlaid with the mixed spice of old-fashioned carnations.

Helena appeared as the first bar of "Whatever Lola Wants" slid through Jo's thoughts.

"Mother." Helena's expression darkened, and her eyes narrowed.

Leo and his posse of Jo's nearest and dearest, plus Gustaf, slid to a halt in a semicircle with their compressed, concerned faces looking down at her on her back, on the snow, again.

Jo looked past them, up into the night sky. The sun would come up soon, but for now the snowflakes drifted down on her like hundreds of falling stars. It was impractical to stay there, the cold seeping up through her coat, but it was a welcome change from the inferno she'd escaped. Correction. The inferno that Mary, Jesus's mom, had coaxed her out of.

That was going to take awhile to digest. She'd pledged no fealty to Leo's god, and she had zero connection to Mary aside from her best friend in third grade being draped in a blue blanket for the nativity play at her grandmother's church. Jo had refused to participate, but Grandma had dragged her to the Christmas Eve service anyway.

"What happened?" Vesna's breathless voice ended Jo's childhood reverie and pulled her hand out of the warm grip of her grandmother's.

Jo's jaw was uncooperative for a moment, but the words found their way out. "I'm not sure exactly, but I can offer you a firsthand account of being burned at the stake." She pushed herself up with her good arm and looked over the faces of her family. She guessed that included Matjaž now, too, and even Gustaf, if begrudgingly so. He could be the crotchety uncle she'd never wanted. "I think I need to revisit Dr. Struna."

Leo and Faron helped her up, avoiding her bad arm.

Matjaž approached her with an expression that was impossible to parse. "I think you're in good hands. Is Helena here now?"

Jo nodded.

"She and I need to see to Mother." Clearly, Matjaž had not missed the cloying perfume clinging to Jo's clothes and hair.

"I should go with you." Goran stepped in closer, adding to the number of people in Jo's personal space.

"You are welcome to come, but I don't think your services will be needed." Matjaž looked like he wanted to laugh but knew the moment was wrong. Church giggles. Jo had them enough times herself to recognize the signs. Matjaž leaned in and kissed her on the cheek. "Get your arm looked at and get some sleep."

———

Matjaž could smell the floral funk of his mother's magic before he reached her front door. He'd never seen the aftermath of a broken compact and wasn't sure what he was walking into. Helena's presence felt near, but it could have been wishful thinking.

He opened the door with his key. The air in the flat embraced him with a crush of rotting lilies. The door to Avgusta's studio stood open, offering a glimpse of her altar and a line of salt on the floor.

Whatever had happened to her was partially his responsibility, but he hadn't seen any other way to keep her from continuing her campaign of harm. He stood in the door and took a deep breath.

Avgusta was still alive, but she wouldn't be for much longer. Her body lay half inside the salt circle. She'd broken her own spell, but the damage was already done.

Matjaž crouched beside her and pulled her to a sitting position against the solid altar in the center of the room and her broken magic.

"What were you thinking?" He pushed her fine silver hair off her face.

"Is she dead, then?" Avgusta coughed, but her gaze didn't waver.

"No." He picked up a handful of the salt and let it fall between his fingers. "You made a compact with me, and you broke it."

"There was interference."

"What did you think was going to happen?"

"I would die, but I would take that woman and any ability Dušan had to live any kind of mortal life with me." She coughed again and closed her eyes.

"You have been so blinded. Dušan had no intention of

possessing Jo." He wouldn't tell her the rest. The night's events were Jo and Faron's story to share.

"You're a fool. Why would Dušan want to continue living his pathetic charade when he could have a mortal life?"

"That's amusing coming from someone who wanted nothing more than for one of her children to be immortal."

"You never understood." Her voice was fading.

"I didn't, and I never will." He moved to sit next to her against the altar and took her hand. There was no closeness between them, but she was still his mother.

Avgusta died, her head on his shoulder. A perfect, white lily appeared in her open palm. Matjaž looked for Helena, hoping he could catch a glimpse of her. The flower had to be her doing; Avgusta's powers left her the moment she released the spell against Jo.

He was the only one left of his dysfunctional family. His sister lingered as a ghost, but he was the only one with breath. The temperature dropped around him, and a comforting chill settled on his other shoulder and over the hand that held Avgusta's.

CHAPTER 29

Faron sat in the breakfast nook of his flat. Ivanka poured tea into a chipped cup and slid in across from him.

She smiled up at him over the rim as she took her first sip. "I'm not going anywhere."

"I can't ask you to be part of this, not after–"

"Not after all I've been through? That's exactly why I'll stay." She smiled again.

"That doesn't make any sense."

"Of course it does. I already know the world is full of ghosts and monsters and humans who can do things humans aren't supposed to be able to do. Do you think I can just forget that?" She set her cup down and looked out the window before looking back at him. "Besides you need me to help you get a handle on this white god stuff."

"I don't mean to be a shit, but honestly, what do you know about it?"

"Nothing. I know you. And I think I can help you remember who you are, at least for awhile."

She had a point. But. "I won't age. I'll have to leave at some point to avoid people figuring that out. And ..."

"And I will get old and gray and you can tell people I'm your grandmother. Or we'll fall out of love, and I'll move on and leave you to mope for all eternity over me. I'm not going anywhere now, though."

She was back to being the Ivanka she had been before her parents had died, yet different. Maybe it was all the time she'd spent with his mom and Vesna at the teahouse. Maybe she was a stronger person than he had given her credit for. Either way, he was inclined to believe she meant what she said.

She finished her tea. "And now I need to get going. Goran said not to be late."

"Late for what?"

"He agreed to train Veronika, but only if Ana and I also studied with him."

"What?"

"Witch sisters come in threes or something like that. Besides, if I'm going to stick around, I'd like to be able to defend myself against the shit you and your mother attract." She stood up and kissed him on the cheek.

Faron stared as she collected her backpack and headed out the door. He stood up to watch her from the kitchen window. She coasted into view on her bike and headed away from the building, her dark hair blowing behind her. He watched until she disappeared down the street.

———

Vesna finished her coffee and took her and Igor's mugs to the sink. She washed them and set them on the drainboard. When she turned around, Igor was there, close enough that she had to look up to speak to him.

"And what are your plans today?" Igor pulled her into a hug and kissed her on top of the head.

He'd showered before breakfast, but there was always a hint of paint about him. "Help with prep this morning. Jo isn't back for a couple of days."

"She's been gone a lot. Leaving you with more to do." He leaned back to look her in the face.

Vesna nodded. "I think there will probably be more of that."

"Is that a good thing or a bad thing?"

"For me or for Jo?" Vesna smiled up at him.

"Both. Either."

She extricated herself from his arms and leaned back against the sink. "Both for both. I miss her when she's gone. I don't have the chops to actually replace her in the kitchen, but I kind of like scheduling the bands and working more with Fred on menus. Gregor already suggested turning the day-to-day accounting over to Olga if we need to."

"And Jo?"

"I think that's her story to tell."

He nodded. "Fair enough."

"I have a question for you this morning, too." Her smile faded. She was probably making what Jo called her "serious mom" face.

"I already know what you're going to ask." He took both her hands in his.

"Well, then?"

"Ask anyway. I think you need to." He wasn't laughing at her, but the twinkle in his eye revealed that he found this all slightly amusing.

"Were you going to tell me you are a seer?"

"Were you going to tell me you are?"

"Eventually." It came out more sheepishly than she had intended.

"Same." He laughed.

"But the mural with Jo and the tea. How did you–"

"I didn't. It doesn't work like that for me. I start a piece, and the images come together in my mind. I don't 'see' what they mean until later. And you?"

"Auras mostly, but sometimes I know things. Usually things I wish I didn't know."

"And what do you 'know' about me?" He pulled her back to him.

"I knew you were a seer the morning I met you at the shop with Jo. And I thought you were more into her than me."

"So sometimes you are wrong."

She laughed. It hadn't been her intuition that was wrong. Her extended "dry spell" had whittled away at her self-esteem a bit, and Jo had shown a little bit of interest in the graffiti artist. To be fair, Jo seemed to take interest in everyone, or she had before things had changed so irrevocably.

"I'm glad you were wrong. I like Jo, but her life is far too chaotic for my taste. And besides, I don't share very well." Igor nuzzled into her neck and kissed her shoulder.

"Mmm. Me, either." She would've happily dragged him back to bed, but she had sandwiches to make.

CHAPTER 30

"Of course I came back."

Jo set her backpack inside the door to the Novak family farmhouse. The mudroom was musty and would need some spring cleaning before she left. "Though it was dicey there for a bit, whether it would be Shade Jo or Alive Jo who returned."

"Do I want to know this story?" Henry laughed.

"Maybe. It can wait though. I, we, have work to do." She jammed a knit cap in her pocket and pulled a flask out of her backpack.

"You just got here. You could sit for a minute. The bus ride, the walk …"

"Weren't so bad, really." Dr. Struna said her arm had healed miraculously well and quickly. Jo chalked it up to whatever Achelous had done to it when they were chatting under the river. "They've been waiting for me." Henry had been waiting for her, too, though he wasn't one to admit it.

"Okay, then." He grabbed the camp chair from the corner. "The blankets are kind of musty."

"I'm good." It wasn't exactly warm out, but the snow had

melted except in the shadiest places. There were patches of crocus. Even if it wasn't that much warmer outside, it looked like it was. That was enough.

Henry was unchanged: the same heavy fisherman's sweater, the same rakishly long hair. He was a 1950s advertisement for "manly" men everywhere and seemed to have the same inability to let that shit go. He wouldn't have to worry about it much longer. If reincarnation was a thing, maybe he would come back next as a sensitive ponytail guy.

He followed her out to the meadow, now snow-free and vibrant with that spring green color from the sixty-four-crayon box. With the snow-covered peaks offering the perfect backdrop, she expected to see Julie Andrews pirouetting through any minute.

Instead there were more ravaged and frozen soldiers for her to name. They approached her in disbelief. The first one to greet her was the Austrian who had offered to let the others know she would return.

"You came back, Jo Wiley." His accent was so like Gustaf's. He must have been Viennese, as well.

"I made a promise. It just took me a little longer than I'd planned." She extended her hand to the man. His fingers were black with frostbite.

"I'm sorry you had to wait for me."

"Days are not much in the memory of years." He smiled, revealing gleamingly white teeth as he took her hand.

"What is your name?"

"Franz Müller, but don't speak it yet. I would like to stay until you are finished with the others."

Jo cocked her head at him. Franz seemed like a good guy, and his eyes weren't preternaturally green or anything. This was out of her, admittedly brief, standard procedure. "If you wish."

"It's only that, like your friend," he nodded at Henry, "I wish to see these men at peace."

She would have to trust that was all.

The others came then. Short and tall, dark and light, whole and broken, young and old, but mostly young. So many lives cut short, their family trees savagely pruned. Like the soldiers in her dreams of Winifred and Rebecca, the faces were smooth but the eyes were old. She tried not to think of Faron, but it was impossible to push what had happened to the back of her mind. He would always look young, too.

She stood for hours but finally sat in the camp chair as the sun got closer to the mountains. Henry asked her how she was doing as he recorded name after name in the notebook.

Franz stood with them, his cold-burned hands at his sides until the gloaming when the last few soldiers made their way to the center of the meadow to touch Jo's sleeve or face and disappear into the Next behind her. Josef and Anthony were the last two, and then the meadow was empty except for Jo and the two shades who flanked her.

"I would go now, Miss Wiley." Franz moved in front of her and took both of her hands. "My grandmother told me stories of Valkyries, the choosers of the slain who escort the favorites of the gods to a great hall."

"I don't think I am a Valkyrie. I would choose that no one die as you and the others had to die."

"War is a human failing, but one that must entertain the gods." Franz was older than most of the others. She guessed he'd been in his thirties when he died.

"You've had a lot of time to think about this." Jo looked up at Henry, but he was quiet. He'd shoved the pen and notebook into his pants pockets. He had already written Franz's name in the book.

"I had time to think of it before the war. I was a lecturer at the university." He looked over her shoulder, out to the meadow beyond, before returning his gaze to Jo.

She stood. "Franz Müller, I hope you find peace in the Next."

A door opened behind her, its pull as clear to her as if it had opened inside her.

"I wish peace for you, as well, Jo Wiley. I do not know who comes for a Valkyrie. When it is your time, I wish you a guide as faithful." He kissed her cheek and walked behind her to disappear.

Jo didn't turn to watch. "Henry, if you're ready."

She wasn't ready to send him off, but she couldn't ask him to wait.

He didn't answer for a few heartbeats. "I would like to stay with you tonight at the farmhouse, if–"

She nodded. "Please."

"I didn't bring anything to cook. I didn't expect to be up here as long this time." She pulled the cheese and other provisions out of her bag and unwound a bottle of wine from the towel she'd cushioned it with for the bus ride.

Henry pulled wine glasses from the cupboard and set them on the table. Jo arranged the bread, *pršut*, and cheese on a board with two small jars and sat down.

She opened the first jar and spread fig jam on a corner of bread before slicing a whisper-thin portion of cheese to lay over it. She hadn't been hungry until she'd unwrapped the food.

"What happened in Ljubljana?" Henry speared an olive from the other jar and waited for her answer.

"Short or long version?"

"Short. Curiosity has the better of me." He ate the olive.

"I died on my birthday. My son brought me back from the dead, giving up his mortality in the process. On the way home a witch tried to magically burn me at the stake. Oh, and I broke my arm, but it's fine now."

Henry would have choked on his olive if he had any breath in his body. "That's all, then?"

She laughed. "Never a dull moment."

"Valkyries lead interesting lives." Henry braved a piece of bread smeared with the jam.

"I am not a Valkyrie. I am definitely not a demigod. Voices are mortal women, remember."

"Mythology only attempts to explain. Perhaps Voices are many things to different peoples. Your kind could be the Morrigan of Irish myth or any of the other ushers to the underworld."

That was not a comforting thought. "There are only three

of us left. And two of us are definitely not working in the field."

Henry took a sip of wine. "What do they do?"

"My aunt mostly keeps it to herself but does 'readings' if she's asked. I have no idea what my mother does. She's in and out of the hospital and institutions." Jo pushed some crumbs around with the tip of the jam spreader.

"And there are no more?"

"Not that I or the Board know of."

"What happens when the three of you are gone?" Henry clasped his hands around the stem of his wine glass in front of him and stared into Jo.

"I don't know." She had to look away. His gaze felt accusatory.

"I am a betting man, and I wouldn't take odds on you against nature keeping things in balance."

Faron was now the counterpart to Dušan. He would be the white god to Dušan's black and would escort the fallen to the Next. The universe found its balance on the back of Jo's family. She wanted to rail and cry, but the cold of the dead had seeped into her and sat like a hollow where her anger had been.

"That contest has already finished. I would say I lost, we lost." She got up to clear the table and wrap up the food for breakfast.

Henry leaned against the counter while she washed the dishes. Jo dropped a knife and grabbed for it as it fell. The blade sliced across her palm and the web of her thumb.

"Shit." She held her injured hand balled up inside the good

one, blood oozing between her fingers. "I know better than that. 'A falling knife doesn't have a handle.' I've said that to Faron a thousand times."

"Maybe there are some bandages in the bathroom." He headed that way, and Jo followed.

Henry flipped the light on by the mirror and rummaged in drawers and under the sink. He produced one nearly finished roll of gauze and some cotton makeup swabs. "I don't think these are sterile. Do you have any alcohol besides wine?"

"There's an old bottle of vodka in the cabinet next to the glasses."

"I'll be right back."

Jo stood facing the sink and opened her hand to assess the damage, hoping it wasn't deep enough to need stitches. There wasn't a gash, only a red line from the edge near her thumb to the center as if she'd scratched the tip of the blade over her skin.

Henry came back and looked over her shoulder. "That doesn't look bad. Where did all the blood come from?"

"I don't know."

"It can't hurt to clean it." He held her hand over the sink and poured the vodka over.

It didn't even sting.

"I thought I'd cut it worse than that." Jo flexed her hand and dried it off with a clean towel. "I'm glad. I was racking my brain trying to figure out how we'd get to a doctor to have it sewn up."

"We?" He laughed.

"Well, me, I guess." He was standing very close and was colder now even than Helena.

Henry took Jo's face in his hands and kissed her. He ran his hands over her shoulders and down her arms before taking her by the waist and pulling him into her.

She kissed back. There was Leo and there would be Leo, but not yet. There was no bird hex this time. She was going to miss Henry. He had helped her understand what she was. It was taking goodbye sex to a very different level, though.

"I'd rather not do this in the bathroom." Henry ran his thumb over her temple.

"Agreed." She led him back to the bedroom.

Henry unbuttoned her sweater, stopping at each button to brush his lips over hers again. His slowness reminded Jo with every movement it was his last night on earth, or at least this plane of existence. After he crossed the threshold of his door, he might not even be Henry, or whoever he was, anymore.

Jo stopped him before he kissed her again. "You know you are going to have to tell me your real name for me to open your door."

"We will get to that in good time." He covered her mouth with his before she could say anything else. He walked her backwards toward the bed.

Jo sat on the edge and pushed herself back. He followed her until they were stretched out beside each other.

Henry put his hand on the side of her face and ran his thumb over her cheekbone. "Where does a Valkyrie find her peace?"

"I don't think she gets peace until the end." A man with inhuman eyes comes for her. Henry's eyes were dark brown and thoughtful.

"I am sorry I cannot offer you some measure of what you have given me."

"You have."

———

Jo stretched her arm out expecting to make contact with Henry's chilly form, but she was alone in bed. After a rummage through her bag for a robe and socks, she padded into the main room. Henry sat perched on the edge of the couch.

Jo yawned. "You look like a man who is ready to go somewhere. I'll get dressed and we can go outside. The setting is nicer than a musty house."

"The door is there." He nodded toward the front door. "It's been there since we came in last night."

"Why didn't you say?" She hadn't sensed a door open, but then again she hadn't opened Henry's door.

"I wasn't ready to leave." He stood up.

"But you are now?"

"Yes. It's time."

She hugged him, and he put his arms around her. Shades usually carried no scent, but with her face buried in Henry's sweater, Jo could smell the sea.

"I think I know your name." She leaned back from him, still circled in his arms.

"Does it matter who I was?" There were too many emotions registered in his expression to pick one out, but he did look amused.

"Not really. If Achelous is right, it doesn't matter who I am, either. We were supposed to be here, for whatever reasons the Fates devised." The Fates could be kind then, as well as cruel. Henry had accomplished two things she couldn't have done alone.

He laughed. "Do you believe that?"

"I'm not sure what I believe right now. I have a lot of new information to sift through. But whatever the reason, I'm glad things worked out like they did."

He nodded. "Thank you, Jolene Wiley."

She smiled and sighed.

"Will you walk out with me?"

"I'll walk you to the front door. It's bad form for me to see another's door, and I seem to have a penchant for going through ones that don't belong to me." She pulled her robe around her more tightly and pulled at the loops on the bow at her waist.

"You have a purpose to live for. Don't wish your life ended." His expression darkened. She had forgotten he had taken his own life.

"I think it's a hazard of the trade, but you are right, I have a reason for all this now. Despite the grimness, it makes more sense to me. I have you to thank for that."

"You would have gotten there on your own."

"Maybe. Let's say your timing was good." She opened the

door for him. She could sense it, but it didn't pull at her center like the others had.

Henry kissed her for the last time and walked out into the bright morning. Jo closed the door behind him, expecting tears, but there were none. She was sad to let him go but happier that he had found the peace he had waited so long for.

She went back to the bedroom and sat on the edge of the bed, staring out of the window. Her sketchbooks had been neatly stacked on the bedside table. The top one had two sketches of Henry in it. On top of that, Henry had left a book from the collection in the main room.

Jo picked up the battered Slovenian translation of *A Farewell to Arms* and thumbed through to the page he'd marked.

"*Za vse ni razlag* – There isn't an explanation for everything."

———

Her bag was packed, and the house was aired and cleaned before Jo heard the car on the gravel drive. Leo was early. He'd probably given himself an extra hour after the last trip up in the snow.

She met him at the door and welcomed him in. She'd seen him in street clothes before but it was still jarring. The Leo in her mind's photo album was a man in black, cassock and all. He ducked under the lintel and pulled her into a Leo-sized hug.

"Did you think I wasn't going to be here or something?" It was nice though, and he was warm. She probably felt like a shade to him.

He started to say something, then stopped. "Let's just say it's always a good surprise to see you."

She smiled. An awkwardness had developed between them since the river and Avgusta's attempt at burning her at the stake. There was a tacit commitment on both their parts to see where this led, but they were taking it very slowly. Vesna had made an offhand comment about neither her nor Leo having any clue what a healthy relationship looked like. Jo couldn't argue with her, but it still stung.

"Is this all?" He picked up her bag.

"I'm traveling light these days." She shooed him back outside, locking the door behind them. She wouldn't come back until the renovations were finished and Gregor was ready to open the *gostilna* and inn. It would be different enough then. Even with cosmetic changes, she knew it would still remind her of the ghosts she'd put to rest and always of Henry.

The drive down the mountain back into town was much less fraught than their previous trip, though they were both almost as quiet. Jo had watched for her Mary of the Crossroads on the bus trip up, but she hadn't seen her. It was hard to remember where it was, as all the landmarks had been hidden under the snow when they saw her the first time.

"Stop!" She was there, at the corner of the crossroads where she had been last time. There had been nothing there when Jo had looked from the bus. She was positive.

Leo pulled the car half off the road into the grass.

"I'll be right back." Jo opened the door and started to get out.

"Do you want me to come with you?" Leo unbuckled his seat belt.

She shook her head.

"I feel like we have traded places." He smiled but buckled himself back in.

Jo closed the door and made her way through the sprays of early spring flowers surrounding the shrine. It was the Mary of the Flames. She was smiling, eyes downcast, looking at the crowned heart she held in her painted hands.

"Hi. I still kind of suck at this praying thing, but I wanted to say thank you." Jo placed a stone from Achelous' river on the shrine among the melted candles and wilted flowers. Something about serving two masters floated up from her deep memory of attending church with her grandmother. She would add that to the list of shit she needed to sort out.

As Jo started back toward the car, a flash caught her eye. She turned to watch as the used-up candles caught and came to life. Little yellow flames barely visible in the bright sunlight flickered in between piles of fresh carnations the color of blood.

Mary's eyes were open now and looking out, past Jo, down the road, back toward the mountains. Jo could hear a voice like her grandmother's in her head.

"You are not obligated to me, Jolene. That is not the nature of faith."

Jo nodded.

"Leo is a good man."

He was. Better than she deserved.

"That is not the nature of love."

She had a lot more to figure out.

"You will go to Mary. She will need you at the end."

Her mother Mary. The other Mary. There was an obligation there.

"Yes."

When Jo looked up at the shrine, the statue was looking at its hands and the pile of dirty candle wax and browned flowers again. Jo's stone was gone.

Jo got back into the car.

"You okay? You look a little pale." Leo put his hand over Jo's hands folded together in her lap.

"I don't think you need to worry about your god punishing you for leaving the church. I think Mary's got you covered."

Leo pulled back onto the road and headed through town to the highway back to Ljubljana. Watching him drive with his legs folded up like a praying mantis made her wonder if she should get her license.

Her phone rang in her bag. She dug through the dirty clothes and sketchbooks, answering it just before it went to voicemail.

Her aunt didn't even say hello first. "You need to come home, Jo."

"I know. I already got the message."

Our Lady of the Various Sorrows

LOOKING FOR MORE FROM VICTORIA?

The complete *Voices of the Dead* series is available now from 1000 Volt Press.

Who By Water - Voices of the Dead: Book One

Like A Pale Moon - Voices of the Dead: Book Three

Strange as Angels - Voices of the Dead: Book Four

Sign up for the Notes from the Dead Letter Office at victoriaraschke.com for information about upcoming book releases, author events, and an exclusive *Voices of the Dead* short.

THE ZOMBIE CHURCH IS REAL

The Trans-Universal Zombie Church of the Blissful Ringing is a real organization and registered religious group in Slovenia. The church supports the rights of refugees and regularly works to combat the rising tide of white supremacist nationalism in Europe. They also run a pro bono clinic in Nova Gorica, Slovenia, that mostly serves patients with chronic illnesses like diabetes and high blood pressure who can't afford ongoing treatment but aren't deemed ill enough to receive free emergency services.

You can support their work at the clinic by sending donations by mail to:
Hiša dobrot
Vipavska cesta 104
5000 Nova Gorica
Slovenia

Or by international transfer to:
SWIFT: BAKOSI2X
SI56101000053803567
Refrerence: CHAR
Banka Intesa Sanpaolo d. d.
Pristaniška ulica 14
6502 Koper
Slovenia

To learn more about the church go to their public, English language group page on Facebook.

ABOUT THE AUTHOR

Victoria Raschke writes books that start with questions like "what if you didn't find out you were the chosen one until you were in your forties?" When she isn't holed up in her favorite coffee house to write, she can be found at the nearest farmers' market checking out the weird vegetables or at her home where she lives with a changing number of cats and her family who supports both her writing and her culinary experimentation — for the most part. Her first book, *Who by Water,* was published in 2017.

www.ingramcontent.com/pod-product-compliance
Lightning Source LLC
Chambersburg PA
CBHW071754110726
47908CB00006B/1800